QUEEN OF THE ROAD

Recent Titles by Helen Cannam from Severn House

A CLOUDED SKY
FIRST PARISH
THE HIGHWAYMAN
AN HONOURABLE MAN

The Diana Poultney Series

FAMILY BUSINESS
QUEEN OF THE ROAD

QUEEN OF
THE ROAD

Helen Cannam

This first world edition published in Great Britain 2000 by
SEVERN HOUSE PUBLISHERS LTD of
9–15 High Street, Sutton, Surrey SM1 1DF.
This first world edition published in the USA 2000 by
SEVERN HOUSE PUBLISHERS INC of
595 Madison Avenue, New York, N.Y. 10022.

British Library Cataloguing in Publication Data

Cannam, Helen
    Queen of the road
    1. Family-owned business enterprises - Fiction
    2. Domestic fiction
    I. Title
    823.9'14 [F]

    ISBN 0-7278-5586-7

Typeset by Palimpsest Book Production Ltd.,
Polmont, Stirlingshire, Scotland.
Printed and bound in Great Britain by
MPG Books Ltd., Bodmin, Cornwall.

Acknowledgements

Many people have helped me gain some inside knowledge of the haulage industry for the purposes of writing this novel and its predecessor, *Family Business*. Thanks, as always, to Crook library for finding me obscure but helpful books. I am grateful, too, that my researches led me to Lorna Brough, whose own experiences as a female lorry driver are just a small part of an extraordinary life, better than any fiction. Ted Hannon's encyclopaedic knowledge of the haulage industry throughout its history was an invaluable resource. Last but not least, thanks to John Mairs, who led me both to Lorna and to Ted, and whose fund of amazing tales and fascinating information provides me with fortnightly entertainment throughout the winter months when he delivers our coal!

Finally, I should add that any errors of fact are entirely my responsibility.

For Lorna Brough

One

Carol had no warning at all of what her mother had done, until afterwards. No one consulted her, so she was taken completely by surprise. As far as she had known, the business was to be sold, after which her mother – Diana Armstrong – would very likely go to live in Surrey, near her parents. Not that Carol cared about any of it, or so she told herself. She had turned her back on everything: the haulage business, the garage in Wearbridge, the flat over the petrol station; and her mother, newly widowed. In one way or another they had all let her down, and were now in the past. She was no longer Carol Armstrong, but Mrs Byers, and her life was here, on the family smallholding beside the young river, where Kenny had lived since his birth eighteen years ago.

The river had flooded badly only a few weeks ago, at the end of the bitter winter of 1963, covering all the adjacent land – which included the eleven acres or so of the smallholding. Now the waters had receded and a few clear cold days had allowed the ground to dry out a little, though a residual tangle of sticks and grasses formed a kind of rough nest round the base of each tree, and the smell of floodwater continued to drown out the early scents of spring. Carol still needed wellingtons to keep her feet dry as she went out after dinner to give the lambs their afternoon bottle. The Byers family had lost a good few lambs to the cold and wet weather, but there were still two motherless creatures to be fed. Carol, four months pregnant and developing a maternal instinct of her own, felt responsible for them, particularly as no one else seemed to care very much. If

1

the lambs were left to other members of her new family they would be unlikely to live, she thought; none of the Byers family had any conception of regularity or responsibility. Carol, used to being criticised all her life for her untidiness, disorder and lack of organisation, suddenly found herself – unnervingly – the one orderly person about the place. She was convinced that the lambs depended on her for their very survival.

So, without fail, she spent several hours each day – and night – of that cold April out in the small field beside the house bottle-feeding the lambs, who, after three weeks of her care, were at last beginning to show signs of thriving. It was something purposeful, useful, something she could do well, with no help from anyone else, a salve to the raw wound of her anger, hurt and resentment at this marriage that she had never really wanted.

She had not consciously or deliberately made a decision to marry. It had burst from her at the moment of her expulsion from school last June, when she was just sixteen – nearly a year ago now. She had been furious at her father's refusal to allow her to work in the garage workshops, or as a driver in his haulage business – the two things that were all she had ever wanted to do with her life. Since her father claimed that to marry and bear children was the natural end of every woman's life, then that, she'd exploded, was what she would do – and Kenny had been there, willing enough to be swept – bullied? – into marriage.

Yet she had never dreamed that it would actually come about. Right to the last moment some part of her had been certain that her parents would step in and prevent it, somehow. Instead, her father, at first bewildered yet amused, treating it as a joke, had quickly convinced himself it was precisely what she wanted and had supported her in carrying through the decision, even entering gleefully into the arrangements. Meanwhile, she had been sure, within herself, that her mother knew she had not the remotest wish to marry Kenny, that it was all being done out of pique. She knew her mother did not like him, where her father only felt a certain inevitable sense that, like any potential husband, he was not quite worthy of his daughter. Her mother, she felt certain, would make quite sure that the marriage did not happen. But her mother had failed her. Diana had been, through it all, so restrained, so cool. She had murmured to Carol that she would have all her support, should she wish at any stage to back out of the marriage; she had gently hinted at what she really felt – but never in terms strong enough to make her daughter feel she could retreat without losing face. What Carol had wanted above all was a storm of protest. Her mother should have raged and screamed and shouted, even locked her in her room – anything rather than allow her daughter to go through with it. Instead, Diana's ingrained politeness had held her feelings in check and allowed events to take their course. She had not been much older than Carol was now when she had become an Armstrong – by name. At heart, though, she had remained, throughout the whole horrible business, the good-mannered doctor's daughter of her girlhood. And so, ever since the August day when her own impulses had somehow been allowed to trap her into a marriage she had known was not right for her, Carol had raged inwardly against her mother's middle-class restraint.

Now, nine months later, her father was dead. Carol tried not to consider what difference it might have made, if she'd known his death was to come so soon. None, probably; after all, with the business sold, she would still not have been able to work in the garage. On the other hand, she would not have had her father's unwanted support for her marriage. Her mother might more readily have opposed it, had that not meant openly setting herself against her father.

Bradley Armstrong's death had not brought Carol closer to her mother – on the contrary. She had known her parents' marriage was not a happy one, that there had been unbearable strains between them for a long time. An only child in that small flat, she could not help but feel the tension and hear the arguments, even though her mother's sense of decorum generally kept her from open explosion. Carol had hated her father's frequent drunkenness. Yet she had loved him, deeply, whatever their

3

differences, and when he was found dead under the wagon he had overturned one drunken morning she had been devastated. If her mother had felt the same, the death might have brought them closer, but she knew that Diana could not begin to feel as she did, that there must even have been a measure of relief in what she experienced. They could not even comfort one another with shared memories, for their predominant memories were so disparate. It had been her grandmother, her father's frail mother Elsie Armstrong, to whom Carol had turned for fellow-feeling in her grief; and her new family with whom she had tried to forget it, since they very quickly did.

The first lamb, already fed, was nudging at her legs, while the second tugged urgently at the bottle, almost pulling her over with the force of it. Carol laughed. "You greedy little beggar, you!" Then the first lamb shot away from her, without warning, and, braced against him as she had been until then, she pitched sideways, just putting her hand out in time to break her fall and stop herself from being coated in mud. Out of the blue a hand grasped her, steadying her and helping her to her feet. She looked up at the person who had startled the lamb. Her mother: Diana Armstrong.

Carol blinked, as if the figure beside her might not have been a figment of her imagination after all. Standing there in the clear windy sunlight, Diana looked so elegant, so assured – she had such an odd shining look about her. No one would have thought that this youthful-looking woman in the camel coat that skimmed what was still a trim figure was only two weeks a widow. To Carol, there was something shocking about her appearance, as if her husband's death had been, for Diana, neither a grief nor a loss, but, entirely, a step into a bright new future.

Once secure on her feet, Carol faced her mother, resentment at her own wrongs mixed with anger at the affront to her father that she perceived in the happy woman – for Diana was clearly happy, unequivocally happy. Smiling, she said, "I've bought up the business, all of it. From this morning."

4

Carol stared at her, not understanding. The second lamb, finding the bottle suddenly held just out of reach, bleated his protest. "What business?" Carol asked, stupidly.

"Armstrong's, of course – haulage business, garage, petrol station, all of it. I've bought out Uncle Jackson's share. I shall get the lorries back on the road and make Armstrong's a force to be reckoned with again."

Carol abandoned the lambs altogether and stood up. "What, you, by yourself?" Diana nodded. "But – how? Who's going to run it?"

"Grandpa's given me a loan. And I'm going to run it, of course."

"But you're not a mechanic. Or a wagon driver." She felt a sharp pang of envy. *I am a mechanic*, she thought; *and I could pass my test tomorrow, if they'd let me.* So much better qualified, yet excluded – so far excluded that her mother could come and simply present her, like this, with a *fait accompli*, a decision in which she had no say, which she was powerless to influence in any way!

"I drove during the war," Diana reminded her. "In any case, I don't have to do everything to manage a successful business. I do know a lot about running an office. And what I don't know I shall learn."

Carol stared in amazement at the confident woman standing before her, who was scarcely recognisable as her own mother, the green eyes so like her own in an oval face that was not like hers at all, framed with the heavy, glossy dark hair that would scarcely allow itself to be pinned into tidiness. "You know what Dad would have thought of that." She still felt sore at her father's rejection of all she had learned from early childhood in the repair yard behind the petrol station, and his refusal to allow her to make a career there.

For a moment the shine left Diana's face, and her mouth had a wry twist. "He was hardly the model of a successful businessman," she said.

Indignantly, Carol flew to her father's defence. "He did well enough to pay for me to go to St Margaret's." She knew she was on slightly dangerous ground; she had after all managed to get herself expelled from that genteel convent school after five less than glorious years.

"So he did, when he laid off the drink long enough," Diana admitted drily. "And so long as Ronnie Shaw looked as if he might steal a march on him."

"Ronnie Shaw never played fair." Carol recalled the dark charming man her father had hated so much, not least because he had learned his mechanical skills as a boy at the family farm at Ravenshield, the place he had been evacuated to from his native Sunderland during the war. It had outraged Bradley Armstrong when Ronnie, already owner of a profitable repair business in Sunderland, had bought up a failing haulage concern in the Dale and set up as a rival to Armstrong's, which he'd tried more than once to buy up too.

"There was never any evidence of that, as far as I could see. It was just your father's excuse for his own failure. After all, he had the advantage over Ronnie Shaw, right from the start – he was born and bred here, he knew the Dale and everyone in it. He was respected for his father's sake. I never heard your Grandad Armstrong make excuses, when things went wrong – as they did, sometimes, though rarely because of his fault. He just got on with it and did what had to be done."

Carol had never before heard her mother speak so candidly about her father and his failures. It shocked her – these were disloyal words and they were coming from someone who generally kept her feelings hidden beneath a veneer of seemliness. She could not concede the truth of what Diana said, for that would only add to the betrayal. "You never gave him a chance."

"You know nothing about it! I gave him chance after chance, and he let them all go, every time." She stopped, and said more gently, "You loved your father, and that's quite right and I don't want to spoil it. But if you doubt my ability to run the business, just remember one thing: your grandfather Armstrong made sure a part of it was left to me in his will. He knew what I could do, better than anyone."

Carol shrugged and bent once again over the now hysterically bleating lamb. It tugged furiously at the bottle, while she glanced over her shoulder at her mother. "It doesn't matter to me what you do."

The shining look had gone from Diana's face. Carol could see that her mother was hurt and was glad about it, though she turned away to watch the lamb.

"I thought you'd like to know what plans I have," Diana said. She sounded tentative, unsure. "You might have some suggestions to make."

"Don't pretend you care what I think. It's a bit late for that. You've managed quite well without me till now."

There was a little silence. Carol knew her mother was watching her, thinking about what she could say to win her over, but she refused to look round or offer Diana any concession.

The bottle was empty, but Carol still bent over the sucking lamb, her back to her mother, who must have realised that there was nothing further she could say – for having quietly urged her daughter to look after herself, she walked away. Carol could feel the hurt she'd caused, but felt no remorse. Her mother deserved it, all of it.

She waited to return to the house until she was sure Diana had gone. Only when she saw her father's old blue van jolting away over the track towards the bridge on the main road did she begin to walk slowly back towards the untidy jumble of buildings: the stone cottage, with its worn external staircase to the second storey and its lichened stone-slabbed roof, was now overshadowed by outbuildings constructed over the years from a random selection of whatever lay to hand – old bits of wood, left-over bricks and slates, corrugated iron.

As she reached the patch of trampled earth – not quite so muddy now – which the family referred to as the yard, Kenny's motorbike roared on to it and exploded to a halt a short distance away. He did at least acknowledge that she was there, with a nod in her direction – after all, he could hardly miss her. Then he pulled off his leather gloves and knelt down beside the bike and began to tinker with it. He had probably put her out of his mind already.

It was the bike that had first attracted Carol to him, as far as she had been attracted at all. She had loved its power and grace, she had loved sitting behind him as it roared through the countryside. She had longed to be allowed to ride it alone, but he would never allow that. "It's not a girl's machine," he would say, echoing her father's view of mechanical things. She would have liked to tinker with it as he did, to explore the mechanics of it, but he would not allow that either. It was, she knew now, the only thing in life that really interested him. His initial attraction for her, she realised, had been as an accessory, the one thing previously missing – a pretty girl to carry on his pillion. Later, if marriage to her had appealed to him at all – as she supposed it must have done, since he had married her without the usual coercion of pregnancy – then it was because it assured him of the convenience of having a personable woman to bed when the urge came to him, and an extra pair of hands to wait on him, certainly more efficiently than his mother did. He had no interest at all in Carol as a person, in her feelings or her needs. He was not even very interested in the coming child, except perhaps as a gratifying sign of his potency, which also provided an excuse for not taking her on his pillion any more – she suspected that was more for appearances' sake than from any concern for her well-being. A heavily pregnant girl was a different proposition from a slender teenager, rather a halter than a trophy.

On the other hand, it was still too soon to write him off as a husband, especially as for the time being she was tied to him – they had, after all, been married less than a year. She went over to him. "My mother called."

Kenny pulled a spanner from his saddle bag. "Passed her." His bent head obstructed her view of what he was doing.

Carol tried again. "She's taking over the business, all of it, even Uncle Jackson's share."

At that, he did look up, sitting back on his heels to do so. "I didn't know she had that sort of money." There was avidity in his eyes; she knew – and wished she didn't – that he sensed an unforeseen advantage for himself.

"She borrowed it."

Disappointment sucked away curiosity; he returned his attention to the motorbike. "She must be mad then. She'll never make a go of it."

That might have been more or less the view Carol had just expressed to her mother, but she could not allow Kenny to voice the same criticism. "She knows more about it than you think. She's a good head for business." Yet if that were true, she had seen no evidence of it and had only her mother's word to go on. Her father had certainly not shown that he thought such a thing.

Carol wondered if it were true that Grandad Armstrong had wanted Diana to have a share in it, even above the claims of his sons. If so, that was indeed a strong endorsement: Grandad Armstrong had died before she was born, but his business skills were a family legend. On the other hand, Nana Armstrong had never even hinted that her husband had respected Diana, and she herself disliked her daughter-in-law. Carol had realised very early in her life that her kindly and much-loved Nana Armstrong reserved a special set of mannerisms for Diana, which involved pursed lips, a cold light in the eyes, a wondering shake of the head, and a tendency to pay little or no attention to what her daughter-in-law said to her. Carol was glad that Kenny's mother, a cheerful slatternly woman who took life as it came, had never treated her like that – not that she herself cared much for Mrs Byers, who had a permanently grimy look and smelled terrible, but that was another matter.

Kenny seemed to have forgotten she was there. She studied him, considering this boy who was now her husband, taking in his deficiencies with eyes that had never been dazzled by affection, still less by love: he had a small pale face – ferrety, was the word his features brought to mind – pale blue eyes hidden at this moment by thick fair lashes (his one remotely attractive feature);

a thin gangling body, lacking in muscle, and shoulders hunched from too much bending. In bed, he was no better, an awkward grunting boy, getting his pleasure as quickly as he could. If she had not been excited simply by the idea of what they were doing, there would have been no pleasure at all in it for her; as it was, there was very little – a moment of near forgetfulness, if she was lucky, followed by the tedium of waiting for him to finish. Was this really all that life had to offer her, day after day of marriage to Kenny? She had thought of the marriage as a way of punishing her father for his rejection of her – except that she'd not thought it would come to this, never expected it to become a reality. She felt rather as if she were the one who was being punished.

Would it be any different when the baby came? Would Kenny suddenly become a doting, loving husband and father, concerned for them both? Was that even what she wanted? Would she actually find life easier and more pleasurable if he came to want to spend more time with her? The thought, at present, rather revolted her.

She turned and went into the house, unnoticed by Kenny. She tried not to allow herself to wonder what her mother was doing now, what those unspoken plans were for the future. She did not, after all, want to know.

Diana had looked forward to telling Carol what she'd done, of talking over her plans with her daughter. She had, she thought, genuinely wanted to have Carol's views. She had expected the girl to be full of enthusiasm and excitement – not perhaps as much as she herself was, but enough to keep her in the buoyant mood of the morning. Enough, also, to close the painful gulf that Bradley's death had opened up between them.

Instead, it looked as though her attempt to share had only made things worse. What was it Carol had said? "Don't pretend you care what I think. It's a bit late for that. You've managed quite well without me until now."

The words turned themselves over in her mind, nagging at her, accusing. It had never occurred to her to consult with Carol before making her decision. Carol was her daughter, her child, someone who could be told of adult decisions but was not to be involved in them; one did not, after all, expect mature consideration from children. Yet now, suddenly, painfully, Diana realised that to Carol that must seem like nonsense. She might not yet be seventeen, but she was a married woman, soon to be a mother, an adult who had a right to a say in what might affect her. Might she even have wished to play some part in the new business, if her mother had set out to involve her from the start? *I'll never know*, Diana thought. For Carol was right: it was a bit late for that. She recognised now that it had not really been Carol's views that she'd wanted. She had not thought her daughter's views could be of any real use. She had only hoped that, because of Carol's enthusiasm for the garage, the news would restore some kind of closeness between them and heal the rifts of the past year. Instead, it had simply made matters worse – and brought sharply to her attention that, like it or not, her daughter was now effectively an adult.

An adult, she discovered, living in a squalor Diana wouldn't have wished on her worst enemy. She'd understood, in theory, that the Byers family were a feckless lot, since Bradley – not exactly the most orderly of men himself – had always said so. But until today, she and Carol had only met in Wearbridge, at the flat at the petrol station, in the street, or, sometimes, at the Armstrong family farm at Ravenshield, not far from where Carol now lived. Never invited to call at her daughter's new home, Diana had been scrupulous about keeping away. Sometimes she'd glanced in passing at the smallholding, glimpsed across the river, and been conscious of loose slates and walls in need of repair, but this was the first time she'd called at the house, where this morning she had asked for Carol. The total air of decay and neglect, combined with the stench the moment the kitchen door was opened to her by an indolently welcoming Mrs Byers, had seemed to hit her full in the face. She had declined the offer to step into the chaotic interior, and had been relieved to be told that Carol was out of doors. Though she was no model housewife herself, Diana had been appalled by what she found. Was this a fit place for a young girl to bear a child and raise it? It was not in the least what she wanted for her own daughter. But what could she do about it? Carol had made her choice and it was too late to change it. This knowledge was like a sharp pain at the heart of Diana's excitement at the new enterprise, shadowing her enthusiasm as she made her way home in the van, along the road that followed the line of the river, back to Wearbridge and the neat little flat above the garage.

Over a lunch of beans on toast Diana deliberately shook off her unease about Carol, so that by the time she went downstairs to the office her mind was clear. It had to be; there was a great deal of thinking and planning to be done, now that the business was truly hers. She couldn't afford to waste time on regrets and anxieties about things she couldn't change. She unlocked the office door and went in and for a moment she simply stood, looking about her. She was reminded suddenly of how she had felt on the spring day in 1940 when she had first found herself as old Jack Armstrong's employee in the hut at the quarry that served as an office for the haulage business. She'd been new to everything then, wholly untried. Now, twenty-three years later, she had a wealth of experience behind her; and not just that of an efficient office clerk. Of course, she was good at keeping accounts, writing letters and dealing with customers, but she had also made herself keep abreast of every piece of government legislation and regulation to do with the transport industry. And her eyes and ears had always been open to take in everything to do with the running of the business. But for all her close involvement she had never really been more than an assistant, to her father-in-law or to her husband. Technically, she had of course been a partner in the business since Jack Armstrong's death, but Bradley and his brother Jackson had at all times combined to ensure that she had no voice in what was done. If ever she'd wanted them to take up her ideas – as they did, on occasion – she had to make them somehow believe that they were their own ideas, that they had nothing to do with her. More often, she simply fumed inwardly as she saw them make stupid decisions, take unwise actions – or, more often, fail to take wise ones – knowing she could do nothing to change things. She had itched then to make her voice heard – longed to take control.

Well, now she had her wish; she *was* in control. This unimpressive room – with its small window looking over the forecourt, its desk which needed folded paper under one leg to stop it wobbling, its two hard chairs and its shelves cluttered with a few bags of sweets for sale, the cans of oil, battered ledgers and account books – was hers alone. *This is my office*, she thought. *My responsibility. The heart of my new business.* The thought was at once exhilarating and terrifying. The carrier's business that had developed and changed over more than a hundred years in the Dale, had now found its focus and hope in her, an outsider with what seemed to her at this moment alarmingly little experience. She was Jack Armstrong's heir, and it was in her hands to restore the firm to what it had once been – or to fail.

She was not going to fail. As if to underline the point, she set herself the task of putting everything in order, so that in an instant she would be able to lay her hands on whatever she might need. She could have done all this work before today, while Jackson was still considering her offer, but she had preferred to leave it until she was certain it was to be hers – superstition, she supposed, for fear that to presume too much should make it all fall flat.

That done, she sat down and opened the weekly account book at a fresh page; the first page of her business. She would have liked to start an entirely new book, a fresh start in every way, but she had to keep costs to a minimum. A new account book was in no sense a necessity. She inscribed the date, and then underneath printed her own name in neat characters, underlining the words with care. Then she put the book aside and considered the two pieces of paper dealing with business still outstanding; the one, drawn up by herself, recording details of a car that had been in for major repairs when Bradley died and was still not put right; the other, a scrappy note in Bradley's writing which she had found at the haulage depot, concerning an agreement to transport furniture in two days' time for an elderly widow who was moving to a smaller house but could not afford a proper removal firm. Bradley would have done the work for cash in hand, no questions asked, no records kept; Diana had no intention of getting on the wrong side of the law before she even had a carrier's licence in her own name, but nor would she leave the old woman in the lurch – she would do the work without charge, as a goodwill gesture.

There was also a note she'd made the day before Bradley's death, when she'd heard that the steel works at Meadhope were looking for a new contractor to carry stone from one of the quarries that supplied them, now beyond the reach of the railway line. She'd meant to tell Bradley about it, in the rather vain hope that he might be interested – her wartime contacts with the firm might be useful, particularly since she'd also known the manager socially before the war. But that had been two weeks ago, and by now he might have agreed the contract with another firm. It was worth investigating, though – once she was sure that she would have at least one more-or-less reliable driver still working for her, and a lorry fit to use.

That was her chief task, to win over the three men who had worked for Bradley, to convince them that there would be no hazard in working for her instead. They'd been instructed to come to the petrol station tomorrow morning, to learn their fate; Diana knew they'd be expecting to be given their final wage packets and told that their services were no longer required, or at least not by Armstrong's. She had no illusions about the men. The most skilled workers had long since left a firm that was clearly failing, and those who were left probably stayed because no one else would have them. She was going to have to attract other, better mechanics and drivers if she was to make a success of the business. But that was for the near future; for now, she still had to depend on these men, and needed their support for what she was doing.

She pulled paper and pencil towards her and wrote down everything she wanted to say to them, word for word, with much scratching out and rewriting, until she was reasonably satisfied that she had included everything. Later, after supper, she returned to it, spending the evening in front of her dressing table mirror, trying various stances, reading the words over and over until she had more or less committed them to memory. Then she wrote her little speech out again, this time simply with headings to jog her memory. After that she recited it over a few more times, until she felt she could speak with ease. But it would of course be different tomorrow morning, when the men stood before her, and she had to speak directly to them.

It *was* different. After a night of fitful sleep, she felt quite unable to eat any breakfast. She dressed with great care in the neat moss-green suit that she used to wear to Carol's school functions, clothing that could be guaranteed not to embarrass her daughter. She recalled with some surprise that the last time she had worn it had been at the meeting with Ronnie nearly two years ago, which she did not now want to recall in the least. It was the one single occasion when she had come close to being unfaithful to Bradley. Lust, she thought now, with a sense of disgust; and frustration, because Bradley had for a long time been too persistently drunk for sex. That was all it had been, though at the time she knew she had begun to think it was love. She still felt a surge of anger whenever she thought of Ronnie. She had not thought him capable of such insensitivity, to approach Jackson when his brother was not even buried, to ask him, at that most vulnerable of moments, to sell the business. She knew she had in the past come very close to loving him; now she despised him, and regretted that she had ever felt so close, had once even allowed him to kiss her. Very likely he had only done that because he hoped in some devious way to use the attraction between them to his advantage, to further his business interests. Well, now she would exorcise the memory, linking the clothes she had worn on that day with this new venture.

She was just dusting her too-shiny nose with powder when she heard the steps of the men crossing the forecourt. A final swift glance in the mirror, and then she descended the stairs, hunger and terror churning together in her stomach.

Out in the yard, reached through an archway below the flat, she found the men standing in a huddle, talking, though they looked round as she emerged from the archway and fell silent, turning to face her, their expressions braced for what she had to say.

Stan Hall, the garage mechanic, she knew well: a cheerful, easy-going man, father of three young children. He was willing enough, but too little concerned that he often misdiagnosed what was wrong with a vehicle, or got behind with his work. Norman Peart, a short square-set man in his fifties, had first been employed in the repair yard at the garage, but for some years now he had been driver-mechanic for the haulage side of the business, run as always from the disused quarry where Diana had first worked for Bradley's father. She knew little about him, except that he lived near the quarry, and that his nephew Colin, at sixteen a younger version of himself, worked there too as an apprentice mechanic.

Stan Hall greeted her with what seemed to her a rather nervous cheerfulness as she came up to them. The Pearts simply looked at her without a word. Expecting to be dismissed, they must have been as nervous as she was, with more reason perhaps. There was not a great deal of alternative work in the Dale, especially for those without exceptional skills.

"Good morning," she said, and then came to a halt, her mind suddenly, alarmingly, blank. All the carefully prepared words had fled. In their place what came into her mind were Jackson's words to her after they'd agreed the sale: "You'll be bankrupt within a month," he had predicted, with scarcely concealed relish. He had never liked her, of course, from a mixture of jealousy and resentment of her abilities and her high standing with his father. But that did not mean his prediction was wrong. *What have I done?* she found herself thinking.

But she had done it. There was no turning back. She forced a smile and took a deep breath, and, deciding abruptly that a set speech was quite the wrong approach, found new spontaneous words to say what she wanted. She began by telling them that she had bought the firm, watching astonishment break through the resignation of their expressions. "It's not going to be easy,

16

I know that," she admitted. "You'll know as well as I do what a way we have to go to get Armstrong's back to anything like what it was in the old days. But with your help and support that's what I mean to do. We're going to need more men, more vehicles and a lot of hard work by every one of us. There are going to be many changes for us all to face.

"And there's one thing above all that's going to change, and stay changed: anyone who works for this firm lays off drink while he's working, whether it's in the yard, the depot or out on the road – and no one under any circumstances comes to work drunk either. Anyone who does is out of a job, just like that. Is that understood?" There was a murmur which she hoped was one of agreement, or at least of aquiescence, though it might have been tinged with resentment too. She moved on swiftly to her final words, which she knew would prove more palatable to them. "I'm keeping you on at the same wages for the present. But if we do well, if things go as I hope, then there'll be benefits for all of us. Anyone who plays a part in making this firm a success will be sure to feel the benefit in his pay packet. That's a promise I make to you, and one I intend to keep."

She waited for the murmurs of approval, the smiles, the relief and satisfaction; even, perhaps, the congratulatory handshakes. Instead there was a long silence. Norman Peart's head was bent, as if he were still trying to take in what she had said; the boy was looking at him, seeking a lead perhaps. Stan Hall did look at her, but shiftily, only half meeting her gaze, and eventually blew through pursed lips and said, "Why, that's a turn up! Who would have thought it?" Then he too bent his head, and shuffled his feet uneasily.

Diana felt sick, disappointed, hesitant. What now? There was work to be done, but she had not planned the next step, to move the men from this meeting to the day's tasks. "I'll just set the men on," old Jack Armstrong used to say, and she had known what he meant by the words, having seen him do it often enough. Now she had to "set the men on", and she suddenly had no idea at all how to go about it.

Another deep breath. "Stan, I believe Mr Wilkinson's car's still not ready. Can I count on you to have it done by this evening?"

Stan shook his head, in the manner of garage mechanics everywhere. "I'll see what I can do. Mind, it's in a bad way. Take some doing."

"Then I'll let you get on with it without delay," she said firmly. She turned away from him. "Norman, will you and Colin come with me to the office, please?"

There, she told them of the possible contract with the steel works. "I need your assurance it could be done, if we put in a tender. I don't want anyone to say we can't keep to our undertakings. I know you've made a start on the Foden. Are you going to be able to get it back on the road?" The eight-wheeler Foden was the vehicle Bradley had crashed so fatally. It had been severely damaged, but was the only one of the firm's remaining vehicles to be licensed for general haulage; the other, a Commer four-wheeler, was long past its best.

Norman said nothing, simply stared at her with his dour expression. Was he offended, scornful, dismayed? She could not begin to read his expression. Should she say something more, to prompt a response? But if so, what?

"Reckon so. Could do with more drivers though."

Was that a negative or a positive response? "I know," she said. "And a new wagon, as soon as possible. I'm looking into it. If you know of a first-class driver-mechanic I might approach to work with us, please let me know. But the question is, can we take anything on as things are, without doing all that first?"

Another silence, then he nodded. "Aye, reckon so."

"Good. Thank you. I'll contact the steel works then. Nothing may come of it, but if it does I'll be up to the quarry to see you. If not, there'll be other work, I promise you that. Meanwhile, I'd like you to make sure everything's in order up there."

He nodded, made some mumbled sound which she took to be acquiescence and turned to go. Halfway to the door, he halted, muttered, "You could try Ray Bennet. Cowcleugh man, works for Shaws. Might be tempted. Good driver." Then, not waiting to gauge her reaction, he left the office, the boy at his heels.

She watched them go, wondering if she would ever find them easy to deal with, and indeed if it was worth the effort. She knew little of Norman Peart's abilities. The fact that he lived near the quarry might indicate that its convenience weighed more with him than the efficiency of the firm; he might be more highly skilled than most of Bradley's workforce had been over the years. That remained to be seen. As for Colin, he had given even less indication of what he was made of. His expression was not simply dour, like his uncle's, but blank. She did not have high hopes for him. But at least she knew now what her next move must be. And after that, if all went well, she would try Ray Bennet.

Two

Diana returned from Meadhope elated with her success. It was only a three months' trial contract, but so long as she could prove how reliable and efficient they were, then it would be extended. All she needed now was a new wagon and another driver, so that they did not have to rely solely on a man or a vehicle which might fail in some way, without warning. *All!* she thought, amused at her own temerity. But after the uncertainties of the early morning, she now felt confident and happy, sure of success. She believed in herself, if no one else did.

It was well past lunchtime – nearly two o'clock – and she was ravenously hungry. But having parked the van down the side road beside the garage she made her way across the forecourt towards the office, to sort the paperwork before driving up to the quarry. She would take a Mars bar from stock to keep her going through the afternoon. A proper meal could wait.

Someone was standing outside the office door, clearly waiting for her, a strongly made man of medium height, with thick dark hair and an expression of quizzical affection – a man sure of his welcome.

She felt a rush of anger. How dare he come here, so brazenly, after what he had done, as if he were not aware of wrongdoing, or any possible grounds for offence! Had he no conscience? After a momentary faltering, she strode towards him, her expression frosty, while under the surface more complicated feelings seethed unbidden.

She had not seen him for many months, apart from a distant glimpse at Bradley's funeral. What had happened that day had wiped out any trace of the feelings she had once had for him – or so she had thought. Now suddenly they all came flooding back. Desire surged through her veins, stopped her breath; she felt as if she were choking. His grey eyes – the more pale under the fierce black line of the brows – met hers, and hot colour, unwanted, wholly unwanted, prickled its way through her skin. She tried to make some cutting remark, indicative of her anger, but no words came, none at all. She could only remember how it had felt when he kissed her; remembered, because she felt it again.

"I've just heard what you've done," he said. She had forgotten his voice too until now, how deep it was, yet soft, the lilt of the Sunderland accent. It was a voice she felt rather than heard.

What have I done? she wondered. *What is he accusing me of?*

He must have seen her puzzlement. "I was to call on Jackson this morning, for his answer." There was a hint of a rueful smile. "He told me you've stolen a march on me."

She realised then what he was talking about: her buying of the business. Her mind cleared. She recalled everything that had happened in the past fortnight, the ruthless ambition, unguessed at until then (but he had, after all, built a thriving business from nothing), which had caused him to ride roughshod over all decent feelings, to importune the brother of a dead man, at the funeral itself; he'd not even been prepared to wait for a decent interval to pass, forcing both Jackson and herself into a speedy decision. She did not regret the decision, but she hated the way it had been brought about. And now he had the nerve to call upon her here, as if nothing had changed between them, as if her eyes had not been so brutally opened to what he was! The disorder inside her subsided to a tremor she could easily ignore. "I'm so sorry to disappoint you," she said, in an icy tone that meant the opposite.

Disconcertingly, the tenderness in his expression only deepened. "You couldn't do that. Surprise me, aye; delight me. But not disappoint. I can't wait to see what you make of it all. Tell me, do you mean to expand the car repair side of things? You won't be thinking of getting the haulage business on the road again."

"Won't I? Are you afraid of the competition?"

"Of course not! But you'd not get a carrier's licence anyway."

He had touched on a raw nerve, the one fear she had, but thought she had dealt with, though her tone in reply was confident, defiant even. "Bradley's licence covers me for now. And it's the same business. They'd have no reason not to transfer it to me. I do hope that's given you something to keep you awake at night."

To her astonishment, in spite of the acidity of her tone, he smiled then, a gentle smile, and the eyes that rested so intently on her face were full of warmth. "It's not that keeps me awake, Diana. Just you, whatever you do." His voice tailed off in huskiness. Then he drew a long shuddering breath and burst out: "Marry me, Diana!"

Again, all her equilibrium was overthrown, all her anger. She stared at him, her own breath caught in her throat. It was almost as if what he said made no sense, could not be understood. Then, suddenly, she saw that it did, that it could; only too clearly. Her anger flared up again. "Do you think I can't see your game?"

"Game . . . ?" he faltered. He looked puzzled, bewildered.

"You can't get the business one way so you'll try another! Oh no, you don't lay your hands on it that easily! I'm not a fool."

Was that really shock on his face? He reached out his hands towards her, though she stepped back, beyond his grasp. "I love you. I've always loved you." His voice sounded rough, unsteady. He let his hands fall, his expression suddenly dismayed. "I'm sorry, it's way too soon—"

"Oh, I know that wouldn't stop you!"

"Please," he went on, pleading, "forget I said anything! It just came out, that's all."

"Do you expect me to believe that?" She'd felt so much, too much. She had almost risked her marriage for him. And now this! She fumbled in her bag for the office key. Then she raised her head and forced herself to look him straight in the eye, her voice smooth with ice. "You are a cold, ruthless, calculating man who puts ambition before everything. I don't know why I ever wasted a moment's thought on you, but I bitterly regret it, all of it." She could see he was trying to speak, but she ploughed on relentlessly. "Don't try and deny anything. Actions speak louder than words, and your callousness on the day of Bradley's funeral opened my eyes, for good and all." She shifted her gaze from his face – dismayed, astonished as it looked – and took a step towards him; or, rather, past him towards the office door. "Now, I've work to do, if you haven't. Excuse me."

He caught her arm. "Diana, I don't know . . . Please—!"

She shook him off. "How dare you touch me?" One cold glance from the ice-green of her eyes. "Don't worry; I wouldn't have married you anyway. I've had enough of marriage. But even if I hadn't you'd be well beneath my consideration, beyond my contempt even. You have no idea of what's right or decent, of civilised behaviour." Thinking that sounded rather harsher than she meant – though he deserved it, all of it! – she reached up to put her key in the lock, wishing her hands did not shake so obviously. "Now, would you be so good as to leave? I've work to do."

She did not look round to see him go, but heard his departing steps, the car door slam, the Riley's engine purring into motion. It was a long time before she had her emotions under sufficient control to recall what she had to do next.

Ronnie drove back to Meadhope in a fury of hurt and anger. He was bewildered at the change in her since their last meeting. How could he so have misread the situation? He'd at least thought she had some respect for him – no, more than that, he was sure that she had more than a little tenderness for him. Yet today she had treated him as if he were some menial who had got above himself. True enough, his background was not like hers, but then she'd always known that, known that the evacuee she'd met during the war had been born in the slums of Sunderland, one of bastard twins of a naive girl and a sailor of whom she'd known only the name, Roald – the name that was now his, though it appeared only on official documents. Until today he'd not felt that this mattered. Enchanted by her right from the start, he could not imagine that the adolescent passion he'd felt for her would ever have developed into any kind of adult love without a sense that there was some sympathy between them, that she met him as an equal, that she was even attracted in her turn. After all, once, passionately, they had kissed, and he'd been sure then that she wanted him. Now, abruptly, without warning, it had all changed. He was puzzled, and terribly hurt.

At Meadhope he parked the car in its usual place, brushed past his manager, Bill Akehurst, who had come to meet him, and ran up the stairs to his office – the same office where, once, he had held Diana in his arms and thought the universe was his for the asking – and slammed the door shut behind him. When, a moment later, Bill Akehurst knocked on the door, coming in soon after, he was greeted with an uncharacteristic frown. "Well?" Ronnie's fingers drummed impatiently on the table top.

"Thought you should know, Mr Shaw. We didn't get the steel contract."

The drum beats ceased, fingers poised to resume. "We didn't? Why not?"

"Armstrong's got in first."

Ronnie leapt to his feet, his weight pressed forward on the desk. "Armstrong's? How come?"

There was such an air of scarcely restrained fury about him that Bill stepped back a little before replying, "You know Mrs Armstrong's bought up the firm?"

"News travels fast." Ronnie's expression was as tight-lipped as ever, but unsurprised. Bill could sense the tension that still held him poised for what was to come; it disturbed him, and he shuffled his feet uneasily.

"Why then, she's a woman. You know how women get their way – we can't match them on that. She's still a good looker. I don't doubt she used it . . ."

Ronnie drew in his breath, grabbed hold of a glass paperweight with a miniature Blackpool tower inside it and hurled it in fury

24

at the opposite wall; Bill ducked, though it passed nowhere near him. "Damn that woman to hell!" He glowered at Bill. "We've known about that contract for weeks. Why wasn't anything done about it?"

Bill reddened, then looked defiant. "There wasn't anyone else on the market for it, not with Bradley Armstrong dead. That's what I thought."

"Then you thought wrong, didn't you?" He took a deep breath, and calmed himself a little. After all, it was a small contract, and there was plenty of other work, both outside and inside the Dale. "Next time, don't hang about. I don't want Armstrong's getting a hold."

"No, Mr Shaw." The sharpness was still there in Ronnie's tone, and Bill was uneasy. He'd never known his boss to lose his temper like this before, not in all the time he'd worked for him. Ronnie Shaw was known as a good-humoured, fair-minded man – determined, stubborn, single-minded, certainly, or he would never have got where he had, a man who demanded the best from his employees, as from himself. But bad-tempered? Never! Something had clearly happened today that had overturned all his everyday qualities. Bill didn't know Mrs Armstrong personally, but he knew she was the daughter of old Dr Poultney, now retired. Probably thought herself a cut above everyone else, and had maybe let it show some time; Mr Shaw had never seemed a man to be prickly about such things, but you never knew. "Mind, she's not going to keep that contract long, I'd say. One clapped out old wagon, the other hardly fit for the road, and only Norman Peart to drive – how long can that last?"

As he turned to go Bill saw that the remark had appeared to cheer his boss, but as he descended the stairs it occurred to him that she might possibly have money behind her from somewhere, beyond what was needed to buy out her brother-in-law. In which case it might in the end be a different story, requiring some kind of effective action . . .

Diana returned to the flat late in the day; she was exhausted and very hungry, her eagerness for the success of the firm a little deflated by a confrontation with the inadequacies of Bradley's legacy to her. It looked as if Norman would get the Foden back on the road, but it was never going to be as good as it had been, and the Commer was quite inadequate for the work they would be doing, and in any case needed a new licence. If she were to be able to meet the demands of any contract – even the limited one she had just signed – she must buy another reliable wagon, very soon. Certainly she'd allowed for such expenses in agreeing a loan with her father, but she'd rather hoped she could have put that one off for a few weeks, at least. Apart from anything else, there was so much to do at the moment. She did not want to have to spend time examining promising second-hand vehicles, especially as she was going to need to take Norman with her, since he was the only one with adequate knowledge of what to look for.

Norman was the other problem, of course. He was the best – effectively, the only – driver she had and she'd have to make the best of him, but though she judged that he was honest and conscientious, in a plodding sort of way, she wanted her employees to be enthusiastic, as concerned as she was for the good of the firm. More to the point, from things he'd let fall in the course of conversation, and from Bradley's imperfect records, it looked as if he'd recently enjoyed less than perfect health. A driver who was often absent through sickness was simply going to make things more difficult still for her. There was of course Ray Bennet, on whom she intended to call this evening when he returned to his home at Cowcleugh, not far from the depot, but she was not hopeful that a man who was reputed to be one of Shaw's best drivers was likely to be tempted away to work for her.

Halfway up the stairs, Diana heard the phone ringing inside the flat. Resisting the temptation to ignore it (something might be wrong with Carol), she ran to unlock the door, flung it open and seized the receiver. Through her own gasping breath she heard a voice so tremulous with feeling that it took her a moment or two to realise it was her brother-in-law. "Diana," Jackson said, "I thought you should know. Mam had a stroke this afternoon. She's dead." Then, "It's my guess she didn't want to live, with Bradley gone. It broke her heart, that."

Another funeral, so soon after the last. From a sense of duty, Diana went to pay her respects – though that was hardly the word, when there had been such mutual dislike between her and the dead woman. As she drove towards the Methodist chapel at Ravenshield, where all the significant stages of the Armstrong family had been marked (except her own marriage to Bradley, which been held in the chilly beauty of Wearbridge parish church), she recalled her last confrontation – the last of many – with Elsie, on Monday when she'd signed the documents to buy the business. Jackson had predicted disaster for her, clearly relishing the prospect. So had Elsie, but she had added her own sharper gloss on the day: "You needn't think to come to us when things go wrong. You're not one of us anymore. Not that you ever were, if we had but known it." The words had been, Diana knew, her dismissal from Ravenshield, the farm, the life there and the family. In the past, she'd longed to be excluded from the inevitable Sunday dinners, the constant demands made on her life. Now, perversely, she'd felt hurt, and angry too.

Today, five days later, she tried to push away her anger, tried to recall the very early days, when she had first known she was pregnant and Bradley's family had welcomed her unquestioningly, with little sign of the condemnation that her parents had shown. That in the end it had been her parents who had supported her most must not make a difference today, when she was going to Elsie's funeral. Somehow she had to cling on to that solitary cause of gratitude to the dead woman. After today, that would indeed be the end of it.

Carol was already in the church, looking pale and sad. She sat with her Armstrong cousins, fenced firmly in so that there was no place near her which her mother could take. There was no sign of Kenny. Nor of Ronnie, who she'd been afraid might be there.

27

Diana wept during the service, but for her own hurt, not for her mother-in-law. Her brief moment of gratitude had not lasted. She was glad that Elsie had gone.

Outside, after the burial, she went up to Carol, trying to ignore the immediate shutting up of her daughter's expression, the coldness in her eyes; she was not, then, forgiven for her omission the other day. She forced a smile, said quietly, "Let me give you a lift back."

"I'm going on to the farm," Carol said. There was an implied rebuke in her tone, at her mother's failure to observe the niceties. Not that she would have been welcome at the funeral tea, Diana knew. But it was another marking of the barrier between the two of them, and it hurt.

She watched Carol walk away to where her cousin, Jackson's younger daughter Susan, was waiting for her. Then she made her way sadly back to the van. Would it ever get better? Or would she find that even when her grandchild arrived she was still excluded?

As she drove home she tried to keep her mind on business matters – where she was going to find a good reliable second-hand wagon, how she might entice drivers and mechanics to work for her, without paying them more than she could afford. Such thoughts might present her with problems, but at least they brought no hurt with them.

Back at the petrol station, Stan Hall came to meet her as she got out of the van. He was waving a copy of *Commercial Motor*. "There's a Leyland six-wheeler in here, A-licensed, five-year-old. Darlington firm selling up. Air brakes too. You'll have to be quick, mind."

She could, almost, have embraced him. It looked as if one problem might be within reach of a solution. All she needed now was an answer from Ray Bennet, who was "thinking about it." She had no idea which way he would decide, but dared not be hopeful.

When the funeral tea was over, the washing up done, the dishes

28

put away, Carol's cousin Irene, Jackson's eldest daughter, a sensible young woman married to a farmer whose land adjoined the Byers' smallholding, walked back with her over the river meadows. At first, they reminisced about their grandmother, but when they paused to negotiate a stile, Carol asked suddenly. "Is it true that Grandad Armstrong left part of his business to my Mam?"

Irene looked at her sideways. "Didn't you know? Of course, you weren't born then, and no one wanted much said about it afterwards. But I can remember the fuss about it. Oh, there was a fuss too! Dad was furious – why, you can see how that would be. Doing him and your dad out of what was rightly theirs, that's how they saw it. It was too, of course." Questioned further, she explained how old Jack Armstrong had left his business equally three ways – to his two sons, and to Diana, the wife of his younger son.

"Then shouldn't she have had a say in it all this time? I thought she just worked for it sometimes, because she was married to Dad."

"Aye, well, my Dad and yours could outvote her every time. So long as they worked together, she counted for nothing. There was only one time she ever made a difference that I recall – it would have been Coronation year, when Ronnie Shaw wanted to buy us out. Dad wanted to take his offer, but Uncle Bradley didn't – and your Mam backed him, so he won. You don't forget the sort of atmosphere we had at home then, I can tell you."

Before Carol could say anything, the roar of a motorbike interrupted her thoughts. She glanced across at the point where the road was just visible, and saw Kenny shoot along it. Clearly, unmistakably, she saw that he had a passenger behind him, a girl with a pony tail flying behind her. She saw how Irene glanced at her, concerned; she had seen it too then. Carol tried hard to look nonchalant. "Grandad must have thought highly of Mam, then," she said, as if nothing had happened.

"Aye, he must have done. But Dad would never have agreed

with that. In any case, she was just his daughter-in-law. It wasn't right."

They parted where a plank bridge crossed a muddy stream that led directly to the yard, where Kenny was by now bent over his bike as innocently as if nothing out of the ordinary had occurred. There was no sign at all of any passenger. Perhaps, Carol thought, with a mixture of alarm and fury, for him there had been nothing out of the ordinary. Perhaps he habitually took other girls on his pillion.

Kenny glanced at her as she came up to him, but did not ask how the funeral had gone. She suspected he'd already forgotten where she had been, if he'd ever gone so far as to register her grandmother's death at all. "Who was that on your pillion?"

She had his full attention now, and his fair skin was flooded with colour. *Guilt!* she thought triumphantly. *Good!*

"I don't know what you mean," he responded, unconvincingly.

"Kenny, I saw her, riding behind you, just a moment ago, passing through Ravenshield!"

He bent his head, schooling his voice to casual unconcern. "Oh, her – just someone I gave a lift to."

"Who?"

"Brenda Kidd."

Brenda Kidd was notorious; she was also blonde and shapely, a sort of lesser Marilyn Monroe.

"You've no cause to be jealous," said Kenny. "That's all it was – just a lift."

Jealous? Was she jealous? Surely you needed to care about someone to be jealous of a rival's attentions? No, what she felt was more a sense of disgust, as if the incident simply confirmed her own low opinion of Kenny; and thus of herself, who had been so stupid as to marry him, freely, without compulsion. And, of course, of her mother, who for all her apparent wisdom had failed to put a stop to it.

She felt suddenly tired, too tired to pursue the matter. What did she care, after all? She shrugged – not that Kenny saw, since he wasn't looking at her – and went up the outside steps to their shared room above the byre. It was a long, low-ceilinged room, plastered once at some long-forgotten period, but now in poor repair with cracks and damp patches patterning the walls, and furnished only with a threequarter bed, an unsteady table and two wormy kitchen chairs that her mother would have condemned as fit only for firewood. It was cold too, for the sole potential warmth came from a paraffin heater, which for safety reasons was lit only when they were using the room for any length of time, which they rarely did. It was not the sort of room that encouraged long use.

It was not the sort of room in which anyone would choose to bring up a baby either. Carol stood looking at it in something approaching despair, trying to see what alternative there might be. She was not used to finding herself in unpleasant situations from which there was no escape. She had, until these past months, always been good at wriggling her way out of any difficulty, whether by charm or guile. This was different, and very much harder.

She changed out of her funeral clothes into her comfortable everyday clothes; or what had been her comfortable everyday clothes. The skirt, gradually getting tighter about the waist, would not easily fasten at all now. She frowned at the top button, not wanting to force it into the buttonhole, for fear of harming the child. Then she remembered that she had an elastic band in her old school pencil case – she used to fasten her pony tail with it, before she had her hair cut last year – and went to find it, among the clutter of her belongings piled in boxes and a suitcase at the far end of the room. She looped it through the buttonhole and then hooked it over the button. Success! She felt better now, satisfied that the small problem was solved. The other couldn't be solved so easily, but there would be a solution, somehow, even if she couldn't see it at the moment. *Give it time,* she told herself. *I'll see what to do.*

On the Friday of the funeral, at which anger at Diana's treatment of him had prevented him from attending in spite of kindly memories of old Elsie Armstrong, Ronnie drove back to Sunderland, after more than a week's absence. He returned, a disappointed man, to the tiny, neat terraced house near the river which had, until lately, been shared with his twin sister, Freda. He was not a man for whom material things meant much, and this simply furnished house, together with the room next to the office at Meadhope with its single bed in which he slept when business took him to the Dale, provided him with all he needed. What resources he had, he preferred to put into the business, here and at Meadhope. It was a strategy that had brought its reward in constant expansion.

He let himself into the house, which felt cold and cheerless. Once, Freda would have been here to welcome him, with a hot meal and bathwater ready for his use. But a fortnight ago she had at last married the man she'd been engaged to without apparent passion for the past ten years. Ronnie had been glad for her, at the time, the more so because the coincidence of Bradley Armstrong's death had brought him new hope. He'd left here last week with that hope setting him aglow. Now the chill of the house only seemed to drive home to him how deeply he had failed. He was not accustomed to failure.

The telephone rang as he was starting to light the fire. He swore under his breath, wishing for once that he'd not decided to have it installed. It had seemed a good idea to be able to be reached at any time by his employees, but this evening that seemed a less than comfortable arrangement. He went to wash the coal dust off his hands, hoping the ringing would cease before he reached the phone. It did not, and he heard the relief in Bill Akehurst's voice as he answered. "Mr Shaw – thought you should know. Ray Bennet's gone over to Armstrong's. Nearer to home, he says, so he'll get more time with his bairns. But it's my belief she offered him better wages too, though he wouldn't say." There was a long silence, after which Bill said, "Mr Shaw, are you there?"

"Aye – aye, I'm here." Ronnie spoke through clenched teeth. "So – she's got money behind her, I suppose."

"There's one thing, Mr Shaw. Didn't think of it the other day. Will she get a carrier's licence – a woman, and the business so rundown anyway? I reckon Bradley Armstrong would have lost his if he'd lived."

"But he died, didn't he? And his widow can operate without for the first few weeks. She seemed confident enough she'd get it after that. Normally, it would be automatic, no objections allowed." His tone sharpened. "Mind, as you say, this isn't normal. If we get the chance, we'll oppose it every inch of the way. I reckon we've good grounds. At the very least that'll stop her meeting the steel works contract. Keep me informed, Bill."

When Bill had rung off, Ronnie gave up on the fire and decided to go out for a pint and a pork pie in the pub round the corner. He wished he had a woman for company, but most of the women whose company he might have enjoyed were married by now. Except Diana, the only woman he'd ever wanted, who on Tuesday had suddenly and inexplicably looked at him as if he were something nasty she'd trodden in. All that softness he remembered, the moment of passion – had that only been a way of relieving boredom, or even of getting a kind of obscure revenge on Bradley for his neglect of her? Whatever it had been, it now seemed to have vanished without trace. Widowed, Diana Armstrong seemed more remote from him than she had ever been as a wife.

Three

In the room over the byre, Carol gave the baby her bottle and put her into the cot to sleep. Her daughter, a peaceful child, immediately closed her eyes. In the far corner of the room, near the smelly paraffin heater, Kenny was slouching in a chair with his feet – clad in grey socks even more malodorous than the heater – resting on the table. A half-empty mug of tea stood within reach, from which he slurped noisily from time to time. He had come in about half an hour ago, but had not troubled to acknowledge the presence either of wife or daughter, except by demanding the cup of tea, which Carol had grudgingly made for him, though sorely tempted to tell him to make it himself. But it was, she supposed, part of being a wife, to minister to the needs of a man just in from work – or what, in Kenny's life, passed for work. He'd taken the mug without a word and settled to drink. Now, suddenly, he decided to speak. "Your Mam's up the creek, from what I hear. That driver she poached from Shaw's – well, he's gone back to them. Can't stomach working for a woman, no matter what she pays him. And Norman Peart's on the sick. She's no one else to drive for her."

Carol only half heard him, aware more of the note of malicious pleasure in his voice than of what he was actually saying. Then the news reached her, first as something that did not really concern her, or even interest her very much; then, as she absorbed it, as something that could be made to affect her deeply. She stood still beside the cot, looking down at the sleeping child but not seeing her at all. "I expect she'll drive herself," she said easily. "She's a good driver, my Mam."

Kenny gave a disbelieving snort. "She's a woman – everyone knows what they're like behind a wheel!"

Carol turned to face him, hands on hips. Even from there, she could smell his feet. *Stupid little runt*, she was thinking with distaste, *how could I ever have married him?* Aloud, she said, "How come I passed my test first time then?"

"Examiner fancied you. They always go easy on women. Fact! Besides, your Mam can't do everything, drive, mechanic *and* run the office. And who's going to give a contract to a woman driver? No one in their right mind."

Carol was on the point of arguing, then decided against it. He wasn't worth the bother. Turning her back on Kenny, she went to tackle today's pile of ironing. Soon afterwards Kenny went out, saying nothing to Carol and leaving the dirty mug exactly where it was on the table. Carol went to open the window to clear the air – just for a moment, for the November afternoon was raw. She no longer wondered where he was going or if he was meeting another girl; she no longer cared. Besides, there were other things on her mind.

Diana had spent part of the day at the depot, trying to keep Colin busy with essential maintenance work – without his uncle's watchful eye on him he seemed almost helpless, and she came close to despair. Tomorrow there would be another load to deliver to Meadhope, and the Leyland had to be ready in time, particularly as, in the absence of anyone else, she would have to drive it, for the second time this week. Her knowledge of the mechanics of the vehicles she owned was sketchy, to say the least. She'd hoped, rather desperately, that Colin might have some idea who else she could approach to work for her; she'd visited Norman on her way to the quarry, but he'd had no helpful suggestions either – she'd already approached everyone he knew, with no success. The best drivers already had jobs, and were not tempted by any wage she could offer, especially as few of them wanted to work for a woman.

She had thought Ray Bennet was the answer. She'd been

delighted when, lured by the prospect of working so close to home and for a slightly higher wage, he'd agreed to drive for her. He'd proved to be a cheerful and reliable driver as well as a skilled mechanic. She'd been impressed, too, by the way he'd faced some initial unpleasantness from his former workmates. Often, in those early days, he would find a Shaw's lorry parked awkwardly across his path when making a delivery, or driving slowly and waveringly in front of him on the Dale road, preventing him from overtaking. But he'd taken it all cheerfully, refusing to lose his temper. "They'll sharp get sick of it," he'd maintained, and since he'd not reported any recent trouble, she assumed they had. She had thought he would stay.

Until Monday morning, when he'd called early at the petrol station and told her, red-faced, that he was handing in his notice. Ronnie Shaw had approached him and offered to pay him exactly what Armstrong's paid; it had been enough to tempt him back. "To be honest, Mrs Armstrong, I'd sooner work for a man. No offence – you're a fair boss. I've no complaints. It just feels more natural, that's all, taking orders from a man."

She recognised by now that even her original employees did not much relish having a woman as a boss. Initially, they had stayed with her because they were not sufficiently skilled – or motivated – to go elsewhere. By now, they had at least begun to grow used to her, but she knew quite well that they didn't expect her to succeed as a businesswoman. It was certainly beginning to look as if they had a point.

Yet she could not wholly understand their attitude. When she'd worked on Bradley's behalf it had been different. They'd seemed to respect her then for her knowledge of the business and her good sense, a respect they did not always accord to Bradley himself. Even more had she been respected when working at the quarry alongside Bradley's father, in the wartime years. Then, even Jack Armstrong had deferred to her on occasions. Why should it be any different now, when she was in sole charge?

The trouble was that their attitude was beginning to sap her own confidence in herself, especially in this latest crisis. *I musn't let it get me down*, she thought as she drove back to Wearbridge. *I've got this far. I'm not going to give up now.*

What was she to do next? Find another good driver-mechanic and pay some wholly ridiculous wage to lure him to the firm? To appear to be using unfair tactics might put her licence at risk and jeopardise the future development of the firm – she was quite sure that Ronnie would seize on even the smallest piece of evidence to use against her. These days she felt as if he must be watching her every move, ready to take advantage the moment she put a foot wrong. She was beginning to understand how Bradley had come to hate his rival, though in those days she herself had not suspected him of underhand behaviour. What had happened since Bradley's death had made her see things rather differently.

By the time she reached the petrol station she was no nearer coming to any useful conclusion, and there she was only reminded of other problems she had still to confront. Because of this crisis, she'd been forced to postpone the interviews she'd been planning to hold tomorrow morning for a part-time clerk in the office here. She'd known right from the start that the distance between the petrol station and the haulage depot at the old quarry was going to be a problem for her. It had not been a problem when Bradley and his brother had run the business, nor, later, when Jackson concentrated on the farm and left things to Bradley, for by then she herself had been allowed to run the petrol station, with little interference from Bradley. Now, alone, she had to run both businesses, at a distance of more than ten miles. She'd tried to manage during the past months, leaving Stan (he now had a fifteen-year-old apprentice to help him) in charge when she was absent, but it had become progressively more obvious that she would have to employ someone to take charge, at least part-time, of the daily business of the petrol station – serving petrol, keeping the books, making appointments for servicing and repairing cars. She needed to be free to keep an eye on the haulage side when necessary, especially as she believed this was the area most open to expansion. Once – if ever – she had a core of thoroughly skilled and trusted employees for that part of the business, then she might feel able to leave them largely to their own devices, with the minimum of supervision, but until then she had to be there as often as possible. And now the need had become inescapable, before she had the necessary help in place.

Diana parked the van and waved to Stan and the apprentice, Kevin, hoping she looked cheerful and unconcerned. As she walked towards the office she overheard snatches of their conversation. They were discussing what they were planning to do this weekend; it was Thursday today, so there was only one more day to go.

The weekend, she thought wryly; now that she was a businesswoman there were no weekends for her in any real sense, only snatched days and hours. Until this latest crisis arrived, she'd been promising herself one treat in the following days, to arrange to meet with Carol and see the baby, her grandchild. It was the one thing that her life lacked, full as it was, enough contact with the new baby, for whom at times she felt a painful hunger that still surprised her by its intensity.

As long as she lived, she would recall the moment two months ago when the phone rang late one Friday night – 27 September – while she was sleepily checking the books before going to bed. With her mind on other things, she'd lifted the receiver.

"Mrs Armstrong?" It had taken her a moment or two to recognise Kenny's voice, by which time the words he'd spoken next had only begun to reach her brain. "The baby's born. A little girl . . . Why, she's fine, Carol's fine . . . We're calling her – what is it now? – Sharon, that's it."

An image had come into Diana's mind then, of a shrub in a gloomy corner of the garden at Dale House, where she had grown up. Unimpressive for most of the year, in summer it would burst into a mass of bright yellow flowers, whose stamens seemed dusted with gold – *Rose of Sharon*, that was its name. "It'll grow where nothing else will," her mother had said once. "The best plant to cheer a dark corner." And now, a child to cheer them all. "What a pretty name," she'd said, thinking how trite the words sounded, how inadequate. But then there were no words that could have expressed the joy she'd felt at that moment.

She'd called at the hospital the very next day, carrying flowers – but not, sadly, a Rose of Sharon – and had been enchanted by her first sight of the red-faced, crumpled sleeping infant, her lashes like gold dust on her plump cheeks. There had been no sign of Kenny. "He came to visiting last night." Carol had said. "Just as well she was born in time, or he'd have gone again, and I'd have had no one to phone up and tell you." Diana had sensed a move at reconciliation in the words – and indeed it was to her mother that Carol had turned when the time came to leave the hospital. Diana had filled the passenger seat in the van with cushions and driven her daughter and her grandchild home in triumph, saddened only that she had to leave them in that squalid room. Since then, she'd only seen little Sharon once, two weekends ago, just before Norman was struck down with some sort of flu.

Fighting a sense of desperation, trying as so often to repress a rising tide of panic, she tidied the office, locked up, and then ran up the stairs to the flat, her haven. Odd, she reflected, that it should be so. She'd hated this place when she first came here, longing to be back again at Fell Cottage, the tiny isolated stone house where her married life had begun and she had lived alone during the happy, fulfilled years of the war. Here, she'd hated the constant smell of petrol, the view of the road, the noise of traffic, longed for the open spaces, the call of the curlew, the wind in her face, the clear air. But since Bradley's death this place too had become her own, the place where she could shut the door on the world and be herself. Even when she brought her worries here with her, they seemed somehow diminished by the tranquillity, the solitude.

Already feeling better, she closed the door behind her, flipped off her shoes and made her way to the kitchen, one hand reaching out to switch on the radio, the other to bring the kettle to the sink. She stood, half listening, as the kettle filled. Part of her mind registered another sound – feet on the stairs; or was it? *We are just receiving reports that President Kennedy has been shot* . . . Shocked, she gave all her attention to the newsflash, while the kettle overflowed, splashing her suit. It was not until the drops reached her stockinged feet that she realised what was happening and quickly turned off the tap. The news report told of a motorcade, shots ringing out, the President slumping over, his wife distraught, the rush to the hospital. It sounded bad, she thought; a shocking thing, in this dangerous uncertain world.

The flat door opened. Dazed, she looked round. Carol stood there, just visible from the kitchen. "President Kennedy's been shot," Diana said. Then, abruptly, her mind switched to what she was seeing. Another shock.

Carol was holding the baby, well-wrapped against the cold and fast asleep, a dead weight in her arms. She was also, with difficulty, carrying a suitcase in one hand, which she dropped with relief to the floor. "I've left Kenny."

Diana ran to her, took the baby, scanned mother and child for any signs that harm had been done to them. There were none at all, and Carol seemed oddly cheerful. "You were right," she declared. "Kenny's not for me. I'm going to come and work with you."

Diana sat down abruptly on the sofa, while Sharon slept on, the peaceful heart of a room where the radio crackled out its message of disaster and Diana's private world too suddenly faced turmoil. She hoped that all she felt did not show on her face, because, beneath the natural concern, there lay dismay, a sense of being drowned by circumstance, of seeing all her new-found independence washed away. She also understood at last how her own mother had felt when she realised that the marriage for which Diana had fought so fiercely had proved to be as disastrous as she had expected. Carol had spoken of Kenny as if he were a mere casual boyfriend, who could be discarded in a moment. But it was not as simple as that, could not be. She had married him, made solemn promises of lifelong fidelity. You could not just turn your back on marriage as if it had never happened – Diana knew that well enough from her own bitter experience. And this marriage had lasted little more than a year, far too soon for it to be declared a failure. Unless . . . she swallowed hard; the marks might not show, but they might be there all the same. It would be reason enough, in her eyes. "What happened? He didn't hit you?"

"He wouldn't dare! He knows I'd hit him back harder. No. But I'm sick of playing second fiddle to a motorbike, and doing all the work while he does nothing. If I ever live with a man again, he'll be a man, not a kid."

"Have you talked about all this with him?"

"Have you tried talking to Kenny about anything but motorbikes? He's just not interested. He's not even interested in Sharon, not really. No, Mam, it's finished, and that's that."

There was, Diana realised, no point in pursuing the matter, at least not for the time being. "So you're coming back here, to live?" *Here, in this small flat which now feels just right for me alone; too small for two adults and a growing child.*

"If you'll have me." There was no doubt in Carol's expression or her voice. She was quite sure of her welcome. *After all*, Diana thought, *she is my daughter and I love her. She's quite right; in the end she means more to me than my freedom.* But the prospect oppressed her all the same.

"There's one thing," Carol said, as she carried her case towards her old room. "I'm driving for you."

Diana stared at her, while her mind struggled with the implications of her daughter's words. "But you haven't passed your test."

"I have, in June, soon as I could. Had to borrow Uncle Jackson's car – you can bet none of the Byers' cars was fit to use. And I could hardly get in the car I was that fat. But I passed first time."

"Why didn't you tell me? You know how pleased I'd have been."

Carol shrugged. "You know now." There was a hint of the dismissive, hurtful rebuffs of the past in her tone, but the next moment she said, "I didn't even tell Kenny till afterwards. I knew he wouldn't like it. Used what I'd got in the Post Office to pay for it. Anyway, I can drive. You need another driver don't you? I heard what happened."

"You can't, Carol. You're not old enough."

"I'm seventeen."

"You have to be twenty-one. For anything over two and a half tons."

Carol looked, not disappointed, but devastated. For a moment she was silent, as if trying to take in the full enormity of what Diana had just said. Her next reaction seemed to be disbelief, for she suddenly demanded, "How old were you when you were driving, in the war?"

Diana had been nineteen, the first time. "Things were different then. They needed every driver they could get hold of. But you wouldn't get away with it now. If I condoned anything like that, there'd be no chance I'd get the full A-licence, none at all. We'd be finished."

Carol slumped on to the sofa. "Haven't you got it yet?"

She didn't sound very interested, but Diana answered the question all the same. "No, only the one for the Meadhope contract. I've applied for the full one, but Ronnie Shaw's objected, though he's no firm grounds, yet. But I'm taking no chances. Not that it'll make any difference whether I get it or not, the way things are. At the moment we're finding it hard enough to meet our existing contract, let alone take on more." Trying to sound positive and encouraging, she added, "I *am* badly in need of a good mechanic. You could be just what I'm looking for."

There was a glimmer of interest in Carol's face, but only a glimmer. The next moment it was replaced by a furious scowl. She jumped up, hooked her foot under the footstool that her father had bought her mother one Christmas and sent it clattering across the room, where it came to rest against the sideboard. "Four whole years! Bloody hell! What the hell am I going to do with myself?"

"Go back to Kenny?" suggested Diana tentatively. Then, sensing the explosion that was about to hit her, added, "You could still work at the depot. Of course, there's Sharon . . ." She tailed off, feeling Carol's resistance.

"I'm not going back to Kenny! Never, so long as I live. You

don't know what it's been like. He doesn't care for me, not in the least and, as for Sharon, he only knows she's there when she cries, and then he gets angry and says I should shut her up. It's not as if she cries much anyway."

"No one forced you to marry him." It was one of those occasions when Diana wished the words unsaid before they were even out of her mouth. "I told you so" was hardly a helpful reaction, in the circumstances. Even her own mother had never quite brought herself to say it, when she saw how unhappy Diana was in her marriage – though Diana would have taken it meekly and Carol, most emphatically, did not.

She swung round on her mother. "You should have stopped me! You should have locked me in my room, shouted at me, anything! Then I wouldn't be in this mess. It's all your fault!"

"Then so is Sharon," said Diana quietly, trying hard to keep calm in the midst of the tornado that was sweeping through her tranquil flat. Her words brought a temporary lull, while Carol glanced at the child – somehow, miraculously, sleeping through the tumult – and then glowered again at her mother, who went on, "Perhaps you'd get on better with Kenny if you weren't living on top of his parents. Fell Cottage is still empty. Why not have a word with Uncle Jackson? He might let you both move in there."

"I don't want to live in the middle of nowhere, especially not with Kenny. Anyway, it wouldn't be any good. Kenny wouldn't let me work for you, not in a million years. He'd say there was enough to do at the farm."

"Is there?"

"Only because he never lifts a finger, except to his motorbike. Mam, I'm not going back. Marrying him was the worst thing I ever did, but going back to him would be the next worst." To Diana's relief she sat down again, heavily, as if the explosion had exhausted her. "What's for supper?"

Diana almost laughed, so incongruous was the sudden change of mood. In a moment, Carol was once again the hungry teenager home from school. But Diana sensed that laughter might only enrage her daughter again – and in any case she did not really feel like laughing – so instead she said meekly, "Let's get Sharon to bed first, shall we?"

Carol's old cot was still folded away in a corner of what had been Carol's bedroom, so they assembled it and put the baby to bed for the night. Then Diana – still rather dazed by everything that had happened – made an omelette (rather small and rubbery) for their supper and they ate in silence in front of the television. Afterwards, she switched the television off, took the dishes to the kitchen – the washing up could wait – and went to the sideboard and took out a bottle of sherry and two glasses. "I need a drink." That was something else she wished unsaid – unthought too, for it reminded her too strongly of Bradley. Was anxiety going to turn her to drink, as it had him? "Besides," she added cheerfully, "I suppose we ought to celebrate your employment by Armstrong's."

Carol took the glass her mother handed her. "I've been meaning to say – that's something that should change."

"What?"

"The name. I've thought all along you should change it, now you're in charge."

"You didn't say."

"You didn't ask. Anyway, I hadn't any part in it then." She grinned. "Do I get to be a partner?"

"Hold on a minute, you've only just walked in the door! One step at a time. Anyway, I don't see why you should object to the name. It's been Armstrong's since it was a carrier's, with nothing but horses and carts. I admit, I did once dream of 'Diana Armstrong, Haulier', but I soon realised it wouldn't do. Nor would 'D. Armstrong and Daughter' in case that's your idea. It would put people off, believe me. They're wary enough of a company run by a woman."

"I've got a better idea. We'll call it 'Queen of the Road'. Because we're women, and it's our business."

"And 'Queen' could apply equally to the wagons, or to us," Diana reflected. "Yes, I like that! Except," and here a note of doubt began to creep in, "we shall have to start all over again, to prove ourselves. We can't depend on Armstrong's reputation."

"It hasn't got much reputation left." Carol was, Diana saw, acknowledging for the first time that there was something for which to blame her father, but Diana carefully refrained from pointing that out.

"No, you're right, it hasn't," was all she said. But still she tried to keep Carol's enthusiasm from infecting her too. "Changing a name isn't that simple. It costs money – letter-headings, signage for the wagons, to say the least of it; and then there's the licence. As things are, there may not be a business much longer – you can't run a haulage company without drivers."

She was afraid that might bring another explosion from Carol, against the injustice of being excluded from driving, but to her surprise Carol simply frowned thoughtfully. "Have you advertised?"

"Every newsagents in the Dale, the employment exchange of course, the *Echo*."

"What about the commercial press – and big newspapers, national ones, something like that?"

"It's no good trying to attract men from further afield if we can't provide accommodation."

"There are plenty of places to lodge in Wearbridge, cheap too."

"It's worth a try," Diana admitted.

"And what about changing the name? Don't you want everyone to see that we're different, modern, forward-looking, the best? Not changing the name is a – what d'you call it? – a false economy."

Diana smiled ruefully. She was finding it hard to keep up with her daughter's swings of mood, but this burst of enthusiasm was infectious, attractive. She was surprised to find, too, how much she enjoyed having someone to discuss business matters with on something like equal terms – though it was a novel experience to find herself on equal terms with her daughter. "If we get the licence, yes, then we'll talk about it again. Though heaven knows what sort of extra paperwork that will mean!"

"Who cares!" Carol raised her glass, clinked it against her mother's. "Here's to Queen of the Road, the best haulage firm in the whole world!"

Diana laughed, a little shakily. "Hold on! Let's walk before we start running." Then she raised her own glass. "Queen of the Road."

"Long may she reign!" said Carol.

The following morning Diana took Carol with her in the van when she drove to the depot, the baby asleep in her carrycot in the back. It was barely six and not yet fully light, and Carol grumbled all the way at being forced out of bed so early. Diana, tired herself – she had not slept well after the excitements of the previous evening, and Sharon had cried for a feed at around four – endured her daughter's complaints for a mile or two and then snapped, "If you want to be a working woman you'll have to get used to getting up in the morning." That reduced Carol to sullen silence, which, Diana thought, was a slight improvement.

Colin was not impressed when he came in to work and found a baby asleep in her carrycot wedged into a safe corner of the garage, and Carol already doing a routine maintenance check of the wagon her mother was to drive. Told that this was his new workmate, he was outraged. "She's a girl!"

"Observant of you," said Diana. "She's also a good mechanic." She felt suddenly a little unsure of herself, and of Carol. She was so used to her daughter's insistence that she knew everything there was to know about wagons, so familiar with Bradley's former pride in Carol's skills, that she had never really questioned them. Last night, she had simply been relieved to find a way of pacifying her daughter which also seemed to offer a partial solution to her own problems. Certainly Carol had spent hours of her girlhood in the garage, tinkering with engines, often under Norman's watchful eye. She must have learned a great deal. But was it enough? Would she be able to hold her own here at the depot, working as a supposed equal with the men, even with the inept Colin? Would she in fact prove to be the asset the business so urgently needed?

It was too late to have doubts. Diana forced them away, looked severely at Colin's red and truculent face – he was surely about to object again – and said, "There's work to be done, enough for both of you."

"Then what's she doing with that wagon? I did it yesterday." Carol's head emerged from under the bonnet. She held up an oil filter. "Then why wasn't this changed? Look at the state of it. Be ready in five minutes, Mam!" she added, and disappeared again from view.

Diana went to get her logbook and papers from the office, worrying now about the baby. They had brought bottles ready made up to keep her going through the day, and nappies for changing her, but the washing facilities at the depot were primitive, to say the least. And even when every care was taken the garage was a dangerous place. Even one day in this place seemed to threaten Sharon with all kinds of harm.

That was another worry to push from her mind, as she came a little later to collect the wagon from Carol. By now her daughter had begun work on the Foden, while Colin stood by, smoking and grumbling. "Colin, you could begin by clearing up the mess you left yesterday, and tidying up a bit in here."

"I'm not a skivvy. Let her do that. I'm the mechanic round here."

"You're an apprentice, as she is. Anyway, I expect to find everything in order by the time I get back tonight." She felt uneasy at leaving them together without other supervision, but she had no choice. There was no one else to lead the load of gannister to Meadhope.

During the war Diana had enjoyed driving lorries, delighted in the sense of power and control, the excitement of doing something new and different. But she had been young then, eager for adventure, for freedom. Now she wanted to manage the business, not end up doing everything herself, and she was conscious all the time of the hundred and one things she should be doing, rather than this – finding help for the petrol station, putting out new advertisements for drivers, looking for work for the firm. Instead, she would be on the road all day, loading, roping, weighing, tipping, making sure logbook and delivery notes were in order; and enduring the banter of workers at quarry and steel works. During the war it had been quite usual to find women doing men's work, and they were generally treated with respect; now it was unheard of, and the jokes and teasing irritated and embarrassed her, though she tried to take them in good part, ignoring the most offensive remarks as best she could.

By the time she returned to the depot she was dusty, hungry, deafened by the noise of the engine, and exhausted. She found Sharon peacefully sleeping, apparently unharmed, Carol putting the finishing touches to the wagon, and the garage as untidy as ever. There was no sign of Colin. "He bunked off home," Carol said, in answer to her query. "Said he wasn't working with a girl."

Diana was too tired to face the problem now; it would have to wait until tomorrow. Why did these things have to happen, one after the other?

Back at Wearbridge, they found Kenny waiting in the shelter of the archway, in front of the locked gates. He emerged into the wet evening as the van came to a halt. "I'm not speaking to him!" Carol hissed into her mother's ear. "You keep him talking. I'll get Sharon upstairs." She was halfway out of the van when her mother caught her arm.

"No, Carol – he's still your husband, and Sharon's father. You ought to speak to him."

Carol turned on her mother with that all-too-familiar look of chilling rejection. "Don't tell me what to do! It's my life – I'll do what I want." Then she was out of the van, round the back, tugging on the doors.

Before Diana could decide what to do, Kenny had reached her. "Carol, you have to come back." He sounded exasperatingly feeble, as if he were reciting a speech learned by heart but not fully understood.

"No I haven't," said Carol. "Go away, Kenny." She lifted the carrycot from the van and began to walk, briskly, towards the flat door. "You're nothing to do with us any more."

Kenny stared after her, but did not move. "Mam says—"

"You can tell your Mam what she can do, with my compliments!" The flat door slammed behind her, though they could still hear the clatter of her feet on the stairs inside.

Diana shook off the numbness that had taken hold of her at Carol's outburst. "You'll have to do better than that if you want her back," she told Kenny.

He stared at her, as if not understanding. *What on earth did Carol ever see in him?* Diana wondered. *But of course,* she told herself, *that's not the point. She married him; freely, in a way.*

"Mam says she has to come back," Kenny said after a while.

"Never mind your Mam. Do you want her back?"

Again, that blank stare. "Course," he said at last, though without conviction.

"Then you'll need to show you can put her and the baby before your own interests, even your motorbike – give them time, care and attention." After all, she reflected, even Bradley, inadequate husband though he was, had done that much, most of the time. His love for his daughter had never been in question.

"It's not right – she's my wife."

Exasperated, longing for peace and solitude, Diana lost her temper. "Oh go away, Kenny! Come back when you've thought about what you really want, for yourself – not what your mother says you ought to want." She locked the van and turned her back on him. "Goodnight, Kenny!" She had an uneasy sense that she was colluding in keeping husband and wife apart, and a child from her father, but at the moment she did not care.

There was little peace upstairs in the flat. By the time Diana reached it Sharon had dirtied her nappy and was crying for her next bottle. While Carol fed, bathed and put her to bed, Diana made supper (a tin of soup and beans on toast, since she had no energy for more elaborate cooking, nor had she had time to do any shopping). After the meal, while Diana was carrying the dishes back to the kitchen, Carol ran herself a bath, taking all the hot water. After that, she settled herself in Diana's favourite corner of the sofa to watch a programme her mother hated. "This is nice!" she said, sipping at a mug of cocoa she'd just made for herself, without offering to make one for Diana too – probably because there wasn't enough milk for two.

It was nearly ten o'clock by the time the bath water was hot again and Diana was able to have the long soak she had looked forward to ever since leaving work. Once in bed, she was too tense with exhaustion to sleep, and in the end, about one in the morning, got up and began to draft an advertisement that might somehow lure new drivers to work for her. It did not make her feel any better.

Four

The following Monday, Diana found time to set about placing her advertisement for drivers in various national papers and magazines, to reorganise the interviews for secretarial help for Wednesday morning, and look into the question of renaming the firm. In every other respect it was not a good day. There were, fortunately, no deliveries to be made until tomorrow, so she planned to spend the morning at the depot office and the afternoon at the petrol station, returning to the depot to collect Carol at the end of the day. While she was in the office, Sharon could stay with her, which was a better arrangement than leaving her in the garage. But even that was not ideal, as she had pointed out to Carol over breakfast on Saturday.

"It's all very well as a temporary arrangement, but it won't do as a permanent thing. It's just not safe. Besides, imagine what the traffic inspectors would think if they happened to look in, which they might well. And it'll be worse as she gets older. Besides, she needs proper care and attention."

Carol's face looked blank, unyielding. "What are you saying?"

"That we're going to have to find someone to mind her, some of the time at least."

Diana saw relief in her daughter's expression and realised that Carol had feared her mother was going to order her back to domesticity. "Why yes, there'll be someone who'll do it," she agreed cheerfully, as if that was the end of the matter.

"What about Kenny's family?" Diana asked, a little warily. "Is there anyone there you'd leave her with?"

51

"You're joking! I wouldn't leave a puppy with them."

She had a point, Diana thought, but that still left the problem unsolved, and it worried at her even as she worked on other things through that Monday morning. The other major problem was Colin, who had not appeared for work this morning, nor sent any message. When there was still no sign of him by lunchtime Diana took the van and drove to his home, at his older brother's farm near Cowcleugh, to be told he'd gone to call on his Uncle Norman. Diana drove the half mile to the sick man's house, where she found the two of them toasting themselves beside the kitchen range.

Invited in, though without enthusiasm, she sat down on a hard chair at the nearby table, taking care to ask first after Norman's health. "No better for what Colin tells me," he said. It was a discouraging beginning, and quickly grew worse. "It's not right, taking on a lass."

"Why ever not, if she can do the work?"

"Because she's a lass. There's language in a garage."

"Then Colin will just have to watch his tongue." Diana took care not to show her amusement. "Though I expect Carol will cope."

"What of Colin, working that close to a pretty young lass? There's no telling what will come of it."

Whatever next? Diana wondered, while she tried to imagine what improprieties her daughter might be tempted into in the company of someone even less appealing than Kenny. On the other hand, perhaps Norman feared that Carol's proximity might inflame the shy and awkward Colin to risk making a pass at Carol – who would certainly repel him with vigour.

"Besides," Norman continued – Diana had never known him so voluble – "She's a married woman, with a bairn. Let Kenny Byers look after her. She shouldn't be taking the bread from the mouths of working men with families. There are married men enough who'd be glad of a job."

"Then how come I've not managed to find drivers or mechanics in months of trying?"

"Aye, well – they won't work for a woman. And I'll say this, Mrs Armstrong: if you take on young lasses like this, Armstrong's'll be a laughing stock. And then there's you driving. I know it's an emergency, but still – it's not right. You'll sharp have no men left working for you, not one. And that includes Colin, and me." Through his pallor, his expression was defiant.

Diana looked in exasperation at his stubborn face. It seemed she was doomed either way, then, simply by the accident of her sex. She almost laughed. But it was not funny to find she was on the way to losing the support of one of the few men still working for her. She groped in her mind for some argument to use against him, one that he would find unanswerable, that would convince him that Carol must stay. She suddenly found herself confronted with a memory of a long ago autumn day in 1947, when Carol, an inquisitive toddler, had found her way down into the yard at the petrol station and been found a little later by her anxious parents examining the engine of a wagon, with Norman at her side. His expression then had been full of tenderness. "When you worked at Wearbridge you didn't seem to mind having Carol around. In fact, you seemed happy to have her there."

Norman made a derisive noise. "She was a bit bairn then, not a grown woman. Why, yes, she used to be for ever asking questions, and taking note too. A proper tomboy. But that's bairns. A grown woman's different. Her place is at home." He glared defiantly at Diana. "Anyway, I've said what I have to say."

It was an ultimatum. What was she to do about it? Instruct Carol to return to Kenny, or at least stay at home with her baby? And what of herself? Was she to risk losing the one contract they had, to spare Norman's embarrassment? Or was she to stand firm and lose both Norman and Colin?

On the other hand, it was just possible that Norman did not mean what he said, that it was a bluff, that faced with firmness on her part he would back down. In that case they would all be the better off. More to the point, she would have asserted her right to run the firm as she chose, to make her own decisions and stand by them. She drew a deep breath. "If you don't like the way I run this business, then by all means hand in your notice. But if you stay, then you do things my way, and accept Carol as a mechanic, and me as a driver, when necessary – believe me, I don't want to drive any more than I have to."

Norman scowled at her. She guessed that she had surprised him, that he had expected her to give in to him at once, though none of that showed on his face. She waited, braced for what he would say next. He opened his mouth, but no words came. She glanced at Colin but, though he was observing the exchange, his expression was as blank as ever. She supposed he would follow his uncle's lead, whatever that was.

She left soon afterwards, wishing Norman a speedy recovery, but no wiser as to what the outcome of the confrontation would be. Next morning, Colin returned to work, and no more was said. As far as Diana could gather, he and Carol bickered all day, and he did little work, but fortunately there was not a great deal to be done for once – it was astonishing how much work had been done in the two days of Carol's employment. In the evening, Carol called on her cousins Irene and Susan, to see if either of them might consider minding Sharon for a day or two each week, but they so clearly disapproved of her leaving Kenny that she came home in a foul temper and made the flat seem smaller and more overcrowded than ever.

On Wednesday, Diana interviewed three candidates for the job of part-time office clerk, and took on Gladys Embleton, a sensible-looking mother of two teenagers, with secretarial experience, whose one-time quarryman husband was unemployed; few of the Dale's quarries were still working. Gladys was able to begin work immediately. What was more, she offered a solution to another problem. "Why yes," she said, when asked, "there's my kid sister, Anne – Anne Nattrass, she's a child-minder. Lives in one of those houses across from Dale House. She loves bairns, but her Malcolm didn't want any more, so when the twins started school she took up minding. I don't think she's got anyone at the minute – tell her I gave you her name."

Anne Nattrass's house, called on that afternoon without prior warning, was found to be spotlessly clean, though cheerfully furnished and full of books and toys. Anne herself seemed shy, but otherwise calm and friendly, just the sort of person with whom a child might feel at ease. Diana and Carol agreed that Sharon should be left with her during working hours on three days a week to begin with, since at present there was not enough work to keep Carol busy full time. "Any time you want to leave her on top of that, just you let me know," Anne reassured them. On the following Monday, Carol, who had been eager to find a minder for her baby, reluctant even to consider working part-time, found leaving Sharon in someone's else care to be much harder than she had expected, but she quickly grew used to the new routine, especially as Sharon seemed to thrive on it.

A week later, Norman returned to work, to Diana's relief. She watched with admiration as Carol set out to charm him, asking him for advice when unsure about some mechanical matter – which Colin, more ignorant than she was, rarely did – reminiscing about past days at the petrol station, when he had taught her something, or there had been some amusing incident. Diana watched the man's dourness melt before her daughter's offensive, saw how quickly he accepted, even welcomed, her presence at the depot. Once, she even overheard him say to Colin, "You'd do well to watch how Carol does this. You could learn something."

By then, Diana had begun to receive replies to her advertisements for drivers. One of the men interviewed as a result evaded her questions and could not even produce a driving licence. Of the other two, Derek was a Ravenshield man eager for a chance to return to his home Dale, and Geoff, from Liverpool, claimed to be escaping from an unhappy marriage. Both came with good references and clean driving licences. She was sitting in the office at the depot considering whether to take them both on at once when the phone rang. "Mrs Armstrong? Philip Cartwright here, Dale Industrial Minerals. You may not have heard but we're opening up a new vein at Cowcleugh mine, in the New Year – fluorspar. Thought you might be interested in tendering for the haulage."

"I thought Ogles had the contract?"

"They're pulling out. Thought you might like first refusal. Armstrong's used to have the contract, and I heard good reports of you from Harold Watson at Meadhope. I'd sooner it went to a local firm."

"So would I," said Diana, trying to sound calm, and businesslike. "Can you let me have more details, then I'll come up with some figures for you?" *Better take both those drivers on!* she thought, triumphantly.

She looked forward to telling Carol the news when she returned home in the evening, though that was the only aspect of going home that she looked forward to. It had been one of Carol's days at home, and Diana knew from experience that she would find the flat in chaos, the floor scattered with baby clothes and toys – scattered by Carol, since Sharon was far too young to be untidy – dirty washing piled in a corner of the bathroom, the sink full of dirty dishes, and some noisy pop record playing. Usually, there would be cigarette butts in the ashtrays too – Carol did not smoke much, but enough to irritate her mother, who was reminded only too easily of Bradley. It was perhaps not quite so bad when Diana was not completely exhausted by a day at the wheel, though she still found it necessary to drive from time to time, simply to prevent Norman from making himself ill again from overwork. But even this evening, at the end of a very satisfactory day, she was tired and would have liked to know she was going back to the old tranquillity. Yet what alternative was there, since Carol refused to go back to Kenny? While the business needed all available resources, there was nothing to spare to allow one of them to move into other accommodation, of whatever kind – in any case, Diana knew that Carol was perfectly happy and saw no need to move out. It was only a week until Christmas, in any case; the time when families were supposed to be together. Last year she had longed to spend the time with Carol, but then of course Bradley had been alive.

She parked the van, locked it, paused to brace herself for the evening ahead. Perhaps Carol would have a meal ready tonight, though she doubted it. Taught by her Nana Armstrong, Carol was a good cook, but she seemed incapable of planning ahead.

Diana made her way slowly up the stairs, aware as she reached the top that she could hear voices inside – two voices, adult voices, one of them Carol's, the other deeper, and not one she recognised. Puzzled, even a little anxious, she pushed open the door.

"Here's Mam now," she heard Carol say, from the depths of the sofa, where she sat with Sharon cradled on her knee. There were two empty mugs on the nearby table, a half-eaten packet of biscuits and an overflowing ashtray. The air was thick with smoke.

A broad stocky figure in corduroy trousers and brown tweed jacket advanced on her across the room, hand outstretched. Diana found herself subjected to a vigorous handshake, while a pair of bright brown button eyes looked her over. "Shirley Coatsworth." The voice was deep and husky, a chain-smoker's voice. "Saw your ad. Been a driver all my life. Bloody good mechanic too. Never worked for a woman though. Like to give it a try."

So abrupt was her manner that it took Diana a moment or two to realise that the woman was applying for a job. She said, "Just let me take off my coat. I'll be with you in a moment. Please take a seat."

It was hardly the conventional place for a job interview, there in the muddle of the living room with Carol and the baby looking on, but Diana was too tired to suggest they went down to the office. Fortunately, Carol showed unexpected tact by offering to make supper and then disappearing into the kitchen, which was still well within earshot. Diana sat down facing the woman, who seemed rather less formidable when seated, and examined the licence that was handed to her, and the two excellent references. She asked a great many questions about Shirley's experience, which seemed considerable, and rather fewer about her health, which was clearly good. She did not need to bring up the question she usually asked: "How would you feel to be working with a woman?" At the end of it, her head spinning, she heard herself say, "If I take you on, it'll be for a month's trial, starting in the

New Year. Do you live locally? No, you said you'd been working in Newcastle."

"Booked in that little B&B round the corner. Start work any time you like."

"I'll let you know tomorrow then, when I've had time to think it over."

Shirley stood up and made a move towards the door, but Carol called from the kitchen, "Are you staying for supper? There's enough for three!"

The woman grinned, but called back, "Thanks, Caz, but I'm expected at the digs. Goodnight!"

Already, she was using Carol's schoolgirl nickname. Diana saw her out, then went into the kitchen. "She's nice isn't she?" Carol greeted her. "A woman driver!" She giggled. "I thought she was a man at first. She has some great stories."

"Maybe she has," said Diana. "But you shouldn't just invite any stranger into the flat. You know nothing about her."

"Oh, she's OK. You will give her a job won't you?"

"We'll see. Probably." Then she told her daughter about the possible contract.

Early in the New Year they heard that they had been granted the haulage contract for Cowcleugh Mine, and a few days later received confirmation that Mrs Diana Armstrong, owner of Queen of the Road, had been granted a full carriers' licence, covering all her vehicles.

Five

The firm now had three lorries – two Leyland six-wheelers and the Foden – painted with the words "Queen of the Road" in a fresh yellow and green. Carol had wanted a little gold crown added above the words, but Diana had drawn the line at that. "Ugh! Tasteless!" she'd exclaimed, with the look of someone sucking on a lemon. Fortunately, Carol had simply laughed; one could never be quite sure how she'd react, whether cheerfully, as then, or with furious resentment or anger at what she saw as a slight. She might be a mother and a working woman, but she was also still very much a teenager, most of the time.

She had also been working full time for the past two months, since their contract started with Cowcleugh mine. Diana knew that there were times when Carol felt unhappy at leaving Sharon in Anne's care so much; but for her own sake, rather than Sharon's – the child was clearly thriving. Which was just as well, because with two contracts to meet and the hope of more, and three wagons in constant daily use, a good mechanic with no other calls on her time was essential to the business. And apart from Carol, there was only Colin.

Diana was on her way to the workshop in search of Colin, who was due for another lecture on his lateness, idleness and general deficiencies of skill. She was pondering how best to tackle him this time – his usual reaction to criticism was to complain furiously that she used Carol as her spy, and that her daughter lied for her own ends – when she heard the phone ringing in the office. Exasperated, she swung round and broke into a run, just reaching the office in time.

She gasped, "Hello!" into the mouthpiece, and then heard an agitated and only too familiar voice at the other end.

"Mrs Armstrong, it's a bad road, there's trees all along and you can't see – nowt to show there's a ditch . . ."

She knew only too well what was coming. "You're stuck again, Derek." It was not a question.

"Anyone would be, Mrs Armstrong."

She interrupted the inevitable excuses to find out precisely where he was, and promised to get help to him as soon as possible. *He's going to have to go*, she thought. Because he was a local man, eager to please, she had given him another chance, even though it was clear by the end of his first month with them that, when manoeuvring to load or unload, he had an unerring instinct for finding the only ditch, the only piece of soft ground in which his wheels would stick fast. Moved by his pleading and promises of amendment, she had extended his trial period by another month, and then another. That third month ended in a week's time, and her patience was exhausted. Not only was she weary of sending help to get him out of trouble, she was also concerned at the frequent damage – so far fairly small – that was being done to the vehicles he drove. It might have mattered a little less if he had been a sound mechanic, but his skills in that line were minimal too. After the second incident, she had transferred him permanently to the Foden, rather than either of the two much better and newer vehicles, but she could not afford to risk any wagon being off the road.

She went in search of Shirley, who had just come back to the depot after finishing her day's quota – unlike Derek, she had proved an invaluable worker, industrious, trustworthy, and competent in everything she did. After an initial wariness, the men seemed to have accepted her, not as a woman, but as a fellow man. Where they would moderate their language in front of Carol, they did not worry with Shirley; though Diana had once heard her rebuking Geoff with savage sharpness because he swore in front of Carol.

She found Shirley standing by her lorry, parked just inside the depot entrance, watching Carol climb up into the cab. It was Carol's one chance of driving, here in the depot, when any vehicle had to be moved into or out of the workshop, and she insisted on her right to that single privilege. They were laughing together about something, but as Diana reached them Carol started the vehicle. "Wait!" said Diana. "I'm afraid Shirley's going to have to go out again – if you don't mind," she added. "I'm afraid Derek's in trouble again. Could you get down to Cowcleugh and give him a tow?"

Carol opened the cab door and jumped down. "Let me go too, Mam – please! Better have two – you know the mess Derek gets himself into."

"I'll look after her," Shirley put in. "Trust me!"

Having seen how consistently protective – motherly, even – Shirley was towards her daughter, Diana did trust her. "So long as you give her a lift back to Wearbridge afterwards."

They cheerfully began to load up the vehicle with old sacks, a couple of shovels, rope and a chain, anything they might need. "You'll have to collect Sharon, Mam!" was Carol's parting call.

It took two hours to free Derek's lorry. "Why don't you just sit tight, the moment you get stuck?" an exasperated Shirley demanded, on first seeing how deeply the spinning wheels had gouged the side of the ditch, causing the wagon to tip steadily further on one side. "All this floundering only makes things worse. You know you can't get out by yourself. Bloody stupid man!" She glanced at Carol. "Pardon my French."

Derek was not in the least grateful for his rescue. "Why didn't she send Norman or Geoff?" he demanded from his seat in the cab, from which he could look down on the two women at work with shovels several feet below him. "They'd have got me free in half the time."

By some miracle, the lorry had suffered only minor damage and, once freed, Derek was able to drive it back to the depot, though Shirley insisted on following him all the way there. "Just to make sure you stay on the road," she said, to his further annoyance.

Later, they dropped him off at his home. "Hope your Mam's going to give him his cards," commented Shirley. "They're long overdue. That's one thing about being a woman in a job like this – it's no use being soft, or you lose respect. You've got to be as hard as any man; no, harder, or the bastards'll just tramp all over you."

"Don't you like men? You seem to get on all right with them."

"They're OK, so long as you remember they're all little boys at heart. You've got to watch them. Give 'em an inch and they'll take a mile."

Carol liked Shirley, but was curious about her. She had a fund of wonderful stories, a wealth of experience on which she could call, but it was all to do with work. Perhaps she enjoyed driving so much that there was nothing else in her life, and never had been. Certainly she always deflected any questions that verged on the personal. Yet she must, surely, have faced difficulties, doubts, obstacles of many kinds in taking up her chosen career – if she had deliberately chosen it. It was possible she had begun to drive during the war, found she enjoyed it, and simply carried on from there.

"I've often wondered," Carol said now, conscious of treading on dangerous ground, "where you come from. I know you were working in Newcastle before you came here. But you don't talk like a Geordie."

"No, I'm not." To Carol's relief, Shirley showed no sign of resenting the personal nature of the observation. She even seemed in what was, for her, a confiding mood. "Place near Manchester, biggish village; you won't've heard of it. Wouldn't want to either. Narrow minded, prying little dump. Couldn't get out of it fast enough. Not been back since I was seventeen. Dad was a farmer."

Carol was surprised. Shirley did not seem to her like a country girl, even in some long ago forgotten life. "I always thought you must be part gypsy!" she said lightly; there was something about Shirley's weather-beaten face and wiry black hair – scattered now with grey – which bore that out.

"No such luck. Long line of bloody stick-in-the-muds. God knows where they got me from. Asked themselves that often enough, I guess." Then, neatly, unobtrusively, she moved on to her experience of transport cafés, bringing in such a wealth of disgusting and quirky detail that by the time they reached Wearbridge Carol was helpless with laughter.

Parting with Shirley near her lodgings, Carol walked on alone, aware that across the road the Meadhope bus had just dropped off three passengers, one of whom, a slight dark girl, ran through a gap in the tea-time traffic, reached the pavement just in front of her, glanced round, and then exclaimed, "Caz Armstrong!"

"Bernie!" Carol recognised a school friend from her days at St Margaret's. "What are you doing here?" She knew Bernadette lived at Meadhope.

"Calling on my Auntie. I'm just back from work. What about you then? I heard you were married."

"Aye – to Kenny Byers. But I've left him. I'm back with my Mam." They agreed they were going the same way and began to walk along together.

"Why, yes, she's taken over Armstrong's, hasn't she? Reckon her ears must be burning lately." She smiled at Carol's questioning look. "I'm in the office at Shaw's. Mr Shaw doesn't like your Mam, especially since she got that licence. Furious, he was."

Carol knew Ronnie Shaw had tried to oppose the licence application, but had not thought he felt quite so strongly as that. "There's enough work for all of us in the Dale. Besides, Ronnie Shaw's main business is in Sunderland."

"I know, but he was doing quite well here till your Mam took over – what with your Dad—" She suddenly realised she was touching on delicate ground, and blushed. "Well . . ." Then she tried to change the subject. "Mind, he's got his eye on the development up at Parkgate. That'd be a contract worth getting, if anything comes of it."

"Oh, what's that then?" Carol listened to what Bernadette told her, trying to look as if she was only mildly interested and ending the talk with more personal matters. "Let's meet up some time!" she cried as they parted.

At home, Sharon, a pink and white angel with flossy gold curls, was bathed and ready for bed, and Diana had a casserole in the oven. Carol kissed the child goodnight – cautiously, so as not to get oil and mud on her spotless face – and shut herself in the bathroom, emerging some time later to amuse her mother over supper with the tale of Derek's rescue, though it was not really funny, when you thought of the time wasted. "So," said Carol at the end, "when does he get his cards? Shirley says you have to be tough, or you'll get taken advantage of."

"I'm afraid Shirley's right," Diana admitted. "I've been too soft with him already. But I'm not going to enjoy sacking him."

"He must know he's had it after this." Carol spooned up the last of the gravy from her plate. "That wasn't bad, for you," she said with a grin. "Mind, I was hungry enough to eat anything." She reached out to stack the plates. "I met Bernie Murphy today. You know what she said? They're talking of building a cement works at Parkgate. Massive scheme, employment for hundreds of men, all that kind of thing. Mam, they'll be needing hauliers for years to come!"

Diana, who had risen to take the plates into the kitchen, sat down again. "I'd heard something too. But I wouldn't get so excited if I were you. The railway still runs through Parkgate. They're sure to use that for any transport they need."

"But they've been going to close that line for years, the bit above Wearbridge anyway."

"What's left of it." Diana could remember when the railway ran almost the whole length of the Dale. "But I imagine if they're building something as big as that's likely to be, they'll keep the line open, at least as far as Parkgate. They'd be mad not to. On the other hand," she continued reflectively, "while they're setting it all up they'll be in need of building materials, all kinds of things – and not all of them necessarily most easily carried by rail. No, you may have a point." She smiled reflectively. "The only trouble is we can't take on more work without at least one more lorry and another couple of drivers. And they'd have to be paid for."

"We're doing well, aren't we?"

"On paper, yes, but Dale Industrials are none too prompt about paying their bills, and in any case we haven't been going long enough to have much to fall back on. There's always the bank." She saw a look of slight puzzlement on Carol's face. "A loan." Puzzlement changed to alarm. "How do you think most businesses run?"

"I thought you had Grandpa's money?"

"That was a loan too, remember – interest free, of course. But the last of it went on buying the new wagon. Don't worry, if I borrow from the bank it'll only be short term, and I shan't take on more than we could cover, if we had to. I like to sleep at night."

"Then you'll go for the Parkgate work?"

"Perhaps. If there is any. I see no harm in making enquiries."

"Before anyone else does – especially Shaw's." Carol decided not to mention that Ronnie Shaw was hoping to get the work.

A little later, when Diana returned from the kitchen, Carol, now curled up on the sofa with a cigarette, said suddenly, "Kenny's going out with that Brenda Kidd. Definitely. For certain."

Diana studied her daughter's face, with its impassive expression – she did not look hurt or dismayed. "I thought there was something like that going on. I've seen them together a few times."

"Can't think what she sees in him. Half the lads in the Dale are after her. She could have anyone."

"Maybe she likes motorbikes," suggested Diana, wondering if it was wise to mention what she was sure had been Carol's reason for first going out with Kenny.

"Could be. At least she can't marry him for it, not unless we divorce. Though I hope she'd have more sense."

Did Diana detect a note of bitterness? She was not sure. "Have you considered divorce?" The words, spoken impulsively, almost shocked her; after all, Carol had only been living apart from Kenny for a mere five months.

"Can't prove adultery, not just on him being seen a few times with Brenda Kidd on the back of his motorbike. Maybe if I ever get rich I'll get a private detective and do it properly. Then he'd be out of my life for good."

"He's still Sharon's father," Diana reminded her uneasily.

"And what difference does that make? He's not interested in Sharon. She's better off without him."

Diana thought it wiser to change the subject.

Dismissing Derek was every bit as unpleasant as she had feared. She had hoped that he would recognise that she had already given him more second chances than anyone could hope for or expect, but instead he raged at her, blaming the fact that she was a woman for the unfairness of his treatment, and including both Shirley and Carol in his condemnation of Queen of the Road and all to do with it. At the end of the interview Diana felt limp with exhaustion. Norman, coming to the office immediately afterwards, gave her a rough pat on the shoulder. "He had it coming. Good riddance. Never thought I'd say it, but that Shirley's worth three of him."

Meanwhile, Diana had begun to make discreet enquiries, which told her that the plans for the cement works were sufficiently advanced to be a certainty, and that the Conway Cement Company, with a head office on Teesside, was the firm behind the development. After that, it seemed a relatively simple matter to make an appointment with Mr Gerald Conway at his Middlesbrough headquarters, to which Diana drove the following week. She dressed with what she hoped was quiet elegance, and knew her air of assured competence impressed him. He confirmed that they would require a certain amount of road haulage in the early stages, while the plant was being built, though he merely assured her he would consider Queen of the Road for the contract, when the time came.

After that, she had a satisfactory meeting with Mr Stephen Hepple at the Wearbridge branch of Bond's bank, whose father had been on good terms, socially speaking, with her own father. She suspected him of believing that Dr Poultney, having advanced her the loan on which the present business was built, could be depended upon to bail her out were she to get into financial difficulties, something she would not dream of asking of him. But she did not mention her scruples to the bank manager, since he seemed happy for her to borrow what she needed to meet any contract with the Conway Cement Company.

By the end of April, Diana had prepared and submitted a firm tender for the work and quickly heard that it had been accepted, at which she bought a new lorry and took on three more drivers, Harry, Dick and Bruce. Harry was a wiry little Cockney in middle age, with a persistent whistle; Dick a burly widower from Stockton; Bruce was big, twenty-two, and brought a rough-coated grey lurcher with him. "Where Smokey goes, I go," he declared.

Three days after work began at Parkgate, Carol and Diana reached the depot one morning to find that Shirley, who should have been on the road by now, was standing by her lorry with her head under the bonnet, though she looked up ruefully as they reached her. "Bloody thing won't start. Turns over, but nothing happens."

"It was OK last night." Carol had checked it herself. "You get in and switch on."

Shirley did so, while Carol watched what happened. Then they both examined the engine again, bit by bit; until Carol cried triumphantly, "That's it – look, the solenoid – the wire's—" her voice tailed off.

"Cut," said Shirley. "Someone's bloody cut it!" They looked at one another. "Norman had a flat tyre last week," Shirley added. "Thursday, starting off from Meadhope after his break. He reckoned it'd been deliberately slashed."

"Then why didn't he say?"

"Once off, you can put up with. Twice is another matter. Where's your Mam?"

They told Diana what had happened. She frowned, looked up at them from her desk. They knew what she was about to say, for the thought had occurred to them too: "Derek?"

There was no proof, of course. At the end of the day, Diana called everyone together to tell them a watch must be kept on the depot through the night. "It'll be voluntary, of course. I'll take first shift, if someone can relieve me later. Of course, I'll not expect anyone up in the night to come in tomorrow morning." That would not, of course, apply to herself.

"I'll take over at ten," offered Norman.

"I'll take next shift, two o'clock till morning," Bruce offered. "Smokey can hear a flea jump a mile off."

It was going to make it difficult to organise everyone for work during the following day, and presumably they were going to have to keep it up for some time. "Let's hope he soon gets tired and gives up," Diana said.

"Or we catch him at it," retorted Norman. They dispersed then. Norman and Bruce walked away together; Bruce lodged with Norman's neighbour, so they hadn't far to go. Diana heard Bruce say, "Someone round here has an old Jowett – haven't seen one of those in years."

"That'll be Bill Akehurst's," said Norman. "Loves that car, nurses it like a babby. Not that it'd take him far from Meadhope."

"It was up this way last night, going past the house, if that's the one it was. Maybe it was another one. Now, is two o'clock OK with you?"

The following morning Diana and Carol set off as usual for the depot, once Sharon had been dropped off at Anne's house. Leaving the village they passed the layby where Shirley always parked her wagon at night, empty by now, for Shirley was an early riser and would have been on the road before dawn.

The road rose a little, then dipped, rounded a bend, rose again to another bend; on which, blocking half the road, they found Shirley's wagon, uncompromisingly stationary. Diana passed it with care and drove on until she found a safe place to park; then they walked back to where Shirley, once again, stood with her head under the bonnet.

"What is it this time?" Diana asked. They'd thought the

wagon would be safe, so near the village, so far from Derek's home.

"Don't bloody know. Started fine this time, went like a bird. Never known it run so well, thought I'd have a job holding it back, not to go too fast. Then all of a sudden – voomp! Stopped, just like that. Dead. Not a flicker. And can I see what's wrong? No, I bloody can't. And before you ask, yes, I filled up last night, last thing."

Carol joined her in examining the engine, while Diana busied herself improvising warning signs on the road, then came back to see how they were getting on. "Any luck?"

"Nope!" Shirley did not even look round.

"Can you manage if I go on to the depot? I'll ring the police from there, to let them know there's an obstacle on the road. Once you get going, come straight up there to let me know."

By midday they had found no clue as to what was wrong, though the wagon still refused to show any signs of life. By then, they had decided simply to strip everything down, as the only possible way of getting to the bottom of the trouble. It was well into the afternoon when Carol removed the fuel pump, giving it a cursory glance, which sharpened into a second, keener look. "Hang on a minute, what's this?"

Shirley, streaked with oil and dust, clearly exhausted, lifted her head. "What?" She sounded as if she didn't really care.

"Look at this. There's no way any diesel could get through this. It's no wonder it stopped. But what is it?"

Shirley came to look. The pump was clogged with a hard, resinous-looking substance; as were all the pipes that led to it. She gave a whistle. "Bloody hell, we're in trouble!"

"What is it?"

"Sugar."

"Sugar!"

"Yup. A bag of sugar, like you get on every pantry shelf. That's all it takes. And you've got hundreds of pounds worth of damage. I've seen this done once before, long time ago. Someone's certainly got it in for us, that's for sure."

"So they put sugar in the fuel tank?"

Shirley nodded. "Mixes up with the diesel. First thing, wagon goes like a bird. Next thing, it stops dead." She made a sweeping gesture under the bonnet. "We're going to need all this replacing, the whole lot."

Carol gazed, appalled, at the innocuous-looking, useless engine. "So Derek must have come all the way down here last night, just for revenge." She could understand – just – how his anger might have led him to slash a tyre or cut a wire, but this was malice on quite a different scale, something beyond any kind of understanding. "What do we do now?"

"We'll need a tow to get this to the depot."

"But what about the police?"

"What about them? There's no proof is there?"

"They might know where to look for some."

So, at Carol's insistence, they walked into Wearbridge and called at the police station, where she outlined her suspicions.

"Derek Bell, now," said the duty sergeant. "Would that be the same Derek Bell who was rushed into hospital with a heart attack, end of last week? He's my brother-in-law, so I should know. Still there, far as I know."

It was, they soon discovered, the very same Derek Bell. On the way to the flat to phone the depot, Carol said, "Then if it wasn't Derek, who on earth could it be?"

Shirley shrugged. "You do well in business, you make enemies – and we've been doing pretty well, I suppose. If you were another haulage business in the Dale, struggling a bit maybe."

"Most of them are one- or two-wagon firms, with enough regular work – except Shaw's, of course." Carol came to a sudden halt, recalling something Bernie had said: "Mr Shaw doesn't like your Mam, especially since she got that licence. Furious, he was." And since then Queen of the Road had won a contract he had very much wanted . . .

Shirley studied her face. "You think Shaw's might have it in for us?" Carol nodded emphatically.

She repeated her theory later, back at the depot, where her

70

mother, Norman and Colin had gathered to examine the damaged lorry. When she came to an end, Norman was the first to speak. "Never did like that Ronnie Shaw. Got out of National Service you know. Said it was his feet, but no one ever saw 'owt wrong with them."

Carol caught Shirley's eye and grinned. Diana said, "He was as astonished as anyone, and we were all glad enough not to lose him, up here at the quarry." She sounded surprisingly annoyed, Carol thought. "Besides, that doesn't make him responsible for this."

"No, but I tell you what," Norman broke in again, "Bill Akehurst's Jowett was up this way two nights ago – Bruce saw it. And last night I saw it again, around midnight, driving slowly past here. Came back a bit later. Thought it was odd, but didn't know then . . ." He saw how Diana looked at him, and added, "You know, Bill Akehurst, Shaw's manager. No kin up this way that I know of. Not one to flog that old car of his either, not without good reason."

"And the best reason would be orders from Ronnie Shaw," put in Carol.

It was a year now since Diana had become disillusioned with Ronnie Shaw, had learned what he was capable of. Yet she still couldn't convince herself that this was his doing. "I find it hard to believe . . ."

"Someone did it!" retorted Carol. "Who else is there? Anyway, I'm going to see him, tomorrow."

"I'll come with you," said Shirley promptly.

"But what proof have we got? We can't just accuse him, not without more to go on than this." Diana fought a fierce wish that this could not be true, that Ronnie would not, could not do this to them.

"Oh, Mam, we're never going to have that sort of proof! Not unless someone spotted him last night, which I bet they didn't. But we can't just let him get away with it. And the police won't be able to do anything, will they?"

"No – no, they won't." Diana pushed her reluctance aside. "No,

71

you're right. If we just leave it, it might happen again, and we can't afford that. But you're not to go and see him, Carol. I know you – you'll just lose your temper. And it still might not be him. It needs handling with care. I'll go and see him, by myself."

"Right," said Carol, "but quickly, Mam. Before he does it again."

"I'll go tomorrow," Diana promised, though she felt sick at the very thought of it.

She did not sleep well that night, and when at last, well after midnight, she did fall asleep, it was to descend into a confused dream in which Ronnie Shaw, at first the tender lover of two years ago, lost shape and definition and grew gradually, inevitably, charged with menace, so that she forced herself awake again.

Six

D iana did not want to confront Ronnie. She would have to phone him first, of course, and even that prospect hung over her like a storm cloud on Friday morning as she dressed and nibbled half-heartedly at a piece of a toast.

Carol left early to get a lift with Shirley in the old Foden she'd been reduced to using while the other was off the road, which left Diana to take Sharon to Anne's house. After that, once back at the petrol station, there was no putting it off any longer. For she knew that Carol was right; every circumstance pointed to Ronnie as the force behind the destruction of the wagon. For this, if he had done it, he had to be brought to account somehow, if only because they could not afford to let it happen again. She knew, as she lifted the receiver and dialled the number of Shaw's Sunderland office (Thursday used to be Ronnie's day for coming to Meadhope – otherwise, except when driving, he was to be found in Sunderland), that a part of her still hoped that he would be able to prove somehow that he could not have done it. Except that, of course, he would then be angry that she could accuse him of such a thing. Odd that she should mind that prospect, when she had thought he had already sunk as low as he could in her estimation.

"I'm sorry, madam," said an efficient female voice. "Mr Shaw's in Meadhope today."

She was about to look up the Meadhope number, when she changed her mind about making an appointment. Better surely to take Ronnie by surprise, before he had time to prepare a denial or an excuse, for himself or any of his employees.

She took the van keys from their hook, gathered up her coat, and set out. It was nearly three years now since she had sat in Ronnie's office in Meadhope, and felt the air alive with the attraction between them, and allowed him to kiss her; might even have allowed more, if circumstances had been different. What would she feel now, were she to find herself in that very place?

Half an hour later she was there, walking into that same office, unchanged as far as she recalled, though there was no sign of Ronnie. Instead, Bernadette was seated at the desk, busily typing away. "Hello, Mrs Armstrong," she said cheerfully. "What can I do for you?"

"I wish to speak to Mr Shaw, if you please. In private."

Bernadette, conscious of something unexpected in the atmosphere, went briskly in search of Ronnie and within a short time he was coming into the office, alone, murmuring some conventional greeting as he did so. Flooded with memory, Diana struggled to push everything else from her mind, to concentrate on why she was here, stirring her anger into renewed life, though she kept her temper well under control. She refused his offer of a chair and remained standing. "I strongly suspect you know why I'm here," she said, at her coldest.

If he did know, he was hiding it well. "No," he said, facing her, too close for comfort. "I haven't the least idea." He seemed to be trying to match her coldness.

"So you have no idea at all who tipped sugar into the tank of one of our lorries? It was a miracle no one was hurt, on that stretch of road." She watched him closely for the expected signs of guilt, however well disguised.

There were none. He simply looked shocked. "Sugar?" He gave a silent whistle. "That's bad." Then, "You surely don't think I'd do a thing like that?" He studied her face. "You do – you actually think I'd stoop so low!" He sat down then, heavily, on the chair facing her across the desk. She could see that he was hurt; that, or he was a consummate actor, something she had not suspected of him.

"If not you personally, then one of your employees on your

behalf." She was aware of an odd mixture of relief and disappointment. After all, if he was not responsible, then who was? And how could she ever hope to discover the truth and prevent it from happening again? "Your manager has been seen near the depot twice lately, late at night. On each occasion damage was done about the same time. Can you explain that?"

Did she imagine some momentary flicker of response on his face? "It's a free country. Bill Akehurst can go where he likes out of work hours."

"Not if it's my yard and he's out to destroy my property."

"Oh, that's nonsense, and you know it!"

"Who else would want to see us fail as badly as that? Who else has been after the same contracts, and failed to get them, as often as not?"

"You sound just like your late husband. When things go wrong, blame somebody else."

"I didn't imagine the sugar in the tank," she said sharply. "And I certainly wasn't responsible for putting it there."

He stared at her, biting his lip. "Fair enough. I accept that's unlikely. But that doesn't make it my fault. There are plenty would like to see you fail – every other haulier within miles, I'd say."

"As much as you would?"

"I don't wish you any harm. Nor would I condone anything so underhand. I play fair. I thought you'd know that, if anyone did. Besides, we've got work enough without the two little contracts you beat us on. We're expanding all the time. Your little firm is no threat to us at all. Much more likely it's someone your own size who'll go under if you expand any more."

"You suggest someone then, who'd mind that much! Because I can't think of anyone."

"Tell you what," he said suddenly. "Let's have Bill up here and ask him about it. Just to set your mind at rest." She agreed, and he went to the door and gave a message to Bernadette. When the manager came, Diana noticed that he halted just inside the door, looking quickly from one to another of the room's two occupants. Did she imagine it, or was there, briefly, a hint of both guilt and panic in his expression?

"Close the door, Bill. Now, come and tell Mrs Armstrong that we don't play dirty in this firm." Ronnie explained what had been done to the wagon, and Diana added details of the other two incidents, while Bill listened intently. Whatever Diana might have seen, there was no hint in the man's expression now of anything suspicious – though neither did he seem troubled by what he heard. "Now, Mrs Armstrong thinks we had something to do with all this. She claims you were seen in the area that same evening. I hope you can put her mind at rest."

"Course I can, Mr Shaw. What would I be doing up there? After a day working for Shaw's all I want is a swift half in the Grey Bull at Meadhope and then my bed. You know that, sir. Ask anyone." He gave an odd sideways look at Diana, half smiling. "Bad thing to happen, Mrs Armstrong. Hope you find out who did it before it happens again."

After that, there was nothing for it but to take her leave, seething with frustration though she was. Some instinct told her that Bill Akehurst was lying; now that she had heard his protests of innocence she was the more sure of his guilt. But there was nothing she could point to, nothing she could put her finger on; nothing, worst of all, to stop him doing the same thing again. All that was left to them was to protect their property as best they could and hope that would be enough.

When she had gone, Ronnie turned to dismiss his manager and was met by a knowing grin. "All right, Mr Shaw?"

An appalled realisation hit Ronnie. "You're lying through your teeth. You did do it!"

The grin remained. "Why, you did say she mustn't be let get the better of us. 'Don't let her get a hold,' that's what you said. If her wagons are off the road she can't meet her contracts, can she? And no proof we've owt to do with it, that's the beauty of it."

Diana returned to Wearbridge feeling drained and depressed. All that effort, all that waste of emotion and energy, for nothing! She was exactly where she had been before she went to Meadhope, with the near-certainty of yet more harrassment to confront over the coming weeks. She would be deluding herself to think they could protect vehicles and drivers for every moment of every day and night, though they would have to try. In the weeks to come more damage would certainly be done, maybe even worse things, if that were possible. It was a wearying thought.

She made herself a sandwich for lunch and then drove up to the depot to make arrangements for security over the weekend. It riled her to have to pay drivers to waste their time doing nothing, when it would mean she could not then ask them to put in the full number of hours doing the work for which she employed them. Next week she would see about hiring a full-time night watchman. For now, with the agreement of those who volunteered for duty, she drew up a rota, which she then pinned up on the noticeboard in the workshop. "Shirl's not on it," Harry pointed out.

"She's not here. No one goes on the list without their agreement." Carol, urgently in need of transport to go in search of parts for the damaged vehicle, had begged a lift from Shirley, who'd finished her day's quota of loads by lunchtime; or so Norman told Diana. "Skiving, that's what she is, as usual," had been Harry's comment, though scarcely audible, probably because he knew it was unjustified. Diana thought it wiser to ignore the remark – he and Shirley had taken a dislike to one another right from the start, but they were equally valuable employees, in their different ways.

Carol returned home in as exhausted a state as her mother, and in as foul a mood. It had been bad enough having to spend the afternoon doing the rounds of vehicle supply shops, dealing with inefficiency, lack of interest, simple failure to meet her requirements and the – at best – patronising attitudes of staff towards a young and pretty woman whom they clearly assumed to be ignorant about mechanical things. Then, on the way back to Wearbridge at the end of a trying and largely fruitless afternoon, the Foden had broken down – not sabotage this time, but simply the result of overstrain on an already old and unreliable vehicle. Between them, she and Shirley had botched up a repair and got the lorry back on the road, and managed to reach Wearbridge in time for Carol to collect her daughter from the minder – it was as well that Anne was happy to keep the baby with her as long as was necessary.

She found Sharon propelling herself about Anne's living room with the support of the furniture. The child reached out a hand towards her mother and laughed, and then looked at the minder and clearly, unmistakably, said, "Anne!" It was the first word Carol had ever heard her say; though she soon gathered from a rather sheepish Anne that Sharon had already said it twice before.

Carol wheeled Sharon home in the pushchair in a mood of even greater vexation. Her baby's first word, and not only had she not been there to hear it, but it had been, not "Mammy" or – unlikely – "Daddy", like any normal child, but the name of her minder! She felt hurt and angry, and burst into the flat with, "I've had a horrible day!"

"That makes two of us," said Diana, which was not the response Carol had hoped for. Mothers were supposed to console and support you.

But at least supper was more or less ready, and soon on the table, and Diana offered to put Sharon to bed while Carol had a bath. Later they sat down together in the living room and shared the day's problems, though Carol was not soothed by the talk; she felt as if they were competing to see who could declare the worst day. Diana seemed to make little of Sharon's first word. "Oh, children always say the wrong thing first. You said 'Daddy' long before you said 'Mummy' – and even then it was 'Mammy', which I didn't like." In case that sounded harsh – after all, Carol still called her "Mam", which she disliked as much – she hastened on, "Though of course I got used to it."

"That's quite different!" Carol retorted sourly. She fell silent, feeling as if no one understood her, and then reached for the

Radio Times, to see if there was anything worth watching. She wanted to shut out her mother.

Diana, who felt she could not endure the clamour of the television this evening, said quickly, "There's a letter from Granny, if you'd like to read it."

Granny Poultney wrote frequently to her daughter, though Carol, allowed to read her letters, did not find them very interesting; they echoed too much with the prim and proper voice of her maternal grandmother. But she reached to take the letter from the sideboard; it was something to do. This time there was less of the plodding day-to-day account of meetings attended, village festivities, church services; Carol found herself more interested than she expected. "This Daphne with the posh meal for her fourteenth birthday," she asked, at the end of the second page, "who is she?"

"My sister Pamela's daughter, the youngest, I suppose."

"So she's my cousin, like Irene and Susan? Then how come I've never even heard of her before?"

"I expect you'll have seen her mentioned in one of Granny's letters. But you know I've lost contact with my sisters and brother."

"It's weird, that. We never saw them when we stayed down there, did we? Yet don't they live near Granny? It sounds like it from this."

"Aunty Pamela does, I think, and Aunt Angela's not far away. I think Uncle Robert's still in London. But they have their own busy lives."

Her mother was being polite again, pulling a veil of decency over family rifts which she never mentioned, but which Carol guessed at from things she had occasionally overheard in the past. She was about to probe a little – something she rarely did, as Diana was skilled at repelling unwanted questions – when, turning the page before her, she saw that the letter had undergone a dramatic change, ending in a heavy and largely illegible handwriting that she did not recognise. "Who's this who's finished it off?"

"Grandpa." Diana smiled ruefully. "I wrote to tell them how well things were going, after we got the Conway's contract. In case you can't read it – typical doctor's handwriting! – he's saying how proud he is of me."

"Oh dear!" said Carol; sympathy for her mother revived a little. "Are you going to tell them what's happened now?"

"I don't know."

This time, Carol detected an alarming note in Diana's voice; she glanced across at her mother's bent head, the anxiety visible on her face even through the fall of dark hair. "Mam, is it serious?"

"It's not good." Diana looked at her daughter, her voice as matter-of-fact as she could make it. "It's going to be very hard to meet all our obligations, with a lorry down and drivers tied up in keeping watch. If we lose any of our contracts we could find ourselves in trouble financially. When I say trouble, I don't mean out on the streets or destitute or anything like that, but we might have to sell wagons or lay off men."

"All because of Ronnie Shaw!" Carol glowered at the letter, as if their rival's face were superimposed upon it. "Why don't we try a bit of sabotage ourselves?"

"Because that would probably only make things worse and in any case it would put us in the wrong."

"Oh, it's all right for Shaw's to try and bankrupt us, so long as we're in the right? Fabulous!" She stood up. "I'm going to bed." She lay awake for a long time, planning revenge on Shaw's; while her mother found her own uneasy sleep troubled by dreams in which attempts at sabotage went disastrously wrong.

The following morning, though it was Saturday, Diana drove up to the depot, where she had put herself on the rota for the entire daylight hours of the weekend; the men had felt that a woman on watch at night was likely to be putting herself in danger, though they made an exception for Shirley. Diana set out an hour before she needed to, because she felt guilty at her privileged position. She couldn't remember who had been on the rota for the last watch of the night, but heard Harry's whistle as she approached the office, which had seemed the best place for the men to be installed, since it was small, easily heated, and had a window overlooking much of the yard, as well as a telephone, in case of emergency.

"Nothing doing, Mrs Armstrong," the man greeted her, getting to his feet, putting his flask and sandwich box away in his haversack. "Not a mouse squeaking." He knocked a heap of files off the corner of the desk, apologised and stooped quickly to tidy them up. "I'll take more water with it next time!" he joked.

Diana took the files from him, and the papers that had fallen out of them. "I'll see to these. I shouldn't have left them in your way." She had thought she'd left the desk clear, but could only suppose that in the disruptions of the past two days her usual clear-headedness had deserted her and she had forgotten to do it. She thanked Harry and watched him walk away towards his battered old Morris Minor, his whistle gradually diminishing.

Mid-morning, the post came, and there was a neatly typed envelope addressed to Diana. Inside, on a single sheet, headed *Shaw's Haulage*, was a brief letter, written yesterday.

Dear Mrs Armstrong,

I find that my manager is after all responsible for the damage that was recently done to your vehicles. I assure you that this happened without my knowledge or connivance.

I deeply regret any inconvenience caused, and assure you that it will not happen again. If you will be so good as to refer any expenses incurred to me at the above address, I will personally ensure that they are met in full.

Yours sincerely,
R. Shaw

Diana gave a crow of delight, made a number of calls to let everyone on the rota know they would not be needed after all, locked up the office and carried the letter home in triumph to Carol. The day was hot and the sun was shining, so they celebrated by taking Sharon for a picnic in a sunny, sheltered dip in the fells about three miles away.

"Do you think he really does mean to pay?" Carol asked, as they lay stretched on a rug beside the burn, with Sharon crawling around between them.

"He's put it in writing, so, yes, I should think so. We shall have to see. Since I've also got it in writing that Shaw's was responsible, I suppose I could take him to court if he doesn't pay up."

"Couldn't you anyway?"

"It'll cost less to settle it this way."

"Do you suppose he really didn't know what Bill Akehurst was up to?"

"I don't know. He's a good actor if not. But that's not to say he wouldn't have let it go if we hadn't found out about it, and been glad enough we were in trouble."

"I used to think you quite liked Ronnie Shaw," Carol observed.

Diana, aware, to her annoyance, that she was blushing, rolled over to pick Sharon up and carry her to the water's edge. "Maybe I did, until I realised what sort of man he is." She reached down into the water. "Here, Sharon, look at this pretty stone!"

That evening, Shirley called at the flat to say that the drivers were meeting up at the Queen's Head, for a celebratory drink; did Diana and Carol wish to join them?

"Oh yes!" exclaimed Carol.

Diana did not, and in any case someone had to stay with Sharon; on the other hand, Carol was very young. She hesitated.

"I'll keep an eye on her," Shirley promised. "Make sure she stays on the orange juice and doesn't stop out too late."

The Queen's Head was the most respectable of the Wearbridge public houses, and the most modern – it even, sometimes, allowed children into a corner of the lounge bar, if their parents were drinking, where most of the Dale's publicans frowned upon unaccompanied women and made sure they were shown how unwelcome they were; some flatly refused to allow a woman across the threshold, even with a male escort. Carol enjoyed feeling that she was one of the men, in a way, though they treated her at first with careful politeness, moderating their language even more than usual; later, many pints of beer later, they became less restrained, more voluble, and as the language ripened, the tales recounted became ruder and very much funnier. Even Shirley drank a good deal, to Carol's surprise, as she seemed otherwise to take her duties as chaperon very seriously, rejecting all Carol's pleas to be allowed just one half pint of beer. "No one will know I'm not old enough!" Carol urged, but Shirley continued resolutely to shake her head.

Later, Carol and Shirley made their way home together through the quiet streets – to reach the garage, they had to pass the house where Shirley lodged. Six pints of the Queen's Head's best bitter had mellowed Shirley into a soft and sentimental mood. She stumbled along with an arm round Carol's shoulder, singing a rude song under her breath, too low – fortunately – for the words to be audible. Carol, caught up by the pleasures of the evening, almost felt as if she too were a little drunk, giggling, light-headed, without a care. Tonight, Shirley was no longer an older woman with a lifetime's experience that Carol envied, as far as she knew about it, and a tendency to mother her. She'd become a mate, a friend – they were two girls together, as Carol had been with her schoolfriends in the days before her marriage, sharing secrets and silliness. She was filled with a mixture of nostalgia and euphoria. "Couldn't do this if I was still with Kenny – he'd never let me out like this. Best thing I did, leaving him."

"So it was, so it was," agreed Shirley, who'd never met Kenny, though Carol had once pointed him out to her as he roared by on his motorbike. "Who needs men?"

"Have you ever been married?"

"Not me, love, not me. More sense. No men, no kids, no ties." She tugged Carol closer to her side, almost throwing her off balance. Then she came to a halt and gazed intently into the girl's face. "You're a love, do you know that? Pretty too, very pretty!" She ran a hand caressingly down Carol's cheek, onto her neck, where it began to move round to the back, fingers thrusting into her hair.

Carol stiffened, suddenly becoming aware that there was something here that was more than just a reversion to girlish sentimentality. The next moment, Shirley had locked her in a clumsy embrace and was making an attempt to kiss her.

Carol broke free, stepped back, with a hasty look round to make sure no one could have seen them. (There was – thank goodness! – nobody about.) The movement of recoil seemed to have gone part-way to sobering Shirley – enough, at least, for her to realise what was happening. Even in the dim light Carol could see that her face had a rueful expression. "You're not interested, are you?"

Carol was not wholly sure what she was supposed to be not interested in, but nodded her head vigorously.

"Stupid question – I knew that anyway. Just my fucking luck. Story of my life that. Sorry, love. Didn't mean to give offence. Forget it happened, yes?"

Carol swallowed hard. "Yes." Then, suddenly sorry for the distress on the other woman's face, she said matter-of-factly, "I'd best be on my way. Goodnight then. See you tomorrow!"

Shirley gave an uncertain wave, said goodnight in her turn, and strode unsteadily off into the night. Carol felt sick, bewildered, filled with a horrible sense that she must now reassess everything that had ever passed between her and Shirley. She had liked Shirley very much, enjoyed her company, looked up to her, envied her, even found herself touched by the other woman's protectiveness towards her. All those simple, pleasurable things now looked very different, almost sinister.

She had never come across anyone like this before, or not to her knowledge. Of course, they had talked about such things at school, whispering and giggling. Many girls had an occasional crush on an older pupil or one of the younger nuns; some were even felt to take this a bit far. But Carol had never been quite sure what was behind the whispers, what precisely was the nature of the feelings between those afflicted by them. She had never once felt the remotest attraction for anyone of her own sex.

Now, a growing awareness had been forced upon her, and she felt acutely uncomfortable. Her mother had promised that as soon as work on the damaged wagon was completed, she could spend a day in Shirley's company, acting as driver's mate. But now she did not know what to do. Tell her mother she didn't want to go, knowing that Diana would be puzzled and would immediately want to know why? She knew she could never tell her mother what had happened tonight, from embarrassment on her own part and from some residual and as yet unexplored sympathy for Shirley. The other alternative was to agree to the arrangement and spend an acutely uncomfortable day trying to keep a distance between herself and Shirley while in an unavoidable physical proximity.

She had still not resolved the question by the time she arrived at the depot on Monday morning, feeling exhausted after two sleepless nights. The first person she saw, to her alarm, was Shirley herself, who would normally be on the road by this time, but who was standing by the workshop, clearly waiting for her. She came to meet Carol as she left her mother at the office and took a few reluctant steps towards the workshop. Carol felt herself blushing furiously, and saw that Shirley too had gone red, though she did not speak until they were close enough to be able to talk quietly, with no danger of being overheard. "Caz, I'm sorry about what happened Saturday. I was drunk, or it wouldn't have . . . It shouldn't have anyway. It won't ever again, I promise. I'll not speak of it again, if you won't."

Carol looked at her, though she glanced round first to make sure there was no one remotely within earshot. "OK," she said. Whatever her misgivings, she found herself believing Shirley, enough at least to give her a second chance. When the other woman held out a hand she hesitated a moment before returning the handshake, and then made sure it was as brief as possible. She watched Shirley walk away, knowing that nothing had really been resolved.

She went into the workshop, where Colin was leaning against the cab of the wagon drinking his first mug of tea of the day. Could he have heard or seen anything? Would he have drawn any conclusions if he had? Colin was neither intelligent nor perceptive, but what of the other men? How many others, more worldly-wise than she was, guessed about Shirley's tendencies – even knew about them? Worse, would they think that Carol shared them, since she seemed to be so much in the older woman's company? And if Carol were to become driver's mate for Shirley, would that not simply reinforce any such view? As she set to work on the lorry she tried to think of ways out of the difficulty. She had so set her heart on this promised treat that her mother would think it very odd if she were to try and back out, and she could think of no plausible excuse to do so, short of the drastic and unthinkable route of sabotaging another vehicle so she would have to stay behind and repair it. Besides, she did genuinely want to ride with Shirley – with anyone, for it was as near as she was likely to come to actual driving for years yet. She thought of a previous occasion when she had ridden with Shirley, of being shown how to rope a load and secure a tarpaulin, of stopping in a café for a meal, of the talk and laughter, all things that now made her feel apprehensive and awkward in anticipation. Then she recalled how other drivers had made complimentary remarks about her, had tried to chat her up, until repelled by Shirley, for which at the time she had been grateful. Well, in future she would reject that kind of help. *I'll just have to bloody well make sure everyone can see I'm not like that*, she resolved. *Let them see I really like men.* Colin finished his tea and came over to give what he regarded as assistance, and, true to her new resolve, she greeted him warmly, with a quick smile. She saw how astonished he was, and hoped he wasn't pleased as well. Life was complicated enough as it was.

A week later the lorry was back on the road and Diana totalled up the cost of the repair, adding a reasonable sum for inconvenience and other consequential expenses, and sent off a businesslike claim to Ronnie. Two days later he drove to the depot and knocked on the office door, though he did not wait for an answer before coming in. "Hoped I'd find you here today. Thought I'd deliver this in person," he said, handing Diana a sealed envelope.

She opened it, watching him warily as she did so. Inside was a cheque for the precise amount she had asked for. "Thank you," she said stiffly.

"It was the least I could do, as you know. I wish it hadn't happened, but at least I hope this can be the end of it."

She had no intention of letting him off as easily as that. She did not even ask him to sit down, though she might have been able to feel more on equal terms with him if she had done so; as it was, she had to look up at him, and he seemed to fill the small room. It was odd, she reflected fleetingly, that his presence felt more benevolent than threatening, considering what she knew of him. "It had better be the end of it," she retorted, the more harshly to repel any lingering warmth she might still feel for him, in spite of everything. "But are you sure Bill Akehurst won't try something like that again? You said you didn't know what he was up to, but I've only your word for it. It's easy enough to plead ignorance afterwards."

"Bill Akehurst no longer works for me."

"You've dismissed him!" She was surprised, and it showed.

"What do you expect? You'd have done the same, wouldn't you, if one of your employees had done such a thing?" Tired perhaps of waiting for her invitation, he pulled the chair towards him and sat down. Diana felt even more uncomfortable then, for he seemed so close to her, facing her across the narrow desk.

"Yes, I would – but—"

"Then let's put all this unpleasantness behind us," he urged. "I admit I was sore with you, especially at first. But it all got out of hand. It shouldn't have done. I was wrong to oppose your licence, especially as it gave Bill Akehurst the wrong idea. We don't have to be rivals – there's room for both of us to do well. We were friends once . . ." He paused, and she wondered if he was recalling – as she was – that they had been more than friends. Then he went on, "I'd like to be friends again." He reached out as if to shake hands, but she left his hand hanging in the air. "What's up now? Is that too much for you to stomach?"

"That chance was lost when Bradley died."

"But why? I know you were angry with me then. I admit that proposal of marriage was much too hasty. I won't make that mistake again."

"Mistake! It wasn't any mere mistake I objected to! Besides, you'd already shown your true colours. It was just another example of the same thing, and not the worst at that."

He frowned. "I don't understand."

"That's just the point. To do such a thing and not even know you could possibly have caused any offence! Once, I wouldn't have believed it of you. Now I know better."

"Diana, I really don't know what you're talking about. What have I done – what did I do?" He was clearly thinking back to the time of Bradley's death. "I came to the funeral, but I didn't think that would offend you. Was I wrong? Is that what you didn't like?"

"It's what you did after the funeral." She glared at him. "You really don't see it do you? *That*'s what's so breathtakingly repellent. You muscle in on the funeral, march into the wake, and the first thing you do is collar Jackson and demand to buy up the firm, before Bradley's even cold in the ground. I had—"

He rose to his feet, leaning towards her over the desk; the chair clattered to the floor behind him. "Here, wait a moment! What did Jackson tell you?"

Not wanting to be put at a disadvantage, she rose too, facing him, eye to eye. "He said you'd made an offer, there and then, straight after the funeral. It's true isn't it?"

"It's true. But only because he came to me and asked what I'd give for the business. *He* approached me, not the other way round. I wouldn't have dreamed of speaking of it otherwise, at such a time and in such a place. Oh, Diana, how could you have thought that of me?"

She felt the force of his reproach, like a blast of fire in her face. He looked and sounded like a man who had been deeply wronged.

But had he? Was he telling the truth? Was it likely? She thought of Jackson, and his eagerness to be rid of the business, to make money to put into the farm; the way he had pressured her for a quick decision. Yes, it was likely, only too likely. She should have known. It was after all the obvious explanation, entirely in character. She looked at Ronnie's face, the hurt in it, that she should have thought so badly of him. She felt a growing sense of shame. Why had she not thought of that? Knowing Ronnie as once she had done, knowing Jackson, she should have realised how it was. She had a sudden desolating sense of opportunities lost, of trust irrevocably destroyed; a recollection of things said which she knew were beyond forgiveness.

There was a long silence, which she felt she must break somehow. But how? She stood before him feeling as she supposed a criminal must feel in the dock, her hands by her sides, her head bent. "I don't know what to say," she said at last. "Except that I'm very sorry, more sorry than I can find words for."

For a long time he said nothing, simply looked at her, as if still not quite able to take it all in. "Does this make us quits?" he asked at last, though she sensed that he was by no means sure of the answer. His voice sounded oddly shaky, as if the force of what she had told him had disturbed him to his very roots.

"No – no this is much worse." She did look him in the face then. "Thank you for the cheque." She resisted an impulse to return it to him, as a means of underlining her apology. Then the phone rang. It was Geoff, ringing from the Parkgate site to say he was having trouble with his wagon, which had failed to start after he'd tipped his load. "I'll get someone down there," she said, trying to sound calm in spite of her irritation.

"I'll be going," Ronnie murmured. She could see the reproach in his eyes long after she'd heard his car drive away.

Seven

C arol woke half an hour before the alarm was due and reached out to switch it off, while her mind adjusted to the day and what it held for her. A weekday, so there would be work in the depot as usual – or was there to be a journey with Shirley, when they'd stop in a transport café and she might come across Dave, or Tony, or one of the other young drivers met on the road who made it clear they admired her?

Last week, at a petrol station near Carlisle, she and Tony had gone to an unsavoury but private corner behind the petrol pumps, and they'd had an exciting snog, coming as near as she'd yet gone to going the whole way. It had been fun, but she couldn't wait until she was driving by herself and could do what she liked, without fear of being observed. Shirley was no longer as protective as she had been before that uncomfortable, revelatory evening three years ago, but it was still hard to escape her watchful gaze when they were travelling together.

Then she remembered, with an explosion of joy: it was indeed a weekday, but no ordinary weekday. This was going to be the best day in her life so far: Friday, 2 June 1967, her twenty-first birthday; the most special birthday she had ever lived through. From today she was fully and completely an acknowledged adult; from today, she would be able to drive. She knew she would burst if she lay still any longer. She sat up, swung her legs over the side of the bed, and then saw the empty cot. Sharon – now a sturdy three-year-old – must have let down the side and crept out, some time before she herself awoke. From within the flat came soft noises, whisperings and gigglings and the occasional clatter; clearly, Diana and Sharon were making an early cup of tea, to surprise her. Carol sighed. She could not bring herself to spoil things for her daughter, so she lay down again and pulled the covers over her, forcing herself to wait, listening, tingling with impatience, for the knock on the door. It came at last, after what seemed an age, accompanied by further soft giggles. "Come in!"

Diana carried the cup of tea, and Sharon's small face was hidden behind a large flat parcel, which she struggled to carry to the bedside, where she toppled it on to the bedspread; an envelope slid off the top of it. Then child and grandmother sang "Happy Birthday to you", while Carol, pink with pleasure and embarrassment, beamed at them. Then there were hugs and kisses all round, until Sharon tore herself from her mother's embrace and squealed, "Open it! Open it!" She clutched at the envelope: "This first!"

Inside the envelope was a card on thick paper, brilliantly if crudely coloured and inscribed with "Love from Sharon" in wobbly uneven writing, under which, much more firmly, was drawn a row of kisses. "Did you make this all by yourself?"

Sharon nodded with enthusiasm, before adding more candidly, "Anne helped me."

Anne again! Carol thought. *It would be!* She placed the card very carefully on the bedside table, putting Anne out of her mind. "I think you're very clever," she said, and again embraced her daughter, who clutched her enthusiastically about the neck until Carol had to break free for her own comfort. "Now, let's see what this is." She began to tear the paper off the parcel. Inside was a new road atlas, marking all the latest motorways. "Wonderful! Thank you," Carol said, looking at her mother with real pleasure, though a small unedifying inner voice whispered that it was a somewhat meagre gift for a twenty-first birthday.

"That's just something to be going on with," said Diana. "There'll be a surprise for you later."

"Oh, tell me what it is!"

91

"Then it wouldn't be a surprise, would it? No, wait until the right time."

"When will that be?"

"Wait and see."

Carol leapt out of bed. "I think 'wait and see' is the most annoying sentence in the whole of the English language."

"Will bacon and egg for breakfast make up for it?"

"Bacon and egg!" crowed Sharon, and skipped after her grandmother into the kitchen. "And tomato, Nana!"

There were more cards at breakfast, one from Diana and several that had come in the post during the previous days, from the few far-flung Armstrong relatives, and from Granny Poultney, widowed since last year. There were, of course, no greetings from any other members of the Poultney family, but at least her grandmother had made up for their deficiences by enclosing a substantial cheque. "Ten pounds!" Carol exclaimed. "Mam, that's a fortune!"

There was a letter too, which she read and then passed to her mother. "She sounds OK, but you can see she misses Grandpa."

"So do I," said Diana. "I still wish I could have got to the funeral." Dr Poultney had died very suddenly of a stroke, just as Diana herself was struck down by appendicitis, for which she had to undergo an emergency operation on the very day of the funeral.

"You got to the memorial service," Carol reminded her. That had been held in Wearbridge, where Diana had been moved to see the church full, realising how many people still had kind memories of the Dale's much-loved doctor.

"Yes, but Granny was the only other member of the family to come to that. If I could have been at the funeral, perhaps I'd have been able to make it up with the others."

"If they can't forgive you for getting pregnant all those years ago, then they're not worth bothering with," said Carol with a new and adult boldness. "That is why they pretend you don't exist, isn't it?"

It was something that had still never been openly acknowledged by Diana, but now she said slowly, "To be fair, they didn't have any choice about it at first, or at least Angela and Robert didn't – they were still children. Mother and Father didn't want them to think it was the right way to behave, and kept us apart."

Carol stared at her mother, trying to imagine how that must have felt. Not having any siblings herself, it was hard, but she experienced a surge of anger towards her grandparents. "That's awful! How could your own parents do that to you?"

"I understand why they did it, I suppose," admitted Diana, uncomfortably red. "Later, I know they tried to bring us together again. I even wrote to all of them, via my parents, but none of them replied, not even Pamela. I think now that my worst sin in her eyes, wasn't the baby, but marrying beneath me."

"Beneath you!" exclaimed Carol. "What do you mean? The Armstrongs were always one of the best-respected families in the Dale."

Diana coloured uncomfortably. It was clear that the views she had accepted – however reluctantly – as commonplace were wholly alien to her daughter. "I suppose they thought a doctor's daughter should have married someone – well, with a professional background, at least."

"Then they're snobs and we're better off without them!" With one of her swift changes of mood Carol's frown changed to a grin. "Come on, Mam, it's my birthday. Forget about them."

Diana smiled. "You're quite right. I'm sorry, my dear." She glanced at the clock. "Time we were on our way!"

The flat was engulfed in the usual early morning rush, after which the three of them found themselves on the garage forecourt, with Sharon in her pushchair, ready for the five-minute walk to Anne's house. This morning they were both to take her there.

Anne welcomed them at the door as usual and, as usual, Sharon, released from her pushchair, ran happily into the house. Anne had a card and a box of chocolates for Carol, who thanked her warmly, though there was an element of gritted teeth in the thanks. Anne was perfection; no mother could wish for a better minder for her child. She read stories to her charges, sang nursery rhymes, and had toys that were both educational and fun to use, so that children loved to come to her. Sharon adored her; which was the trouble, of course, because Carol wondered, often, if her daughter loved her mother as much as she loved her minder. She said nothing of her feelings to anyone, for she sensed they were unworthy. How, after all, could she do the job she loved without Anne? If anything, she was going to need her more than ever in the months to come. And at least she could have no doubts at all that her child was being well cared for.

But today the reflection could cast no more than the smallest, briefest blight over her spirits; today she was going to drive. Her feet felt winged as she parted with her mother – Diana was due to spend the morning sorting out the drivers' wages – and made her way to the layby where Shirley was waiting beside the new eight-wheeler Foden. The older woman pushed a small package into her hands. "Happy Birthday!"

Inside was a neat little travelling alarm clock, covered in green leather. "Oh, thank you!" Carol was touched, recognising that it must have cost a good deal, as well as having been chosen with care. "It's just what I need too." The clock she used now was a spare one of her mother's.

Shirley grinned. "But I know this is what you really want." She opened the door on the driver's side and bowed to usher Carol in. Jubilant, Carol climbed up into the cab, taking that longed-for position behind the steering wheel, while Shirley took the seat in which she had so often sat in the past. Diana had insisted that Carol have a driver's mate for this first experience of driving on the road, though her daughter had tried to insist it was quite unnecessary. Now, she felt glad of Shirley's cheerful, sensible presence as she switched on the engine, glanced in her mirror and up and down the road, and gently eased the vehicle out of the layby. She had driven often enough at the depot, become used to negotiating wagons into difficult spaces. She had been sure that this would be different, and better. It was; but it was also suddenly, momentarily, utterly terrifying. All this power in her hands, and the winding road with who knew what hazards hidden around its corners . . . For a moment she felt something close to panic.

Then it was gone as if it had never been, and in its place was only an immense joy. Now, today, in this instant, all the different parts of her experience of driving came together, fused, found their focus and their goal. The child who had first sat at the wheel of a lorry on her father's knees, with his hands guiding hers on the steering wheel; the girl who had felt confined in the cramped, low space of a car, and almost despised the skill that got her through the driving test at her first attempt – that person came of age now on the Dale road, as she changed gear, steered, took note of junctions and blind bends and road signs and other vehicles, controlled the lorry as easily, as instinctively, as if she had been doing it all her life. Today she was a woman, and she was doing at last what she, who had been that child and that girl, was always meant to do.

Halfway to the depot, she caught Shirley's eye, and the other woman laughed suddenly. "You've got a silly grin on your face. Have had ever since you got into that seat."

Carol grinned even more. "I love this!"

"No surprise. Feels right, doesn't it?"

"Is that how you felt the first time?"

"Aye! Never forgotten that day. You won't either. Nowt like it."

To Carol, everything in the Dale looked different today, from her noisy new vantage point. Every stone wall enclosing hay field or pasture, every freshly green tree, the distant shining glimpses of the river, seemed outlined with a new clarity. In the villages they passed through, women waiting at bus stops seemed to gaze at her with awe, old men turned from talking outside pubs or by field gates to watch her go by. They reached the cement works, open and fully working for two years now, and Carol recognised one of Kenny's friends crossing the yard beyond the gate. She pressed the horn, and saw him glance round, halt, stare; and then wave. She waved back, feeling triumphant. She hoped he would

95

take the news back to Kenny, whom she saw occasionally, but from whom she had heard nothing for months now, not even on Sharon's birthday or at Christmas.

The depot, too, looked different, when they reached it, though it had not in fact changed a great deal in the three years since the firm had faced the results of Ronnie Shaw's resentment. There was new and better equipment in the workshops, and a solid stone building had replaced the wooden hut which housed the office, after it was finally blown to pieces during a winter storm. There were five new wagons too – one of them articulated – so that none of the firm's vehicles was unreliable any longer, and four new full-time drivers, one to replace Dick, who had been dismissed after once coming in drunk to work; they had also begun to take on part-timers. It was just a depot, as it had always been, but today it seemed a glorious, shining place, welcoming Carol as it had never welcomed her before.

She was teased of course, unmercifully, by the men, but with affection (except from Colin, who would probably continue to resent her to his dying day, especially as he had not yet succeeded in passing his driving test). Norman and Geoff had cards for her, and Bruce gave her a present of a record she liked, Procol Harum's "A Whiter Shade of Pale". "From me and Smokey," he said. Carol patted the dog, by way of thanks.

After that, it was a normal working day, though everything was fresh and exciting to Carol. She had done the run from Cowcleugh to the mine's chief customer at the Derwentbank Steel Company often enough before, loading up, securing the load, the tipping, and back again for more; but then she had been only a driver's mate. Now, even with Shirley beside her, she felt completely different, aware of every single moment, conscious both that today the ultimate responsibility was hers alone, and confident in her ability to do the work well. She was astonished when Shirley suddenly said, "Twelve o'clock. Weren't you to be back in Wearbridge about now?"

Disbelieving how quickly the time had gone, Carol admitted that she had promised to go home for lunch, instead of taking sandwiches to eat in the cab during her break, as the drivers generally did. Next week, she would please herself – one ought, she thought resentfully, to be able to please oneself on one's birthday, but her mother had been very pressing, and she supposed she had to keep to the arrangement. She drove to Wearbridge, where, outside the petrol station, she handed the vehicle over to Shirley and watched her drive away. Then, her happy mood souring fast, she went upstairs to the flat.

Diana had gone to a great deal more trouble with lunch than usual. In honour of the day, instead of simply opening a tin of beans, she had prepared a celebratory meal with her daughter's tastes (and her own abilities) in mind – something called *Paella*, from an easy recipe found in a woman's magazine Carol had recently bought (rice, left-over chicken, frozen peas and a tin of shrimps, with onion, tomatoes, green pepper and garlic – the two last triumphantly run to earth in a specialist greengrocer's in Durham the previous week), followed by an instant strawberry pudding out of a packet from the Co-op. There was a bottle of Schloer apple juice standing ready on the sideboard, from which Diana poured two glasses as soon as Carol came into the flat. She handed one to Carol. "I'm sorry it's not anything stronger in honour of such a great occasion, but we've both got to drive this afternoon – I'm not taking any chances with this new breathalyser. You can make up for it tonight." Then, to Carol's surprise, she stood for quite some time with the glass held in her hand and her head bent, as if pondering something, before looking up suddenly and saying, "You know I said there would be something else to come later today?"

Carol nodded, darting a glance at the table: she could see only a pile of cards – this morning's post – to the right of her place, and a thick official-looking envelope to the left, between her place and her mother's. No festively wrapped parcels, no large gifts. Her mother meanwhile had at last raised her tumbler.

"Happy Birthday, and congratulations – to my new partner in Queen of the Road!"

Carol, with her own glass halfway to her lips, froze, mouth

open. What was her mother saying? What she thought she was saying . . . ?

"That's if you agree, of course," Diana added, unable perhaps to gauge her daughter's reaction. That Carol was astonished was clear enough – but pleased too; or dismayed?

Light seemed to spread over Carol's face. "Agree? Of course I agree!" She put down her glass so quickly that the apple juice slopped stickily on to the sideboard. Then she hugged her mother. "Oh, Mam – do you really mean it? I'm to be a partner?"

"It'll be hard work. You'll have to take decisions, and bear the consequences if things go wrong. So far you've given me your opinion often enough, and very helpful it's been too, but in the end you've not been the one to carry the responsibility. As my partner that'll change. And you'll have to concern yourself with tedious things like accounts and balance sheets and government legislation."

Carol stood back, gazed into her mother's anxious face. "I know, Mam. I promise not to leave it all to you. Besides, it'll be much better, two of us doing it. A trouble shared . . ." She took up her glass again and they drank, solemnly, to the future. Then she did a delighted dance about the room. "A partner! Fabulous! Oh Mam, thanks!"

"There'll be papers to sign," Diana said a little later, as they took their seats at the table. "That's why I wanted you back here for lunch. Once that's done, then we'll go up to the depot and I'll make a formal announcement to everyone." They helped themselves to the *paella* and began to eat.

"This isn't bad, for you," said Carol with a grin. "Fit for a business partner."

"There's one thing, the business is in pretty good shape at present."

"Thanks to Grandpa, I suppose." In his will, Dr Poultney had arranged for the loan he'd made to his daughter to be written off, and had also left her a considerable additional sum.

"In a way it couldn't have come at a better time, just when we had to replace those two wagons to meet the new contract. Now we've no debts, plenty of work but not more than we can cope with, not many unpaid bills. So long as we don't get nationalised – and I really don't think that will happen this time – then if things go on like this we'll be making our first really good profit by the end of the year."

"I heard there's another mine opening up again."

"I know. Dale Industrials phoned me yesterday. That's on the agenda for our first partners' meeting."

Carol paused, her fork halfway to her mouth. "Is this it?"

"If you really want to talk business on your birthday," said her mother with a smile. "Though you're not strictly a partner just yet, until you've signed."

Nevertheless, they discussed the implications of the possible new contract while they ate, and by the end of the meal had decided that they could take it on, now that Carol's coming-of-age had given them an additional driver.

Later, at the depot, Diana called the workforce together earlier than usual, to where, in the office, she poured apple juice for them all – ignoring a muttered comment from Harry about "Gnat's piss" – and made her announcement. "You all know it's Carol's twenty-first today. But there's another cause for celebration. From this afternoon she's become an equal partner with me in Queen of the Road. So, I give you my new partner! Carol!"

None of them seemed unduly surprised – it was after all only to be expected – and since most of them liked Carol they appeared to be pleased. But Carol suddenly saw, sensed, a change, small and subtle, but there all the same, in their eyes, their demeanour. She was no longer simply one of them. As a mechanic she had been accepted, and then respected; as a driver, for one exhilarating morning, she had been, almost, one of the lads. Now, abruptly, that had gone. An insurmountable barrier had suddenly been thrust between them. She had become one of the bosses. Queen of the Road might be run informally, with a light touch, but even so the workforce knew that Diana was in charge, and that she was set apart from them for that very reason; she was the boss, "them" to their "us". Now Carol had joined her.

Through all her elation, through her pride, Carol felt a little chill, even a momentary sadness.

Then Bruce suggested they meet in the Queen's Head to drink to her success, and the sadness went. It was still her birthday, still the most wonderful birthday she had ever known. And this evening she would drive herself and Shirley back to Wearbridge in the wagon, to put the seal on this day of days.

Eight

"That child's in a funny mood," Carol observed, as she watched Sharon stand on tiptoe by the bathroom basin, brushing her teeth with more than her usual thoroughness.

"She's looking forward to school," was Diana's explanation, called from the kitchen, where she was washing up the breakfast dishes.

Carol realised with surprise that it was true. She had only the dimmest recollection of her own first day at school, though she knew it had been a place she had accepted as a necessary if not wholly desirable part of life.

Sharon, on the other hand, seemed to be full of joyful anticipation, which in her case meant that she was very quiet, showing her feelings only by an occasional skipping step in her walk – when the happiness became too much for her – and a smiling face that seemed lit from within. Carol was puzzled by this odd child, who felt to her like a creature of another species. How could she and Kenny have given life to a creature so utterly different from themselves? Kenny had emerged from school scarcely able to read, and she, though reasonably intelligent, had never shown any intellectual leanings; from the first her interests had all been outside school. But Sharon could already read, though Anne swore she had done nothing to teach the child, except read her stories from her stock of colourful picture books. She could count up to twenty, too. Walking at her mother's side along a street, she would read shop signs (sometimes with very odd pronunciations), count parked cars, show herself sharply observant in a way that Carol – and Diana too – found startling in a child so young. "God knows where she gets it from!" Carol had said more than once, feeling both awed and a little resentful – after all, it was she who had gone through all the trouble of giving birth to this changeling; Sharon might at least have had the grace to show some likeness to her mother.

"Ready, Mam." Sharon was at her side, neat and shining in grey skirt, white blouse and blue jumper, her patent shoes securely buckled over her white socks. She was irritatingly well behaved; Carol had been an untidy, disorderly, disobedient child, a normal child.

Yet she loved her daughter, and this first day of her starting school was going to be a difficult one. It had been easy enough to arrange to be two hours late for work this morning, so that she could take Sharon to school herself. She accepted reluctantly that she would have to leave that role to Anne after today, but today was important to both mother and daughter. But school finished at three fifteen, and there were several essential deliveries to be completed before then. Even if she made excellent time she could not be sure of getting to the school gate in time, and she did not want to risk leaving the child unmet on her first day.

Anne, with exasperating perceptiveness, had said, "I'll be ready to meet her, but if you find you're finished in time just give me a ring and you can do it. I'll give her tea about four if you're not back by then." Anne was always so understanding, so *right*! And almost certainly it would be Anne, as usual, who would listen to Sharon's first fresh account of the day's events, who would comfort her if she were unhappy about anything or share her joy in what had gone well. As so often, Carol found herself seething with a resentment she rarely voiced, because she felt powerless to do anything about it. In any case, how could you show resentment of someone so perfect, so much the mother's ideal?

At school, Sharon, raising her sweet, spotless face for her mother's parting kiss, allowed herself to be handed over to the ample, smiling care of the reception class teacher without a tear or a backward look. Other children around her howled or whimpered and clung to their mothers, but not Sharon. She was already looking round eagerly to see what the classroom offered. Feeling superfluous and rejected, Carol left the school and made her way to the layby where her favourite wagon, the Foden, had been parked up for the night.

Once at the wheel, turning on to the road, all the sourness, the resentment, the disappointment, slid from her. She was in the right place, doing what she was meant to do, and she was happy. From this vantage point she could only be grateful for Anne's kindly competence, for Sharon's contentment, since they allowed her to drive without guilt or anxiety.

It was not until work ended that the ugly feelings of the morning returned. She did not finish until after five, and it was later still by the time she had parked the wagon and walked to Anne's house. The minder did not come to the door herself, but sent Sharon to greet her mother, keeping tactfully in the background while the child responded to the hug, went in search of her coat, said goodbye and walked down the path to the road, her hand in Carol's. "School was great," said Sharon, as they turned out of the gate. There was a note of excitement in her voice, controlled but unmistakable. Carol questioned her as she walked, though there did not seem very much in her child's account for anyone to get excited about. She supposed Sharon had already told Anne all the interesting bits, and had by now tired of talking of them – typical, that she should get the leftovers. *You're a cow!* she told herself. *You should be grateful she's so well cared for.*

They went together up the stairs to the flat. *Needs decorating*, Carol reflected, looking at the shabby wallpaper; but neither she nor Diana had time for decorating, and any spare cash went into the business. In the sitting room, her mother, still wearing the duffle coat she wore to work – though surely she would have been home for a while by now? – was standing staring at a piece of paper. She looked round sharply as they came in, as if startled out of some unpleasant reverie. Her smile appeared painfully forced, though she held out her arms towards her granddaughter – Sharon seemed to have brought out a previously unrevealed softness in this naturally undemonstrative woman. "And how was school then, my darling?"

"Good!" said Sharon, emphatically, nodding with tight lips and bright round eyes. Then she went to hang up her coat and Diana handed her daughter the piece of paper she was holding. "From your Aunt Pamela," she said; her voice sounded odd, strained. It was a telegram. *Mother died this morning. Funeral Thursday eleven am.*

"What a horrible way to let you know!" Carol exclaimed. "How can she be so heartless?"

"She has at least told me the time of the funeral," Diana pointed out, as if it was a great concession.

"She's your sister, for goodness sake!" Then Carol saw, as if for the first time, the look of desolation on her mother's face. She put her arms about her. "Sorry, Mam. I know you'll miss her."

Not for the first time, Diana had an odd sensation that for a moment her daughter had caught up with her, on equal terms – no, not equal this time, for their roles had been temporarily reversed. For now, Carol was the one giving comfort, doing the mothering, and it was Diana who felt as lost as a little child. How was it possible, at forty-six, to feel suddenly orphaned, because the mother she had scarcely seen for thirty years had died?

"I didn't know she'd been ill," Carol said eventually.

"Nor did I. Well, last winter, yes, she had that bad bout of flu. But I'd thought she was over it. She didn't say anything in her letters. I wish I knew – I wish I could phone Pamela and talk to her."

"Can't you?"

"She hasn't given me her number, and I don't know it."

"What about Directory Enquiries?"

"I don't know where she's living now. She moved a few years ago."

"Isn't there another sister?"

"I don't know Angela's married name. If Mother ever mentioned it, I've forgotten." Carol, accustomed to the sometimes over-demanding closeness of her father's family, felt enraged, and bewildered too. "Makes me glad I'm an only one!" she declared. She recalled then that there had once been a brother, little Jacky who had died on the eve of the war, and hoped she was not obliquely adding to her mother's pain.

But today that old grief was a long way from Diana's mind. She gave a repressed sob. "I always meant to visit her, but there was always too much . . ."

"You wrote a lot, and so did she." It seemed to Carol that all her life there had been letters from Granny Poultney falling on to the doormat, to be read over breakfast or later in the day; and her mother often seemed to be seated at the dining table, writing her long replies, passing on all her news. "That's almost as good." Then: "Here – I'll make us a cup of tea. You sit down, Mam." She helped her mother out of her coat and led her to the sofa, where Sharon soon climbed on to her knee.

Later, over the tea, Carol said, "Shall I drive us there, or shall we go by train?"

Diana, stroking the sleepy child's soft brown hair, looked bewildered. "Where?"

"The funeral, of course. Do you know where it'll be?"

"At Fleetham village church, I suppose, where Father's was. But I don't see how we can go."

"Why ever not? We'd need to go down the day before, I suppose, but we could come back straight afterwards. One night away at most. You can trust Norman to keep his eye on things." Norman had recently been made the firm's Transport Manager – growing rather too old to enjoy driving, he had proved a surprisingly effective administrator. "Train might be best," Carol went on. "I'm not sure I could drive that distance in a car." After driving wagons all day, she found her two-year-old Mini a poor substitute. It felt cramped and confined, and dangerously close both to the road itself and to other traffic.

"But what about Sharon?"

"She can stay with Anne."

Diana gave her daughter a sidelong look. "Thank you," she said gently, and something in her tone told Carol that she understood everything that her daughter felt about Anne. That was the thing about being a mother – you understood other mothers, in a way no one else could. At the moment, the thought of ever losing Diana was suddenly unbearable to Carol, though until now it had never entered her head as a possibility.

The next moment she suddenly smiled. "Look at that child – fast asleep. I'd better get her to bed."

The beautiful mediaeval church at Fleetham was already half full when Carol and Diana emerged from the taxi that had brought them from the station three quarters of an hour before the funeral. The three front pews were empty, reserved for family members, most of whom would come into the church behind the coffin – as they themselves should have done, Carol reflected, if only someone had told them where the family was gathering beforehand. She took her mother's arm and steered her towards the empty pews, installing her at her side at the further end of the very front pew. A sidesman bustled after them, bent over Carol and whispered, "This pew is for family only, I'm afraid."

"We are family!" When Carol told him precisely who they were, he apologised and made his way back to his post in some embarrassment.

Diana sat with bent head, absorbed in reflection. Carol, who had found her grandmother far too straight-laced for affectionate recollection, filled in the time by glancing behind her at intervals to see who was coming into church – not that she expected to recognise anyone, but it interested her to know what kind of people had come to pay their respects to Evelyn Poultney.

For the most part, as she would have expected, they were obviously well-to-do, the kind of people who had several well-made, well-cut outfits in their wardrobes suitable for funeral wear, and were now precisely turned out in clothes that could have been correctly worn for such an event at any time during the past twenty years, with an occasional adjustment of hemline, the addition of a different hat or a new pair of gloves – those "classic clothes" beloved of the more square women's magazines; respectable people of good breeding, with impeccable manners and inflexible principles, who were mainstays of their local Women's Institutes and Parish Councils and knew where, always, to draw the line. She supposed her relatives would be cast in the same mould.

The organ, until now giving an unobtrusive accompaniment to the murmur of the growing congregation (the rest of the church was almost completely full), broke into a more emphatically mournful march, and Carol resisted the impulse to look round again. Family members did not gaze about the church when the coffin arrived; to do so would indicate lack of real grief or – at the very least – good manners. She did not mind that for herself, but she did for her mother. The organ fell silent, the congregation stood and the voice of the priest intoning the funeral sentences filled the church.

Even without looking round, Carol sensed the shocked pause as the funeral party reached the front pew and found it partially occupied. She glanced at her aunts and uncles and cousins out of the corner of her eye. Was one supposed to smile at fellow mourners at a funeral or not? Probably not. In any case no one was smiling at them. Presumably, most of the party had no idea who the intruders were, though there was the softest of whispers passing through it, like a summer wind through ripe corn, heads bending as it went. A dozen or so pairs of eyes stared at them, then looked at their companions in consternation. Then the foremost mourner – a big pale woman – led the way pointedly into the pew behind. The others took her lead, filling that pew before filtering reluctantly into the front one, where they left the largest possible space between themselves and their estranged relations.

As the service progressed, with its soothing words and slow muttered hymns and conventional sermon, Carol managed to see enough to satisfy herself that the rest of what she supposed she must think of as her family were, for the most part, like everyone else in the church, correctly but not at all fashionably dressed. She was a little disappointed in them – after all, they lived within reach of "Swinging London" and all it had to offer, but they might have come from the Outer Hebrides for all the signs of modernity they showed. Even the younger members of the party, some about her own age, seemed to have fallen straight out of the fifties – though one pimply youth did have collar-length hair and looked as if his tie was choking him. She could not see much resemblance to her mother in any of the adults and wasn't quite sure who was a blood relation and who had merely married a Poultney brother or sister. Somehow they all seemed to have a sameness about them, and one that came from another, alien world.

The burial followed immediately in the churchyard, at the grave where Grandpa Poultney had lain alone for a year. There too a circle of isolation set Carol and her mother apart, though Carol thought Diana was too grief-stricken to be concerned, as she had not appeared to notice, either, the space in the pew inside the church. After a moment or two Carol forgot her resentment and edged closer to her mother so she could take her hand, which she thought was as much as her mother would accept in the way of a public demonstration of support. She recalled the open displays of grief at Nana Armstrong's funeral, her daughters sobbing, their husbands hugging them. Here, though the landscape was gentler, the air softer, the churchyard sheltered by magnificent trees, everyone was so cold, so correct, so restrained, with only a tight lip or a vigorously blown nose to indicate the sorrow that was being held in check. But at least Diana's fingers closed tightly about her hand, telling Carol that her small gesture was appreciated.

The burial was over, the coffin lowered into the grave, the gravedigger began to shovel earth on to the coffin. The mourners moved apart, to examine the many wreaths laid about the grave, reform into groups, talk softly and sadly together. Diana, blowing her nose, straightening her shoulders, went over to the large pasty-faced woman who had led the party into church and held out her hands and said, "Pamela!" in a voice rough with emotion. Pamela stared at her for a moment with an expression of complete blankness, as if Diana were somehow invisible, and then turned away, without a word. Instead, she strode towards another, similar, but slightly younger woman who had been looking on, and the group closed about them as they walked out of the churchyard towards the waiting cars, leaving Diana standing there, with the pain exposed on her face for all to see.

Carol gave an exclamation and took a step after them, but then felt her mother's hand close on her wrist. She understood that Diana did not want her to make a scene, that for her it would only make matters worse.

"They'll pay for this!" muttered Carol, as she watched the cars, full of relations, drive away to whatever funeral tea awaited them. "We'll get our own back somehow." Then she realised that the rector had come to speak to her mother and was holding her hand in a comforting grasp. He must have seen what had happened.

He asked how they were getting home, gathered that they planned to catch a train much later in the afternoon, and then invited them to lunch at the rectory. "It'll just be a cold meal, but I know my wife will be as happy as I if you would join us. Then I can run you to the station."

Over the meal, of which Diana ate very little, they learned all the things Diana had wanted to know about her mother's death. It had been sudden and unexpected; one day she had seemed well, the next was found to have an inoperable cancer from which she was dead within three weeks. "We suppose that must have been why she was so ill last winter," said the rector. "In retrospect it was more than just 'flu. And I suspect she may have kept a good deal of pain and distress to herself. She was a brave woman, your mother. And we must be thankful she was seriously unwell for so short a time."

"I should have liked to have seen her again. I wish I'd known she was ill. I would have come."

"If I'd realised no one had let you know, I should have done so myself." The rector seemed genuinely distressed. "But of course your mother was in a coma for most of the last ten days. She couldn't make her wishes known. And if you'd come it would have made no difference to her, I think."

Later, at the station, he had further reassurance. "I'll speak to your sister, and try to do what I can to ease the situation. It's very sad she should be so unforgiving. But perhaps we can see hope in her decision to let you know about the funeral."

"I still don't understand why she did," admitted Diana. "It's obvious she didn't expect me to come."

"Who knows? Let's wait and see." He had already given them Pamela's address, in case they wanted to try and make contact; Angela and Robert lived outside his parish, he did not know precisely where. "You know you can telephone or write to me at any time, if you think I can be of help to you," he added, as the train came into the station.

"Well, he was nice, at least," Carol commented, once they were on their way. She was about to add: *More than you can say for your bitch of a sister*, but knew that her mother would not appreciate so blunt an expression of the truth.

Within a few days of their return home from the funeral, Diana received a letter from her mother's solicitor, informing her that under the terms of her mother's will she was to receive a quarter of Evelyn Poultney's estate. "So that's why they let you know about the funeral," observed Carol cynically that evening. "They'll have known about the will. It would have looked bad if the first you'd heard of your mother's death had been this letter. As it is, no one can say they didn't do their duty." She got up from the table and began vigorously clearing the plates away. "They're swine, all of them!"

"Don't, Carol, it doesn't make things any better!"

Carol was beginning to feel just a little exasperated at her mother's continuing depression. She understood the hurt, but herself felt anger rather than misery. When things went wrong she saw no point in getting depressed; much better to take action. Except that in this case she couldn't see what action to take.

She hated the atmosphere of gloomy restraint, all the things that were unsaid, her mother's eternal niceness. Since the funeral she had made sure she worked only short drives, leaving the longer journeys to other drivers – these days they were often hired to carry loads well outside the Dale, which involved staying away for a night or more. Carol loved the longer drives, the exploring of new places, the people she met, the opportunities for excitement. But concern for her mother kept her, reluctantly, close to home, until, after a week or two of the atmosphere in the flat, she lost patience and ached for cheerfulness, youthful company – in short, normality. Her mother had not actually asked her to stay at home, but it was with some sense of awkwardness that, at the end of their monthly partners' meeting, she said, "You know that job for Southampton on Tuesday, for the steel works?" There was a load of small parts to go from Meadhope to a leisure-boat builder near Southampton.

"Harry's down for that isn't he?"

"I'd like to do it. By myself." She saw something she could not quite interpret in her mother's eyes and felt a pang of guilt. "If you don't mind."

"No – no, of course not, so long as Harry doesn't. There's a backload arranged through his friend in the Midlands – equipment from Birmingham, I think, for somewhere on Teesside. He hasn't given me the details yet." Harry's old friend Fred, manager of a large haulage firm in Wolverhampton which had more business than it could handle, had proved a useful contact when they had a wagon returning empty from a long-distance delivery. "Of course, he may want to see to it himself. I think it gives him an excuse to look up his friend."

"I'll talk to him." Carol was confident of her ability to beguile people into doing what she wanted, if more usual methods failed.

She reached the depot early the following morning, and saw Harry at once: he was standing near the entrance beside a gleaming red sports car. Inevitably, a group of his workmates had already gathered to admire it – though not Shirley, who had never overcome her dislike of Harry (which was not helped by his now referring to her constantly, behind her back at least, as "the dyke").

"Nice car, Harry," Bruce was saying. "Mind, I want to know

what Mrs Armstrong's paying you, affording something like that."

Harry grinned. "Had some good luck on the gee gees."

"Then you know something I don't," Geoff commented. "Anything I back comes in last. How do you do it?"

Harry tapped the side of his nose with his forefinger. "Now that would be telling!" He turned as Carol touched his arm. "Morning, Boss number two. What can I do you for?"

When she told him her proposal, she thought for a moment he was going to reject it. Something close to a frown gathered on his face, though it was quickly gone. Then his dark lively features broke into their customary grin, and he shrugged. "Whatever you like. It's a tricky load, mind, the one from Birmingham – not far off abnormal. You'll need help getting it right."

"Ever known Carol not get any help she needs?" asked Bruce, who had been listening. He put a friendly arm about Carol's shoulder. "Want a driver's mate for the trip?"

Of all the drivers, Bruce (and the inevitable Smokey) was the one she found most congenial – apart from Shirley, of course – but this time she felt the need to be alone, free, in sole control. Bruce took his rejection cheerfully, and Harry promised to look out the details of the backload for her.

She set out early the following Monday, elated by a sense of release: three whole days away from the Dale, and from Diana's misery! She refused to feel guilty about it. She'd been more than dutiful, until now. She deserved a break.

It was a perfect day for driving – clear, fresh and fairly bright, but with only occasional gleams of sunlight and little wind. There were the usual roadworks on the A1, mostly where they were upgrading the road, but she felt less impatient with the delays than usual today. Now and then another haulage driver, recognising her, would flash his headlights at her, or sound his horn. She would do the same in return, or wave cheerfully. She was already becoming known, conspicuous in a man's world. Not that the attention was always welcome. Sometimes men would lean out of their cabs, shouting obscenities as she passed; sometimes they would overtake, cutting in aggressively in front of her. Sometimes another driver would be so full of wonder at seeing her that he would come close to crashing his own vehicle in the astonishment of the moment. She had to be always on her guard, ready to take evasive action if necessary. Once she'd complained of the danger to Shirley. "You can't expect them not to notice you," she'd said.

"They don't do it to you," Carol pointed out.

Shirley grinned ruefully. "They can't tell I'm a woman," she pointed out. "Not till I jump down from the wagon at least." Carol had to acknowledge that she was right.

She saw three Shaw's wagons that day, which was about what she would have expected. Ronnie Shaw was clearly doing well, though he now had very little work within the Dale and almost never came there. He seemed to have resigned himself to finding business elsewhere and leaving the Dale to Queen of the Road. She'd heard he'd opened up several depots in other parts of the country.

She made an overnight stop not far from Oxford, at a decent B&B where she had stayed before. Once booked in and tidied up, she made her way to the nearby transport café where she'd parked the wagon for the night. There she treated herself to several mugs of hearty tea, a large fry-up, a plate of bread and butter and a wedge of fruit cake, at the end of which she could think only of sleep. Outside again, the wind had freshened – even so far south, it struck cold, and she had left her duffle coat in the wagon. She made her way across the shadowed lorry park towards her vehicle.

"Caz! Caz Armstrong!"

She turned to see who had called, though it was growing too dark to make out more than a tall muscular shape coming after her from the direction of the café. She waited, a little wary, until he caught up with her. Then she saw a round boyish face crowned with blonde curls, the gleam of blue eyes, and knew who it was. "Dave! What are you doing here?"

113

"What are *you* doing?"

She told him, and they exchanged news of a trivial kind. She'd met Dave two or three times now on her travels, always by chance, and had liked him from the first. He was unfailingly cheerful, good company, with a ready laugh, and he clearly found her attractive. They had snogged a couple of times and he had made it clear he'd have liked more, and she had been tempted – greatly tempted – but she had brushed him aside with a joke, which he had – fortunately – taken in good part. It was not because he was married, though Carol knew he had a wife back home in Darlington. After all, she knew, because she had seen him in action, that he picked up girls wherever he went, a night here, a night there, for dancing or drinking with, and what came after. She guessed that they meant very little to him, except a bit of fun; they probably knew that too, and so, perhaps, did his wife.

Carol had long ago come to the conclusion that the wives of long-distance drivers were fools if they thought their husbands were faithful. One or two were, but they were the exception. But she knew the dangers such behaviour might hold for her. She was well aware that what was perfectly acceptable in a man on the road would be regarded quite differently in a woman. An occasional snog was one thing, sleeping around was another. She had no wish to get a reputation for being a slag. In any case, most of the offers that had come her way in the year since she had been driving had not been remotely tempting. But Dave was another matter. She could not recall ever being so attracted to anyone before, or not anyone who was remotely available – she had certainly felt nothing like this for Kenny, who was the only man she had ever slept with. But temptation had not so far been enough to overcome her caution.

"Let's go for a drink," he offered. Feeling cold and weariness fall away she forgot about her coat and went with him to a nearby pub, where they found a snug corner and drank and talked, and laughed with some of the other drivers there, though they sat a little apart, together, as if they were a couple. Dave had taken a room at the pub, and had already made use of the facilities to have a bath and a shave – he looked clean and spruce and pink beside the other men, still dirty and smelling of sweat from their long day. She wished she had done more than splash water on her face in the cold bathroom at her lodging, and renew lipstick and eyeshadow, though Dave did not seem to mind. He edged gradually closer, until he sat as close as he could, with his arm resting along the back of the seat behind her, in what was almost an embrace. She was acutely conscious of his nearness, and of a need within her. It was a very long time since anyone had kissed or caressed her – Kenny had only shown any kind of tenderness in the early days of their relationship. And for a long time now she had been stifled by the respectability and constraints of others. It was time to break free, to follow her instincts.

After a time there seemed to be nothing more for them to say, the talk and the jokes died away, though the silence was not strained – rather, expectant, full of things that were not being said. "Let's go," Dave said at last.

They went, he with his arm about her, back towards the café, in darkness now, apart from a single outside light, which only threw the parking area into deeper shadow. "See you safe home," he said, his voice husky.

Her landlady at the lodging house beyond the café was pleasant enough, and apparently unperturbed by having a female lorry driver under her roof, but Carol didn't want to strain her tolerance too far. "I need to get my coat," she said. "It's in the wagon."

The wagon was in the darkest corner of the parking area, screened on the far side by a tall hedge, on the nearer by a number of other parked wagons. Tingling with excitement, she climbed up into the cab. "Are you coming up?"

She could no longer see Dave, but she heard him clamber up after her. More to the point she felt him, a warm presence, breathing hard, very near. Then she turned towards him and his mouth was on hers, his tongue exploring, one hand pulling her shirt open while the other fumbled for the zip of her jeans. Her body seemed to explode in longing and need.

She had only previously experienced sex in bed, with Kenny,

and any pleasure she had known then had been minimal and very soon over. This, tonight, was awkward and cramped, with gear lever and steering wheel pushing hard edges into her flesh. But it was only later that she realised they had caused her any inconvenience. For the time being – and it seemed both a long time and yet a moment – there was only pleasure, elation, fulfilment. And afterwards, a laugh, a shared cigarette; and an easy parting outside her lodging, without guilt or pain. "Goodnight! See you!" She slept well that night.

The next day, feeling alert, alive, happy, she set out before dawn and was well on her way when the sun rose. By midday she had made her delivery and found somewhere to park up and eat and rest. Over her meal she spread the road atlas on the table beside her and took a crumpled piece of paper from the haversack she always carried. It had an address scribbled on it, and she read it through and then gave her attention to a careful consideration of the map.

Then she paid for her meal, took a walk and then had half an hour's doze in the cab before setting out again, towards the north. The most logical route to Birmingham was by way of Oxford, but at Winchester she took a more easterly road and made her way steadily towards the Surrey border.

Nine

It was a longer journey than she had expected, and more complicated. In places she met slow and heavy traffic, and three times took a wrong turn – her map was not much use when it came to the fine detail of country roads. Dusk was falling by the time she reached a select area of potholed private roads, high hedges, dense tree-belts and scarcely glimpsed mansions. By a lucky combination of map-reading and instinct – there were few signs – she found the right place without too much difficulty. Pine Drive was inscribed upon the small sign, half-concealed behind a vigorously flourishing shrub. The Birches was about halfway along, with a garden stretching into the shadowy distance, where she glimpsed a faint glow of light blackly patterned by birch tree branches – it was obvious where the unimaginative name came from. Carol noted with satisfaction that there was a convenient widening of the road just outside the closed gates, so that by parking there she would be able to leave room for other vehicles to pass. *Who could possibly object?* she thought with a grin.

She parked the wagon immediately in front of the gates, with much huffing of brakes and – quite unnecessary – revving of the engine. She was sure that beyond the high hedges and belts of trees, faces were looking out of mullioned windows, wondering what appalling invasion had disturbed their haven. She hoped that the inhabitants of The Birches were among them. There was not very much daylight left now by which to see what had happened.

She was afraid at first that nothing was going to happen. There was no sign of any movement beyond the trees on either side, no sound that she could detect. But of course each house had a long drive, and people might in any case be wary of coming out so late, unless they had good reason.

She switched on the ignition again, set the headlights at full beam, edged the wagon forward a little, then back again, closer still to the gate. She had just checked the mirrors for a last time, braked, turned off the ignition, when she heard the gates clang. The next moment there came a furious tapping on the nearside window. A tidy brown head, streaked with grey, was just visible. Carol opened the door, jumped down and walked round the front of the wagon, startling the woman, who had not seen her coming. Carol grinned with cheerful unconcern. "Hiya!"

It was – jubilation! – the pale woman from the pew in church, the woman who had turned her back on her mother: her mother's older sister, very tidy in a tweed skirt – no miniskirts here – sensible shoes, a pale salmon twin set, pearls. She glared at Carol with undisguised hostility, and that peculiar chill about the mouth and eyes that only the well-bred upper-middle classes can perfectly accomplish (even Diana could do it, when she chose). *She's no idea who I am*, Carol thought.

But the distaste was clear, written in every disapproving line of the woman's face, the way her eyes ran up and down Carol's trim jean-clad person. "You can't park that here. This is a private drive." Her enunciation was as clipped as the hedges, her tone icy.

"I know," said Carol. "That's why it's full of holes."

"Then kindly move that" – she gestured towards the wagon – "elsewhere. There are proper places for such things."

"Aye, there are. But I've a mind to call on my long-lost relations."

"I'm quite sure you won't find them here."

"Oh, but I have, Aunty Pamela." *Let me not be wrong! Let it be her!*

It was. The hostility did not lessen at all, but there was a perceptible moment of hesitation, of doubt, before the woman said, "I beg your pardon?"

Carol held out a friendly hand. "Caz Armstrong, your niece. We didn't get any chance to talk at the funeral – you were so busy, I know. So when I realised I was passing this way, I thought it was too good an opportunity to miss. So here I am!"

"I am not aware of having any relation of that name. Now take that vehicle away, or I shall call the police."

Things are getting nasty, thought Carol. *Now what?*

"Mummy! Are you all right? What's happening?" A voice recognisably like her mother's, but younger, with a hint of anxiety; then a girl emerged from the shadow of the birches and walked towards them. She was about Carol's height, with long brown hair and a high-waisted pink-flowered minidress. (*Fancies herself as Brigitte Bardot,* thought Carol, *but Mummy doesn't approve of the makeup.* Without the appropriate strong eyeliner and pale lipstick she looked half-finished, her face scrubbed and shiny as a schoolgirl's.)

"Yes, *I*'m perfectly all right," said her mother. "This person is about to move her vehicle."

The girl stared at Carol. "Aren't you . . . ? Weren't you . . . ?"

Carol reassumed the confident grin. "Aye. Your cousin from County Durham, Caz Armstrong. Hi!"

Miraculously, the girl grinned, looking all at once like a girl straight from the hockey pitch, as if the clothes were a bizarre aberration or a child's fancy dress. "Hello. I'm Daphne. I remember seeing you at the funeral." She stepped back to gaze admiringly at the wagon. "Is this your—?"

Her mother, who had been making urgent but unavailing signals to her daughter, abandoned subtlety and broke in, "Go back into the house, Daphne. Leave me to deal with this."

By now, two women were striding towards them from other houses in the road, and at that moment a third person emerged from the gate to join them, a stolid man in a respectable suit; Mr Edward Streatfield, Carol supposed, Aunty Pamela's husband. He heard his wife's explanation, interrupted at intervals by his indignant daughter, looked Carol over – his expression was impassive, and besides it was beginning to be too dark to see properly – and then said, "Why don't we go into the house and talk this over like reasonable people?"

His wife was about to object, then looked at her neighbours, who were clearly only too willing to intervene, and gave way. The father bade goodnight to the newcomers and shepherded wife, daughter and niece towards the house, along a winding drive through birches lit by occasional standard lamps.

There was a small and quite unnecessary log fire in the hearth in the spacious carpeted sitting room, several tasteful floral arrangements and a number of flowered chintz sofas and chairs, on which Daphne and her mother sat while the man of the house interrogated Carol. "So you're Diana's daughter? Is that right? But I don't quite understand what the lorry out there has to do with you."

"It's one of ours. I drive it."

"You!" he looked utterly bewildered. "I've never heard such a thing!" He leaned closer, as if trying to see signs in her face that she was lying. "Are you telling me the truth?"

"Oh, you know it's true, dear," his wife broke in wearily. "Mother told us about it, more than once. She always was anxious about the way her grandaughter had turned out. But what can one expect, in the circumstances?"

Edward digested his wife's information, and then returned his attention to Carol. "Then I don't understand what you're doing here."

"Why, I'll tell you," said Carol, suddenly weary of the whole business. "We came to Granny's funeral, Mam and me. She loved Granny – they used to write to each other all the time. But she's always been sad she lost touch with all of you. She hoped that somehow when she was at the funeral she'd be able to make it up with you and get to know you again. Then what happens? You treat her as if she was less than the dirt under your feet. Can you imagine, her mother's just died, and the only family she has left pretend she doesn't exist!"

"She made the choice, years ago, when she married that garage mechanic," Pamela pointed out. She stood up again, as if to assert herself more effectively.

Beside her, Daphne jumped up too. "Oh, Mummy, don't be so stuffy and old-fashioned. Nobody cares about things like that nowadays!"

"Which is precisely what is wrong with this modern age," retorted her mother. "There seem to be no standards left, no proper respect."

"For what? Silly old ideas about rank and privilege?"

Her mother reddened. "And morality. It is also a matter of morality."

"Because my mother was pregnant when she married!" Carol put in. She could see that this was news to Daphne, who was listening with wide-eyed relish. "It happens all the time."

"Not to decent people," said Pamela.

"Don't you think she paid enough, with the baby dying?"

"Is that what happened?"

Carol turned to her cousin, whose eyes were soft with sympathy. "Yes, it is. He was only a few months old, and he just died, no one knows why. My mother had a hard time most of her life. My Dad wasn't the best of husbands, but she stuck by him, right to the end." Odd, to find herself defending her mother in this way, she who had so often been critical. But here in this room so far from the Wearbridge flat, so much the kind of room her mother might once have expected to call home, it all looked very different; as did her mother's courage and loyalty. She knew, because her mother had told her, that Granny had wanted her to have the baby discreetly adopted, so as to avoid what might prove a disastrous marriage, but that it was Diana's own decision to face the full consequences of her actions and marry Bradley Armstrong. "I loved him then, I suppose," she had told Carol once. "Or I thought I did."

Carol, who did not think she had ever loved anyone – least of all the man she had married – and had felt passion only for film stars whose pictures she had pasted inside her desk lid at school or stuck on the side of her bedside table, was impressed by the declaration, yet felt just a little wistful, excluded from something that could make one behave with such a disregard for logic and one's own well-being – though of course she had done just that, with much less reason. Her own impulsive marriage seemed in comparison merely childish and squalid. "Even you must make mistakes sometimes." She made her appeal to her cousin, sensing that there was her strongest hope of sympathy. "Everyone does. It's just that most of us are lucky and get away with it and no one ever knows."

"Lucky! It's not a question of luck – nor of 'mistakes' as you call them. It's a matter of right and wrong, nothing less. But one can't expect someone of your background to understand." Pamela turned to her husband. "This is a waste of time, dear. It's the question of the lorry we came in here to discuss." Then, to her daughter, "I thought you had a letter to write, Daphne. You'd better go and do it." Obedient, dutiful, as Carol had never been, Daphne left the room, while her mother confronted her niece. "Now, are you going to move that lorry, or is it to be the police?"

Carol looked into the pale unforgiving face of her aunt and felt a renewed burst of anger. "You're a lot of cold-hearted snobs, all of you, and Mam's better off without you, if only she knew it!" She began to stride towards the door. "I'm going. But only as far as the wagon. I'll sleep there tonight, and you needn't try to move me on or call the police. You don't want your neighbours hearing our story, do you? I'll make sure they do, if you hassle me. Goodnight!" She went out of the room, shutting the door with a satisfactory snap that was not quite a slam.

It took her some time to find the right door by which to leave the house, and she half-expected someone to come after her, but no one did, and she succeeded eventually in making her way back to the wagon. She felt deflated, even a little sad. For a moment then she had begun to hope that there might be a resolution and, though she had no wish to befriend these relations who had treated her mother so badly, she would have liked a reconciliation for her mother's sake. She still could not put from her mind the hurt on Diana's face that day at the funeral.

She always carried a sleeping-bag in the cab, just in case, as well as two or three small cushions. These she now arranged so as to best protect the angularities of her body, slipping inside the sleeping-bag and settling down to get what sleep she could. At least the road outside was badly lit, with only one inadequate street lamp anywhere near the wagon. Usually she could sleep anywhere, on anything, but tonight she slept only fitfully, waking often to another surge of fury at the way her relations had behaved. The Armstrongs on whom they looked down so disdainfully could, she thought, teach them a thing or two about manners, not to mention Christian charity – something she had never given a great deal of thought to. By the time the first light disturbed her she was feeling cramped and exhausted, not at all prepared for a long journey north – especially now she had come so far out of her way. She was hungry too, and there was no prospect of breakfast until she had been on the road for some time. This was not the kind of area where she was likely to find a transport café.

She folded her sleeping-bag, wetted her toothbrush from the water bottle she always carried and scrubbed her teeth, just to freshen them. Then she opened the door and jumped down into the fresh morning. The air revived her a little, and she walked about a little to loosen her cramped limbs. She glanced several times towards the house, but it remained quiet, only just visible, its windows giving nothing away. She was about to climb back into the cab and go on her way when she realised that something was happening; someone was coming down the drive towards her, a small hurrying figure. As it came nearer she heard a hoarse whisper: "Caz!"

It was her cousin Daphne, her hair tousled, dressed with obvious haste in a shapeless grey skirt and a pink jumper – the first things to hand, Carol supposed. She stood waiting for the girl to reach her, her expression deliberately impassive.

Daphne halted a few feet away; she looked slightly anxious,

as if unsure of her reception. "I hoped I'd catch you. I thought you might like these." She held out something – sandwiches presumably – wrapped in greaseproof paper, and a thermos flask. While Carol took them, her expression wondering, she went on, "Mummy behaved dreadfully. I was so ashamed. I don't know how they can go on thinking like that after all this time. Anyway, I wanted you to know I'm not a snob like they are, and I'd like us to be friends." She glanced up at the wagon. "Can I see inside your lorry? I've never been in one."

Carol shrugged off her wariness and grinned. "You can have a ride if you like."

It took Daphne some time, a great deal of help from Carol and much breathless giggling before she reached the cab. "Right, home James and don't spare the horses!" she then declared, inappropriately. They were both laughing as Carol eased the wagon along the tangle of exclusive drives towards the properly maintained road. Once out there, where there was less need to be alert for obstacles, she was able to listen to her cousin's eager chatter and learn something about her. By the time, an hour later, that they returned to Pine Drive they felt as if they had known one another for ever. In spite of their obvious differences, Carol liked her cousin, without reservation.

By now it was fully light, a bright crisp morning. "You're going to get wrong," said Carol.

She realised her cousin was unfamiliar with the expression, though she quickly grasped what it meant. Daphne shrugged and smiled. "Too bad. Let them say what they like. If Mummy wants to talk about right and wrong I'll have something to say about that for myself. Anyway, thanks, Caz. It was fabulous meeting you." She opened the door and scrambled down. "I'll write," she promised.

"And call in if you're ever up our way!" She watched as the girl disappeared into the trees, and then turned the vehicle and set out for home.

Carol brought her adventure home in triumph to her mother,

pouring out the whole story late at night as they sat over mugs of tea. "Daphne's the youngest," she explained. "She has two older brothers who are working in London. But maybe you already know that. She's going to university soon, to Bristol, to study English. Oh I know it's not what we hoped, but at least she's willing to be friends. Something might come of it, you never know."

Diana, who had said little while Carol told of her adventure – though she had laughed in a shocked sort of way from time to time – now stroked her daughter's hand. "It was sweet of you to try."

Within two weeks Carol had received a long loquacious letter from Daphne, and Diana too received a letter. It came, not from any of the Surrey relations, but from her brother Robert, a commercial artist in London, saying that he had heard of what Carol had done and was both amused and admiring. *This old business has been going on far too long*, he added. *It's time we got in touch again. Do come and see us some time.*

Diana looked up from reading the letter at her daughter, watching her from the other side of the breakfast table. She smiled tenderly. "Well, good's come out of it after all. I may be a bit uneasy about your methods, but they do seem to be effective." She rose from the table. "I meant to ask you, how's Brenda settling in?"

Brenda Gibson was a young woman from Meadhope, in her early twenties, who had recently applied for work as a driver. "I've always wanted to drive wagons," she had admitted at her interview, "but they always said no one would ever take a woman on. Then I saw your lass driving by."

"She's fine," said Carol. "Not much of a mechanic – I don't think she wants to be. But she's a good driver. Mind, I think she's having trouble with her fiancé."

"Oh – why's that?"

"Oh, you know men – don't trust us when they're not around. She's trying to talk him round so she can do that job in Scotland next week. He doesn't seem to mind local work – it's long distance he doesn't like."

125

"Can't you reassure him? After all, you know what it's like."

"Quite!" Carol hoped her mother was unable to read her thoughts in her face – memories, rather, for she was recalling the recent meeting with Dave.

Diana gazed at her for a long time, before saying, "Carol, I do worry sometimes – about your safety. I know you're sensible, and wouldn't let anything interfere with your work . . ."

"Don't worry, Mam. I'm not a slag. Besides, I'm on the pill."

"You're what! Where did you get that from?"

"I've been on it since Sharon was born. I don't think Dr Hewitt has ever realised I've split up with Kenny. So I thought I wouldn't tell him. Just in case." Sensing an argument about to fall on her head, she glanced at the clock. "Look at the time! I'd better go." Some things, she thought, were better not discussed. She could never expect her mother to understand.

Ten

Diana knew Carol would be home by now. Or should be. She suppressed the familiar beat of fear. Of course she would be home safely! Two days away, straightforward mineral deliveries to steel plants in Kilmarnock and Glasgow, roads she knew well – what possible harm could come to her? But Diana knew, of course: a moment of inattention on a busy road; some other driver overtaking where he shouldn't, without warning; a man trying to show his superiority to the woman he saw overtaking him. Ice on the road, snow – though there had been no fresh snow for several days, and she had studied the forecast carefully, relieved, yet aware that forecasts could be wrong and there were always local variations. The fear was something she had to live with, had learned to live with ever since Carol became a driver. There had been other fears before, of course, especially in the early years, fears common, most of them, to all mothers. This, now that Carol was an adult, was a wholly new kind of fear, one which she had not expected. She should be beyond all this now, she thought.

She made herself concentrate on the good things; the daffodils blowing in the wind in their pots on the forecourt; the clear evening air of this March day . . . It was not quite dark enough yet for the lights to be on in the flat, to show her that Carol was there.

But the moment she opened the door on to the stairs, she heard the music – the Rolling Stones' "Honky Tonk Women" – very loudly. She allowed herself to go more slowly, to savour the relief. By the time she opened the flat door and saw the inevitable signs of Carol's return – magazines strewn over sofa and floor, an overflowing ashtray, two empty mugs on the coffee table, coat and shoes left where they had been dropped on the way in – there was room, in place of fear, for her usual irritation at the ubiquity of Carol's presence. The din from the record player hit her with full force as she stepped into the room.

"Hiya, Mam." Carol smiled at her from the depths of the sofa. She looked blissfully at her ease, pink from the bath, stretched out in her old blue dressing gown; a young woman without a care in the world.

Diana bit back all the comments she might have made and went to hang up her coat, and Carol's too. "Good journey?" she asked casually.

"Great." No further information; there rarely was. Instead, Carol looked round at her mother. "You weren't at the depot."

"I had to finalise the details with Dale Industrials, for the new contract."

"Did that go all right?"

"Yes, but I've had some thoughts about it. We'll talk about them later – if you still feel up to facing a partners' meeting after all your travels?" They set aside time towards the end of each month to discuss business matters, usually in the flat in the evening. It was not exactly a formal meeting, but between them they listed all that they wanted to discuss and kept notes of all decisions made or deferred. This month the meeting was a little early, because of the impending Easter holiday.

"So long as you get Sharon for me. And cook supper."

Diana was close to protesting, and then reminded herself that she always waited on her daughter after a long-distance drive. As she made her way to the kitchen, she found herself wishing she had only herself to look after at the end of a tiring day. Even when Carol was away, there was still Sharon to care for. Yet how could she think that, when she had only just been able to put aside her fear that Carol might one day disappear from her life for ever? How could she be so ungrateful?

Later, when they had eaten and Sharon was in bed, Diana

brought a sheaf of papers into the sitting room and laid them on the coffee table. Carol's eyes widened in dismay. "All that!"

"End of year accounts," said Diana, edging herself on to a corner of the sofa, near Carol's feet. "I saw Mr Suggett today too." He was the Wearbridge accountant who ran an occasional eye over their finances. He had prepared a summary for them, which Diana handed to her daughter.

Carol glanced at the totals, then laid the paper down; she was not remotely interested in the intricacies of financial statements. "That looks healthy."

"It is, yes, but look at where most of our business is coming from – Dale Industrials."

"Lucky for us, them opening all those mines up, just when we might have been short of work."

"But that's the point: there *was* a good deal of luck in it. Demand suddenly went right up, prices for fluorspar in particular went through the roof. But it's a very chancy industry. Next year – next month – it could all change; they'll develop new processes, ones that don't use minerals, then demand will fall; or they'll find a cheap source of fluorspar somewhere else. It's happened before and it's certain to happen again, sooner or later. So – we need a bit more diversity, different kinds of business."

"There's the steel works. And we do jobs for other firms from time to time. What about all the backloads, for a start?"

"They're all well and good, but they'd not be enough to keep us going if the mines closed again. And there isn't much else within the Dale. If Queen of the Road is to be put on a really sound footing, then we need a good spread of business and most of it outside the Dale. Unless we're going to be just a little local firm living from hand to mouth . . ." She watched her daughter for the expected reaction.

Carol swung her legs to the floor, sat up. "Oh no, Mam, never that!" She grinned suddenly, acknowledging her mother's teasing. "So we're going to go out and tread on Ronnie Shaw's toes, are we?"

"There's plenty of work for both of us out there." Diana hoped no undue emotion showed in her voice. It was disconcerting to find how much she still felt when Ronnie's name was mentioned, though she hadn't seen him since the day, three years ago, when she'd realised how mistaken she'd been about him. As for him, had he set out deliberately to avoid her, once he knew what she'd thought of him? She could hardly blame him for that, guilty as she still felt about it. But life was somehow a little flat without the excitement, the stimulation of their occasional meetings. "Do you ever hear news of him on your travels?" She tried to make the question sound casual.

"I know he's doing well. You see his wagons everywhere."

That wasn't what she meant; she'd wanted to know if he was well, if he still lived in Sunderland, if he was married. But to pursue the matter further would only arouse Carol's curiosity, so she returned to the question they had been discussing. "Then let's see how we can get our wagons out there too. There are the clearing houses, of course. If they can find us backloads, then it's likely they'll have other business for us too. On the other hand, it's obvious they're going to keep the best work for themselves. And then there's their commission. We'd do much better if we could cut out the middle man. I thought we might go direct to the firms we've carried backloads for – especially the ones we work for regularly."

"Why yes – I've lost count of the times someone's said, 'You can drive for me any time.' Mind, I reckon most of the time it's because I'm a woman and not bad looking."

"That's not to say they don't mean it. Can you make a note of any firm you can think of that's said that to you, or something like it? I'll contact them and see what happens. We've nothing to lose." She glanced down at the notes she had made over the past days, odd thoughts jotted down as they occurred to her. "I did wonder if Harry had any more useful contacts in the Midlands."

Carol paused a moment without commenting, then said, "Shirley thinks he's on the fiddle."

"Oh?" Diana looked alarmed. "Has she any reason to think so? They don't exactly love one other, after all."

"I think it's mostly just a feeling. She has a lot of experience though. Anyway, Mam, how did he find the money for that car, for a start?"

"I thought you said he was lucky with the horses."

"Is anyone ever that lucky?"

"To be honest, I wouldn't know. But there's no sign of anything untoward. I can't quite see what he could be fiddling, or how. He does his work efficiently, and I've never had any complaints. The only thing you could say is that he sometimes takes a bit longer than necessary over a job – I know there are times he's stopped off to look in on friends or family, when he's away. But he's never tried to hide it – he generally clears it with me beforehand – and it's never affected his work. He's never late with a delivery and his log book's always entirely in order." She looked round at her daughter's still sceptical expression, and smiled. "All right, not Harry, not for the time being. But tell Shirley that if she has any real reason for suspicion, she's to let me know at once." Another glance at her notes. "That brings me to another thing I wanted to bring up. I've been finding out about these new tachographs. I'd like to have them installed in all our vehicles, especially if we're doing more long-distance work."

"No!" Diana was astonished at the vehemence of her daughter's reaction. "You know what drivers call them? The spy in the cab! I don't know a driver who'd stand for it. Put them in, and I bet you anything Queen of the Road will have its first ever strike."

"Dear me! I'd no idea you felt like that!" She studied her daughter's angry face. "Right then, I'll let that idea drop. But you know, Carol, they'll come in one day, I'm sure of that. They're a much more reliable method of checking drivers' hours than logbooks. They're already compulsory in many countries, and if we ever join the EEC then they'll be compulsory for us too."

"Then let's wait till then, shall we?" Carol retorted. "If it ever happens." She stood up, stretching. "Fancy some cocoa?"

During the next few days Carol noted down all the firms she thought might be contacted with advantage to themselves. She was also attentive, when out on the road, for any gossip about businesses that were looking for transport. That was how, early in May, Diana came to be driving to Sunderland, to call on the manager of a manufacturer of industrial glassware, who was seeking tenders for the carriage of fine quality sand from a supplier in western Scotland. They were anxious to find someone who could be trusted not only to be reliable and competitively priced, but also to transport the sand with due care. Diana could have dealt with the matter over the phone or in writing, but as always she felt that personal contact might make all the difference. It might even be one of those rare situations where being a woman, with women drivers on her books, might actually prove to be an advantage. She went over her arguments in her head as she drove: *I'm convinced that a firm with the feminine touch is exactly what you're looking for . . .*

A couple of hours later she was sure of it. She left the manager's office in a mood of quiet confidence. She was almost certain their tender would be accepted, while knowing that if they were to fail it was not for want of anything she might have done. Meanwhile, they had already taken on two other new contracts outside the Dale.

Crossing the small car park towards her car, buffeted by a brisk wind from the nearby river, she suddenly realised that among the men – they were all men, of course – passing her or coming towards her was a heart-thuddingly familiar figure. She halted, feeling a sudden need to get her breath; and she saw that he too had done the same, and that he, like her, had reddened. Then they both moved forward, with the awkward, pinched smiles of the embarrassed on their faces. "Hello, Mr Shaw," she said, as she reached him.

"I know we've not met for a while, but I never thought you'd forget my Christian name."

She grinned then, and blushed still more. "Ronnie, then. What are you doing here?"

"Why, I'm a bit closer to my home patch than you are. I'm here on business, as I expect you are. We make deliveries here from time to time. So you're trying to steal a march on me again are you?"

"Oh, all's fair in—" No, that was an unfortunate expression, and not what she meant at all. She faltered into silence, and he laughed, suddenly relaxed, at ease.

"There's a café round the corner. Join me for a cup of tea? For old time's sake?"

The café was clean, if nothing else, and they sat at a formica-topped table in front of two heavily tannic mugs of tea, and for a long while found they did not know what to say, not because there was nothing, but because there was rather too much, a good deal of it perhaps better left unsaid.

"I hear you're doing well," she commented. It was there in his appearance too, in the well-cut suit (not too wildly fashionable, but not old-fashioned either – the flares were modest but distinct), the polished shoes, the gold signet ring which she did not recall having seen before – not on his wedding finger, she noted, after a momentary lurch of dismay; it was on the other hand.

"Oh, we're constantly expanding. Business is good. But then I gather you're not doing so badly either." He seemed to be looking her over, judging her. "In yourself too. You look very well." His eyes said more than that, more warmly, and she found herself blushing again.

"I am," was all she said. Then: "You're not in the Dale much these days. At least I haven't seen you or heard of you."

"I've got a good manager this time – I don't need to stand over him." He recognised the scepticism in her face. "Truly! I double-checked him before I took him on. I've no qualms about leaving him in charge. Besides, most of our business is further afield these days. I've opened depots in Leeds, Wolverhampton and St Albans, with more in prospect. I've got my eye on Europe too. Now de Gaulle's gone it looks as though we might even make it into the EEC at last, with all the opportunities that would offer. What about you then? Have you got ambitions?"

"Not like that, not grand ones. Just to build up a good sound business, with a good name for reliability and efficiency." She smiled. "Very modest. Of course, I'd like us to be a household name, but I'm not one for taking undue risks. I don't like being in debt."

"Sometimes you have to take risks to succeed."

"And I have done, more than once. I'm just more comfortable making a profit, however small. Mr Micawber, that's me."

"Me, now, I like being on the edge – that feeling of risking everything, knowing you lose the lot if you fail, but win undreamed-of riches if you succeed. And *believing* that you'll succeed."

She was fascinated by this sudden glimpse of what lay beneath Ronnie's outward steadiness. She had always known that as a businessman he was vigorous, enterprising, ready to spot an opportunity and seize it, but – as she now recognised – without the unscrupulousness that would allow him to trample over those who stood in his way. Now she saw that he had a romantic, adventurous side to his personality as well, a gambler's instinct. She gazed across the table at the grey eyes keen and shining below the dark brows; yes, it was there in that face, if one studied it. "Ah, there's the Viking in you – I can just see you sailing your dragon boat into a stormy sea, in search of new lands to plunder . . . At least, I've always assumed you had some Viking in you, with that name."

"Who knows?" he asked ruefully. "I certainly don't."

"Have you and Freda ever tried to find out about your father?" The words had come on impulse, though she wondered at once if she had gone too far.

"Freda – no." He gave no sign that he found the question obtrusive. "She says there's no point. She's right, of course. Where would we start? Even our Mam knew next to nothing about him. What chance have I got? A sailor in port for a night or two, from a ship no one ever got the name of, still less where it came from? It's not much is it? Roald's a Norwegian name, or so I'm told, but that's not much help. We don't exactly look Norwegian, do we, Freda and me? But we're not like our Mam either, so where does that get us? No, we have to accept we'll never know."

"Do you mind?"

"I did once. Not now, not for a long time. I am who I am, that's all." He began to give all his attention to his mug of tea, pouring in sugar and stirring it vigorously, as if to emphasise his rejection of anything that verged on introspection.

Diana, gazing at his bent head, pondered what he had told her. How would it feel to know nothing of what went into making half of what you were? What if she had never known that Dr Poultney was her father, not even known who he was, where he came from; what if even her mother knew nothing of him? It took a leap of imagination that was beyond her to put herself in that position. She could only sense that there must be a great hole left where that knowledge, so much an accepted part of every human being, must have been. Would you not wonder, when you felt discontented with the way things were, if that came from the father you did not know, if the gifts you had, the yearnings, the intelligence, or lack of it – if all those things had been your father's legacy to you? Only, wondering would be no use, for you would never know, or have any hope of knowing. She supposed you would only learn to live with it by looking, not back, not into yourself, but ahead, to the future and what you could make of it – which perhaps explained a good deal about Ronnie.

He raised his head then and caught her watching him, and smiled. She felt as if her insides had turned a somersault, just as they had that first time years ago, on a day just after the war, when she had suddenly realised he had grown from a boy to a man, and an attractive one at that. Whatever anger might have come between them since then, whatever misunderstandings, the attraction had never wholly gone. Now it was back in force. She wanted to look away, rejecting what she felt. She liked her life as it was, without emotional complications. But she could not remove her gaze from his, nor still the turmoil in her body. He had not moved, but her body was responding as if he had touched her, even caressed her. Of course, it was a very long time – years – since she had been physically close to any man. That must be all it was, a need like hunger, which had long gone unsatisfied, and which could be met and satisfied, easily, by anyone at all, if she chose, if she were that kind of woman, which she was not. She gulped down the last of her tea, without tasting it, pushed back her chair, stood up. "I really must be going. It's been good to see you again." She fumbled with her handbag, half held out her hand to him and then drew it back, and turned to go. She heard the scrape of his chair behind her, and then felt his touch on her arm.

"Diana!"

She looked round. They were close now, very close. She was acutely conscious of his face, his mouth, his nearness; she was conscious of nothing else. If they had not been in a public place, standing by the door of a busy café full of working men, she knew she would have moved even nearer to him, brought her mouth to his.

She felt his hand on her elbow. "Diana." Before, he had spoken sharply. Now his tone was soft, the word scarcely audible, though she seemed to feel it in the deepest part of her. He said nothing more, simply steered her towards the door, and she went with him, meekly. Of course, that was where she had been intending to go, so there was nothing odd about that; except that out in the street she did not turn towards the glass works where she had left her car, but allowed him to guide her the other way, along the road, round one corner and another, into a little terraced street, to a trimly painted blue door. "My house," he said, as if speaking was difficult. "Come in."

She went in; she was beyond doing anything else. Once inside, with the door closed on the dark little hallway, she turned, without word, without sound, without conscious choice, into his arms. A little after, he led her upstairs, to a bedroom screened by net curtains, and a three quarter bed where they lay down together, with no need for invitation or acceptance.

She had no recollection of the journey home, later that day, though she got back somehow, in time for a late lunch in the flat; except that she had little appetite. Her body was drenched now with fulfilment, at peace; but her mind was not. Did she wish it hadn't happened? She was not sure. Every moment in bed with Ronnie had been pure pleasure, a shared and equal pleasure, such as she had never known with Bradley, even in the early years, before he became a drunk. If that had only been all . . .

Afterwards, Ronnie had kissed her tenderly, murmured, "Thank you, hinny," and then they had dressed, pausing for kisses, and he had seen her downstairs again. It was in the little hallway as they paused for a parting embrace that he had suddenly said, "Marry me, Diana!" His tone was urgent, his eyes held hers, imploring; his hands grasped her arms. "Please! I've never wanted anyone but you. I never will."

She had felt as if the door had unexpectedly opened on them, allowing in a cold blast of air. She had stammered some sort of reply: "I don't know . . . No, I don't – I need to think. I need time . . ."

There had been a long silence, while he continued to gaze at her. Then, with the hurt not quite cleared from his voice, he said, "You know my phone number. Ring me when you've an answer. I'll not trouble you till then. It's your choice." Then he added, "If it's no this time, then I'll not ask you again. That'll be it." She thought he was also saying that if her answer was no, then there would be no future for them of any kind, no room even for a meeting like this.

Through what was left of the afternoon, her head seethed with a tangle of confused emotions as she wrote letters and sorted paperwork – though whether anything she did made any kind of sense she had no idea. She was completely unable to think clearly. She even forgot that she had agreed to collect Sharon from Anne's house today, something that had never happened before, and which ensured that Carol, coming home tired to find her daughter was not there, lurched immediately into a bad mood. "What if I'd been away?" Carol demanded, as her mother, horrified by her neglect, grabbed her coat and moved towards the door, car keys in hand; there was no time to waste. "What would have happened to her then?"

Diana was not so full of guilt as to allow that to pass. "She's safe at Anne's, you know that."

Carol, on her way to the bathroom, grunted, conceding nothing. Sharon, on the other hand, had not even noticed that no one had come for her.

Only when the child was in bed and they were eating their supper in front of the television did Carol relent enough to ask her mother how things had gone in Sunderland. It took Diana a moment or two to realise she was asking about the visit to the glass manufacturer and not what had happened afterwards, which was all that now remained uppermost in Diana's mind. With an effort she dredged up a recollection of the morning's business and gave a brief and unemotional account of it to Carol, who at first thought something must have gone wrong, since her mother seemed cool about it, even for her.

Once reassured, Carol moved on quickly to a project of her own. "You know we agreed we need three more artics, with all the new business? Well, I've been asking around who thinks of going for this new HGV test."

Forcing interest, Diana smiled. "I imagine you're top of the list."

"Of course." She had sometimes been able to drive their existing articulated lorry, but not as often as she would have liked; certainly not for the consistent six months which would have exempted her from the test. "I think I could do with a few proper lessons first, too. Geoff and Harry won't need to take the test, with all the driving they've done. But Frank wants to take it, and so does Bruce."

"Shirley?"

"No. She says she's happy as she is. Oh, and Brenda says she's leaving."

"Leaving? But why? Is this anything to do with her getting married?"

"Yes. Whatever his name is – her fiancé – he says she's got to give up or he won't marry her. Doesn't trust her out on the road." From the little Carol had told her – doubtless omitting

138

some of the more alarming details – Diana felt she could hardly blame him; but Carol was not sympathetic. "If any man did that to me I'd tell him to get stuffed, but then I'm not Brenda."

Diana smiled faintly; talk of marriage made her feel even more uncomfortable. "No. Still, it's going to leave us short of a driver." She felt chilled, dispirited. "What about the mechanical side? Norman seems to think we could do with another mechanic or two."

"Then we get a good driver/mechanic to replace Brenda, don't we? Anyway, here's the list for the test." She handed Diana a piece of paper. "It costs a fair bit, but—"

"I know." Diana smiled. "It's an investment. I'll make some enquiries for you."

"You could look at these too." "These" were a number of brochures advertising the latest models of articulated lorries, gleaming monsters photographed against wild landscapes. "Whatever we get, it must have a sleeping cab."

Diana knew from her expression that Carol was already looking forward to the adventures ahead of her. But she herself felt tired, unable to catch her daughter's excitement. In some way Ronnie seemed to have come between them. Was this to be the pattern in future, was he to come between them even more? Was that not inevitable if he were to become in any way a permanent part of her life? She put down her plate, with the meal only half eaten; she had no appetite this evening.

Carol, on the other hand, was relentless, her head clearly bursting with projects and suggestions. "I tell you another thing we have to think about. Space. You know what it's like up at the depot. We've got fourteen vehicles up there now. There never was room for more than ten, and even that was a tight fit."

"I know," agreed Diana wearily. "I've had another complaint about our parking in the layby at Cowcleugh, from the police this time. But now the Denebank idea's come to nothing, I don't know what else we can do." The old lead mine site at Denebank, close to the river and easily reached from the Dale's main road, and several miles nearer to Wearbridge than their existing depot, had seemed an ideal place. But before they could do anything about it, Dale Industrials had bought it up and turned it into a lead processing plant, now in full production. "It was always on the cards, I suppose, demand for fluorspar being what it is." Diana felt too weary to face the firm's problems, but forced herself to consider the question, if only because it provided a temporary distraction from the problem of Ronnie. "There's always Fred Emmerson's old quarry at Ravenshield. I expect he'd sell. We could use it as an overflow yard. There'd be room for eight vehicles there, I should think."

"It's four miles from the depot," objected Carol, "and still too far from anywhere we want to be. But it would do, I suppose." She shovelled a mouthful of shepherd's pie into her mouth then said rather indistinctly, "That letter that came this morning was from Daphne. Says she saw one of our wagons down in Bristol last week."

"She can't have done. We didn't have anybody down that way then."

Carol shrugged. "Oh well – doesn't matter. Anyway, she says it gave her an idea; she wants to come up here in the summer – vacation work, if we've got any for her. She says she'll file things, serve customers, answer the phone, whatever we like."

"I'm not sure we'd have that much work for her – except when Gladys goes away. And it's somebody reliable we'll need then, not an inexperienced student. Besides, where will she stay?"

"Here?" Carol looked round the room, grinned and shrugged. "She could sleep on the sofa." Diana felt a waft of despair; the flat was already too small, too cramped. But Carol clearly considered the matter settled, for she had moved on to something quite different. "I'm getting divorced, Mam; I've decided. I've made enquiries. I have to wait till next year, but then it should be easy. We've been apart more than two years, and I don't imagine Kenny'll have any objection. Then I'll be well and truly rid of him. Free at last!"

Why did all conversation seem to come round to marriage tonight – but only negatively, underlining its disadvantages?

Carol had finished eating, so Diana stacked the plates and took them to the kitchen. She was washing up when Carol appeared in the doorway, cigarette in hand. "One other thing – once the divorce is through, when all that expense is behind me, then I'll find somewhere else to live."

Diana looked round. "Why? Don't you like living here?" She was not sure why she asked – after all, she had been longing for a return to her old privacy ever since Carol first moved in. On the other hand, she'd thought Carol was entirely happy with the way things were.

"Sharon needs a room of her own. She's not a baby any more. And you wouldn't have to put up with my music – or this." She grinned, waving the cigarette. "I know you hate it. To be honest, I could do with my own place too, somewhere I can please myself. We'll all get on better for not living on top of each other."

Diana could think of no possible argument against that, so did not try to find one. She simply gazed at Carol for a moment and then returned her attention to the washing up. The lack of reaction must have alarmed Carol, for she came and slipped an arm about her mother. "Something's up, Mam. What is it? You've been in a funny mood all evening."

"Nothing's the matter, nothing at all. But I am a bit tired. I think I'll go to bed soon." It was only half past nine, but Carol made no comment. Grateful, Diana made a small concession: "I'll take those brochures with me and look them over."

Once in bed, safe from Carol's observant gaze, Diana did not sleep. She lay propped on the pillows with the brochures scattered unread on the worn crimson satin quilt, and went over and over the morning's events, trying to discover what she really wanted, what she should do.

On the one side there was the fear that by the choice she made she might cut herself off from any chance of ever seeing Ronnie again. Until today she would not have believed that could matter to her; now she knew that it did, that she wanted him to have some part in her life, for there always to be the possibility they might meet, and talk – and make love together?

She remembered Carol saying once that nowadays women, like men, could have sex without guilt, without fear – "now we've got the pill everything's changed, for ever," she'd said. "If you're not going to get pregnant, then you can enjoy yourself. Men had better watch out. We're not going to wait around whining to know if they love us. Unless we want babies we don't need a man once it's over. Take your pleasure and move on, just like they've been doing with us since the world began." Diana had been shocked at the words, but now she wondered if that was what she wanted. Yet if that was the case, why did she now feel so guilty, so anxious and afraid? She was a mature widow, without other ties. In sleeping with Ronnie she was betraying no one, doing no harm. There should have been no guilt in it at all.

Except that she was not, like Carol, on the pill, and her periods were still regular and normal. Even at forty-eight it was perfectly possible to become pregnant, if not very likely. It would also be dangerous, not only to her, but to a possible child, who was more likely to be abnormal in some way than one conceived by a younger woman. She was appalled at the very thought that she might bear a handicapped child. It would be a burden she could never lay aside, which would be with her as long as she lived and would almost certainly make work impossible. But even the most normal and healthy child would mean years of commitment, and she was no longer young. She did not want to start again with disturbed nights and nappies, tantrums and endless chatter. She had coped with her grandaughter sharing the same small flat, but only because they had a good child-minder and she had not ultimately been responsible for Sharon. Her own child would be another matter. Of course, if she were to marry Ronnie they could, presumably, move to a larger house, employ good child minders, provide the best. But she did not want to marry Ronnie simply to provide a father for her child, in the way she had married Bradley. Simply, she did not want to marry Ronnie, or anyone.

She'd had enough of sharing her life with a man. Ronnie was not like Bradley, of course, but that did not mean he would allow her to go on working as she was now, without interference.

Certainly, with Ronnie she found a companionship, a meeting of minds that she had never known with Bradley. But marriage changed people, especially men, who had set expectations of what a woman's part was once she became a wife. She had no reason at all to suppose that Ronnie was any different from other men. Besides, what would her remarriage mean for the business, especially if her new husband were a haulier himself? A huge and expanding enterprise in which she – and Carol – would play an active part? Or the sucking of her business into his, the swallowing up of it, so no part of its identity remained, in spite of all that she and Carol had put into it?

Yet if she were to refuse him then she would lose all hope of enjoying his company or sharing his bed. He had made it clear enough, if only by implication, that to have the sort of easy, casual relationship that Carol might have looked for was not an option. Odd, she thought: it had always been women who wanted commitment, and men who avoided it. Perhaps there was something to be said for the new reversal of roles, if only it had been offered to her.

She heard Carol going to bed in the next room and the flat fell silent, like the street outside. Still she was no nearer making a decision. "Ring me when you've an answer," Ronnie had said. "If it's no this time, then I'll not ask you again. That'll be it."

She put down her book, switched off the light, lay down, but there was no room for sleep. She had time, she told herself; she did not need to come up with an answer immediately. One day she would have to, if only for Ronnie's sake. But not yet, not yet! *Who knows?* she thought. *Perhaps if I do nothing, it will all resolve itself somehow.* She could not see how, but the possibility consoled her enough to let her sleep at last.

Eleven

D iana switched off the television halfway through the news, unable to bear the relentless daily reports of war, famine and corruption abroad, strikes and terrorism at home, and – most worrying of all – still more cuts in Middle Eastern oil supplies. There were already shortages, and the petrol station was running low – like many others, it might be forced into closure before long. The haulage business was not as yet greatly affected, except that they had been compelled to put their prices up twice within the past six months, which would make it harder to take full advantage of the threatened rail strikes.

Things had been going so well, too, before all this started. During the past years, the business had grown – not recklessly, but steadily, wisely, so that even in these troubled times they had a solid financial basis on which to depend. It ensured that they now had a fleet of twenty reliable and efficient vehicles of various kinds, to enable them to meet the different needs of their customers, that Queen of the Road's drivers and mechanics were paid above the average for their above-average skills, that they now had a wide range of business throughout the country, yet that everything could still be managed from the Dale, albeit from two overcrowded depots. Diana knew that things would have to get very much worse for very much longer before they would be deeply affected; but still she worried.

Trying to push the anxiety from her mind, she sat down on the chair near Sharon, who was stretched on the floor in front of the fire, reading *The Hobbit* for the third time. At ten, Sharon had somehow become elongated; a thin gangly girl with awkward

144

angles, she was still quite unlike her mother and grandmother. Yet, however orderly and serious-minded, she was also liable to sudden flashes of humour, even wit, that would set them all laughing. Her present position was a typical one, reading being her greatest passion. She spent all her pocket money on books, demanded that almost every birthday and Christmas present should be a book, and always took her full quota from the library, only to have them read and returned and a new selection brought home within two or three days. Her bedroom in Carol's small terraced house two streets away was filled with books, even though she kept a large stock here too for when, as now, she stayed at her grandmother's flat while her mother was away.

"It's after nine," Diana said. "Time you were in bed, my lass." Carol, at Sharon's age, would have argued, prevaricated, found all kinds of excuses not to go to bed yet; Sharon simply closed her book, marking her place with a bookmark she'd made in needlework at school, got up, kissed her grandmother goodnight, and made her way quietly towards the spare bedroom. A little later, Diana looked in on her and found her lying in bed – face washed, teeth brushed – ready to put out the light. "Where will Mam be tonight?" she asked, as she always did when Carol was away; she liked to trace her mother's journeys in the atlas kept on the bedside table.

Diana perched on the edge of the bed. "She should be – now let me see? – she had a delivery to make to Sheffield yesterday, then a load to take from there to Luton, and then a backload to pick up in Watford. She'll be parked up somewhere between Luton and Watford, sleeping in the cab."

Sharon ran her finger over the route in the atlas and then settled to sleep. "It must be great sleeping in a wagon." All but one of the firm's articulated lorries now had sleeping compartments, which made long-distance deliveries much more pleasant. Carol always maintained there was nothing better than spending the night on the road, curtains closed against the world.

Diana kissed the child, put out the light, gently closed the bedroom door; and returned to the sofa, today's copy of the *Northern Echo* – no comfort there – and the effort to keep her thoughts in more cheerful channels. After all, she told herself, there was a great deal to be thankful for. It was foolish to think about what might go wrong, before it did. She set herself to think of the good things – Carol and Sharon, the men and women who worked for them, and those of her own family who were part of her life again, after all these years. Daphne had come to stay for her last two summer vacations, and proved a lively and willing, if not always efficient, worker; she was now working as a reporter on a local paper in Bristol and wrote long enthusiastic letters about her experiences. As for Robert and his family in London, they had twice welcomed visits from herself, Carol and Sharon, and her brother had become a friend as he had never been in their childhood. Remembering the last visit to London, the sights seen, the shows enjoyed, Diana eventually fell asleep.

She was woken, abruptly, by the shrill ringing of the phone. Dazedly, she went to the sideboard, lifted the receiver. "Mrs Armstrong? You won't know me," said the male voice at the other end, accurately. He sounded fairly young, with a south Durham accent. "My name's Dave. I'm a friend of your Carol's." Diana felt her heart thud painfully in the moment before the man went on; he was speaking with great gentleness, which frightened her still more. "There's been an accident. It's all right – don't worry. She's not badly hurt. But they're keeping her in overnight, just to be sure. I'm phoning from the hospital, at St Albans. The wagon's safe – not much damage. It's still roadworthy."

"What happened?" Diana's voice sounded faint, shaky.

"Some idiot at a roundabout – old man in a Morris Minor, came right out in front of her, not even looking, I think. She had to move quickly not to hit him. Wagon jack-knifed. She was thrown out."

Diana did not waste time asking how he happened to know about the accident, but simply asked for all the details she needed to be able to go to her daughter. "I'll stop till you get here," Dave promised.

She looked in on Sharon, who was sound asleep, and then telephoned Anne Nattrass, apologising for the lateness of the hour, deeply thankful for the woman's calm in a crisis: "That's fine, don't worry. I'll pack a bag and come round at once. Don't wake Sharon – I'll stay the night. Then I'll take her home with me tomorrow. You can collect her when you get back, when you're ready."

Diana packed her own bag, trying to repress a sense of panic. Dave had said there was no cause for worry, that Carol was not badly hurt. But was he simply placating her, would she find when she got there that in fact Carol's injuries were serious? And who *was* Dave? She rather thought there'd been a card from a Dave on Carol's last birthday, her twenty-seventh, that rude one her daughter had hurriedly attempted to hide behind the others on her mantelpiece when her mother called round. Just to think of Carol, alive, happy, was painful, when she had no idea what she would find at her journey's end.

When Anne arrived, Diana gave her a reassuring note she had written for Sharon, and then drove through a flurry of snow to Carol's house and packed a bag for her daughter too. From there, she went on to pick up Bruce, whom she'd also phoned from the flat. It was in his company, and that of his now aged dog, that she set out to drive through the night to her daughter's bedside.

In the murky light of the November dawn they passed the transport café where the damaged Scania wagon was parked. "Looks OK from here," said Bruce, which was not much comfort. It was not the state of the wagon that worried her.

On the outskirts of St Albans they passed a Shaw's lorry, going the other way – hardly surprising, since Ronnie had a depot here. For a moment anxiety about Carol was displaced in Diana's mind by an older disquiet, a familiar pang of guilt and regret. It was three years since their meeting in Sunderland and his subsequent proposal, and she had still not telephoned him. She had always intended to ring, if only to say no, just as soon as her decision was made. But somehow the decision never had been made. She knew – she was sure – she did not want to marry him, but neither did she want to drive him out of her life. So she had done nothing, putting off the decision once again every time she had considered it. She had been aware all the time that she must be causing him pain. He had, on the whole, been true to his intention not to contact her, except that each Christmas he had sent a card, one of his firm's official printed ones, with no personal message. She knew it was the nearest he would ever come to nudging her into action.

Then they were at the hospital and Ronnie ceased to matter at all. Outside the ward, they were met by a large, curly haired young man, who approached them at once, shaking hands, repeating his reassurances. He handed Bruce the keys to the wagon, and man and dog went on their way.

"Visiting's not till this afternoon," Dave explained. "But the sister seems OK – I think she'll let you in. Not yet though. The doctor's doing his rounds." He suggested they go to a café near the hospital, where Diana could have some breakfast. She was not hungry, but agreed, because it would at least pass the time.

"She really is all right?" she asked. "You're not fobbing me off?"

"That's what they said. They thought she had a touch of concussion – that's why they kept her in. But she's tough, your Carol. Take more than a bumped head to finish her off."

"And how do you know her? How come you happened to be here?" In case that sounded churlish, she added quickly, "Don't misunderstand me – I'm very glad you were."

He shrugged. "Oh, you get to know other drivers. Known each other for years. This time we met up by chance, yesterday, at Newport Pagnell services, found we were going the same way. I just happened to be following her when the accident happened. Good thing I was. I don't think she knew who she was when they first found her, not for a minute or two."

"And what about the police? Will there be charges? Was anyone else hurt?"

Dave shook his head. "No, only Carol. I'd guess they'll have the old fellow up for driving without due care and attention. It's obvious enough he was at fault – not fit to be behind a wheel, doddery old fool. So they'll be wanting Carol as a witness some time, I suppose. But that's all." He glanced at his watch. "Let's go back, shall we? I reckon they should let you in now."

He was right, and they did. "Just a few minutes," warned the sister. She told Diana that they intended to keep Carol in for another day, just to be quite sure. "She's had some dizziness. Nothing to worry about though."

Carol, propped up in bed at the far end of the ward, looked alarmingly pale, but managed a smile for her mother. "What a fright you've given us!" Diana scolded, as she pulled up an unyielding hospital chair.

"I know, Mam. I'm sorry. But the doctor says I might be able to come home tomorrow. Can you stay?"

"Of course." A little pause; then she said, "Dave's been very good. I like him."

"He's nice," Carol agreed. "He's also married."

"Oh." Diana hoped her disappointment did not show. She so much wanted Carol to find a suitable man, now that she was securely divorced from the wholly unsuitable one. "I thought – well!"

"Mam, I don't need a man, not a permanent one. I'm fine as I am."

Not a permanent one – did that imply there was some not-so-permanent relationship with Dave, even though he was married? Diana realised she did not really want to know the answer to that, because she guessed she wouldn't like it. She would only be reminded once again how very different her daughter's principles were from her own . . . Or were they, when she had kept Ronnie hanging on for her answer for such a very long time, when what she really wanted from him was just the kind of casual undemanding relationship that she suspected Carol had with Dave, and others too, very likely?

At the start of afternoon visiting, Dave looked in briefly to say goodbye to Carol and then went on his way. By then, Diana had booked a room in a convenient B&B which he'd recommended and from there telephoned Anne to give her news of Carol's condition. The following afternoon, mother and daughter made their way north by gentle stages, staying overnight in a comfortable hotel at Newark – no expense spared – and reaching home by the middle of the next day, which was a Friday.

Diana saw a weary Carol into bed in the flat ("where I can keep an eye on you"), telephoned Anne, to tell her they were home and ask her to keep Sharon with her for a day or two longer, and then called Shirley, who had been the firm's transport manager since Norman's retirement last year. Bruce was safely back, Shirley confirmed, and all the minor damage to the wagon had been put right. Then, when Diana asked, routinely, if everything else was in order, Shirley replied by asking after Carol, and their journey, and the accident – almost as if, Diana thought, she were trying to avoid giving an answer. There was an odd note in her voice too, as of something momentous witheld. "Something's wrong," Diana said at last.

"I didn't want to trouble you with it now; but maybe—" Shirley paused. "I'm sorry. Can I come round?"

She apologised again when she reached the flat. "But I don't want you hearing it from anyone else." Another ominous pause. "Had a phone call yesterday afternoon, from West Midlands police. Harry crashed his wagon into the wall of a school in Wolverhampton. Two kids hurt – not badly, thank God! But it's serious enough without that. Harry's been arrested, but they're saying the wagon was unfit – dodgy brakes." She studied Diana's appalled face. "Sorry. Last thing you want, I know."

"But every wagon's checked before it goes out, routinely?" It was a question rather than a statement, since it was Shirley who was now responsible for day-to-day maintenance checks at the depot.

"Aye, and this one was, along with the rest. And a record kept. That's not all, though. Did you give him a job to do down that way?" Diana shook her head. "I thought not. Then what was he doing in the West Midlands? He was meant to be in Leeds yesterday, and home with a backload this afternoon."

Diana, recalling Shirley's doubts about Harry, never fully defined, certainly never proved, gazed at her, knowing what they were both thinking. "Have you asked Brian, or Geoff? They might know." They were Harry's closest friends among the drivers.

"They don't. Or so they say. Anyway, the police are coming up to investigate us. I'd guess they'll be pretty thorough."

It was an unpleasant prospect, setting Diana's stomach churning. The whole thing was horrible. She hated to think that any of their wagons might have caused injury, however slight, to any child. Yet she could not believe the wagon would be found to be at fault, on closer examination, for she insisted on the highest maintenance standards, as did Shirley. After all, Carol was among the drivers whose lives depended on them. As for what had taken Harry so far out of his way, there was probably some perfectly reasonable explanation, which would soon emerge. Or so she tried to tell herself, while she struggled to find some reason for hope in the whole grim situation. She could not quite drive out the suspicion that it had all been too good to last, that they were now having to pay for the success of the past years. The fuel crisis, Carol's accident, now this . . .

Yet Carol had been all right in the end; perhaps this too would prove to be less of a setback than she feared.

She had known that the following weeks would be hard, but they were harder than her worst nightmare. It was not just the police interviews, though they were gruelling enough, and involved not only long hours of questioning both in the office, at the quarry and at the Wearbridge police station (which caused an uncomfortable amount of interest locally and set Sharon complaining bitterly about its effect on her and what her schoolfriends would think); but also meant enduring the police going through every piece of paper, every ledger and document in both the offices, including papers that had been stacked away in boxes at the back of the cupboard since the days when Bradley was in control of the business.

In the middle of December, the whole investigation suddenly slowed down, but not in any way that offered relief. The Prime Minister, Edward Heath, announced a three-day week, to deal with the crippling combination of fuel shortages and industrial unrest. Even without the present crisis, Queen of the Road's business would have been drastically reduced, what with limited working hours and lower speed limits. Power cuts condemned everyone to frequent evenings of candlelight and no television. Somehow it made it all worse, to sit in semi-darkness for hours on end with no distraction from worrying thoughts. Reading newspapers brought no comfort, for they were full of Harry's accident, the risk to the children, the poorly maintained vehicle.

None of the firm's papers had revealed anything improper, but a thorough investigation of the wagon had demonstrated that the brakes were indeed faulty. It was clear, too, that Harry had far exceeded his permitted hours of driving. Detective Inspector Witney, sent north to conduct the investigation, told Diana this at the second of his lengthy interviews with her at Wearbridge Police Station (delayed until the week before Christmas, because of the three-day week).

"That's all that matters to you, isn't it – making a good profit?" he accused, leaning over the desk towards her. He had bad breath, she noticed bleakly, and a large wart on his chin; two small unpleasantnesses among so many great ones. "You've been cramming in as many jobs as you can, never mind safety, your drivers' health, any regulations."

"That's nonsense!" Diana retorted. "I've always demanded the highest standards. My own daughter's a driver, after all—"

"And a partner. I don't doubt she's in on it too."

"You've seen the records – you know everything's in order."

"On paper, maybe. But then that trip wasn't on paper, was it? An extra hundred miles or so, cash in hand, no questions asked, and never mind if the lorry misses its service, or the driver's so dead beat he doesn't know what day it is. Come on, admit it, that's what's been going on, isn't it? You want the work, but you haven't enough lorries or drivers, so you push the ones you have to the limit – beyond the limit. That's right, isn't it?"

"Of course it's not. I would never ask any of them to do anything illegal, never!"

"We know better than that. Harry's told us all about it – and there are others who back him up." That, Diana guessed, would be Brian and Geoff, though who knew who else there might be? She felt helpless, as if she were floundering in the dark, not knowing quite what she had to deal with. She knew, too, how it would look to Inspector Witney, if forced to choose between three ordinary male drivers and their middle-class female boss. It was obvious who a policeman, with a background similar to theirs, was most likely to believe. Would a court do the same? For it was beginning to look increasingly likely that the case would come to court, and that Diana would be the one to be charged with the more serious offence, with Harry facing only lesser charges.

The policeman returned to the attack. "That's what you ask, isn't it? Admit it – they do the work and keep their mouths shut, or they're out of a job." He waited, watching her while she simply sat shaking her head, too weary now to deny it all in words. Perhaps he realised that his previous approach wasn't working, or perhaps he thought he'd found a weak spot, for he suddenly changed his tone, became sympathetic, full of understanding. "Oh, I know you're not the only haulier who bends the rules, breaks them even. We all know how hard it is to make a living these days. That's it, isn't it? Keep to the rules and you go bust. You haven't any choice, as you see it."

"We've been doing well enough without that. We don't need to break the rules."

Perhaps it was disappointment made him say nastily: "We'll have to see about that, won't we? I rather think the taxman might like to take a look at your books too."

Diana had heard enough about the rigours of an Inland Revenue investigation to feel sick at the very thought, even though she knew she had nothing to hide. "He won't find anything," she said wearily. She knew her voice lacked conviction, and she felt only despair.

Afterwards, she went back to the garage, which was temporarily closed for lack of petrol, and sat in the office pretending to work, though in fact she did nothing, simply sat at the desk doodling on the corners of the car repair book, which had only one recent entry. It looked as if the whole sorry business of Harry's accident was already affecting the business, before any conclusion had been reached. It was a relief when the phone rang, though not for long. It was Shirley, reporting that Brian and Geoff had just told her they were leaving the firm. "They don't want references," she added; and then, before Diana had time to reflect on why they might regard a reference from their current employer as undesirable, Shirley went on to talk too brightly of how they were managing to meet their obligations to their clients, in spite of the current difficulties. She could still not disguise the fact that there was less work for Queen of the Road than there had been for a long time, and that some long-standing customers were beginning to look elsewhere.

The next day – the Wednesday of the school Christmas party – Carol was (for once) making a long-distance delivery, the last before Christmas, so Diana brought Sharon home to the flat at the end of the day. At lunchtime, she had bought a small Christmas tree and put ready beside it the box of much-used decorations from the loft. Sharon set to work to decorate the tree, methodically, carefully, but rather as if it were a duty she had to complete as quickly as possible, before being allowed to do something more congenial; in other years, decorating the tree had been a treat, the first real sign of Christmas. Asked how the party had gone, she simply said "OK," and changed the subject. She had never been a particularly talkative child, but she had her own way of demonstrating happiness or excitement; there was not the slightest sign of either this evening – on the contrary, she became steadily more silent, more gloomy. It was clear that something was troubling her deeply. After a while, when she had given no indication at all of what was on her mind, Diana challenged her: "What's wrong, Sharon?"

"Nothing," was Sharon's first response. When her grandmother persisted she burst out: "Everyone's talking about it!"

Diana drew the child down on the sofa beside her. "About what, my darling?" she asked, though she knew full well.

Sharon, sitting stiffly upright, as if she feared contamination from Diana's arm about her, replied without looking round. "They say you're a bad boss. You make people work like slaves so you can be rich."

Diana gave a bitter little laugh and gestured round the flat. "Oh, you can just see how rich we are!" Gently, she forced Sharon to face her, took the child's hands in hers. "Sharon, have you ever seen any sign that we treat our workers badly or break the law in any way? Or heard us say anything that would give that impression?"

"No, but you might do it when I'm at school."

"That's true, I suppose. But if I tell you here and now that none of those stories that are going round have a grain of truth in them, who are you going to believe, me and your mother, or your friends at school?"

"It's in the papers."

"I know. But you can't believe everything you read in the papers either. They print anything that seems to be a good story and they don't mind if it's not true." She stroked the child's hair. "I know it's very hard for you, and you're going to have to be very brave. But what I'm telling you is the truth."

"Then you won't have to go to court?"

"I don't know, darling. It's beginning to look like it, I'm afraid. You see, it's my word and your mother's and Shirley's against quite a different story from three of the drivers, and I think they believe the drivers. There's no real proof either way."

"Will they send you to prison?"

"I don't think so, but I don't know. They might impose a very heavy fine though, and if they do that then I think we may lose our licence. And if that happens then things are going to get very difficult, for all of us. But let's just hope for the best, shall we?"

Words, she thought, brave words that she did not believe. She could see no real cause for hope. She wished that Sharon did not have to be involved in any way, but what could they do about it? When the tree was ready at last, the coloured lights shining, its festive appearance seemed a mockery.

The next morning brought two letters; one, for Carol, which she at once brought round to show her mother, having dropped Sharon at school on the way. The business had now closed down until after Christmas, partly because of government restrictions, but largely because there was little work in any case. "Thought you'd like to see this, Mam," said Carol, handing Diana the letter. It was from Daphne, who expressed outrage at the stories in the papers and declared that she was quite certain they were all lies. "I suppose that's one journalist on our side," Diana observed drily. "I bet it's not her paper's view though, if it has one."

Her own post always arrived a little later than Carol's; she heard the bang of the letterbox just as she was going to the kitchen to put the kettle on for coffee. Carol ran down the stairs to pick up the single letter. "Christmas card," she said. "Don't know who it's from."

Diana brought the full mugs to the coffee table and examined the envelope. It was addressed in what seemed familiar writing, though she could not think whose it was. Inside, there was a card, showing a fat Father Christmas, but also a message, written on a single sheet of paper: *I don't believe a word of it. If you need someone to speak for you in court, I'm your man. Keep your chin up. Ronnie.*

Diana stood reading it over and over, with tears blurring her vision. Once, she had believed the worst of him; yet now, when she was accused of something much more serious, when so many people she had thought of as her friends were turning against her, he did not doubt her. She felt a pang of remorse that she had left him waiting so long for her answer, that she had caused him pain, made worse because, in spite of the way she had treated him, he was still able to give her this support that meant so much. If she had been alone she would have gone to the phone at once and ended the long silence there and then. But Carol was there, watching her with interest and concern, and she had to smile, try to look calm herself, hand over the note for her daughter to read. "Someone else who still believes in us," she said, with what she hoped was casualness.

"That's really nice of him!" Carol exclaimed. "Who would have thought it, after everything that's happened!"

Who indeed? thought Diana, but could not trust herself to speak. A little later, once she had herself under control, with the note folded away in its envelope and the card set up among the others on the mantelpiece, she sat down beside her daughter, took a sip of coffee and then told Carol about Sharon's unhappiness, adding, "We can show her these letters, so she knows not everyone thinks the worst of us. That should help."

At Carol's suggestion, they spent the day Christmas shopping in Bishop Auckland – cautiously, economically – so that it was not until the evening that Diana found herself alone again; Carol had offered to cook for them both, but she declined. For once, she wanted to be alone with her thoughts.

She thought she would eat first, something simple, like beans on toast. But she could not face food, not until she had done what must be done, what should have been done months, years ago.

She went to the phone, lifted the receiver and dialled the number Ronnie had given her; the number of the little house in Sunderland where she had last seen him. *He won't be there,* she told herself, as she listened to the ringing tone. *He'll be out enjoying himself.*

Two rings, and panic set in. She moved to slam down the receiver. Then she heard the voice, familiar, yet made unfamiliar by the phone line. "Ronnie?" she faltered, wondering what she could possibly say. Hating herself, she heard her most coolly businesslike voice chirp stupidly into the mouthpiece. "Diana Armstrong here. I wanted to say thank you for the note in your card."

157

"Oh – oh, don't mention it." He sounded perturbed, flustered, taken by surprise. Then, apparently pulling himself together, he added, "I meant it. If I can help, in any way . . ."

"Thank you." How inadequate that sounded! Diana too struggled to get herself under control. "I owe you an apology. No – that's not quite what I mean. I always meant to phone. I didn't want to leave you without an answer all that time. It's just—" Just what?

Ronnie answered for her. "I know. You don't want to marry me."

"Yes. I suppose that's it. But that's not because I don't feel anything. I do. All this time, I've missed you." That must sound so insincere, she thought, yet it was true. Somehow she had to explain more clearly, without making him feel even more rejected; she owed him that much. "I didn't phone, because I knew if I said no to your proposal, that would be the end of everything. I didn't want it to end. So I put it off and put it off. I suppose I hoped something would come along, and there'd be no need to decide."

"As it has, in a way," Ronnie suggested, his tone a little dry. "Though I don't imagine it's quite what you had in mind. I love you too much not to want to help you, if I can. You must be going through hell. But my feelings haven't changed. I want all or nothing. I can't offer less, or more."

"I know," she said, gently. But she felt a sense of increased misery. Why did life have to be so complicated? Yet she ought to be comforted to know that for this time at least he was willing to put aside his feelings. She thanked him again and he repeated his offer of support and then the conversation ended, with nothing resolved.

Twelve

It was worse than being in hospital. At least then she had felt ill and could not have done much if she'd wanted to. Now Carol felt restless, full of an energy that had no outlet, for there was little work to do. She longed to be alone in the cab of a wagon, driving long miles, putting all troubles aside, leaving them behind. Even the Christmas holiday, when Sharon had been at home and – in theory at least – in want of entertainment and distraction, was not enough to still the need for activity. In spite of her edginess, she was anxious about Sharon, who, never at best an exuberant child, seemed unusually subdued, and had been deeply hurt when Rachel, her closest friend, failed to invite her to her birthday party just after Christmas. Carol was furious, almost prepared to storm round to the offender's house and complain.

Then she was made to realise, in the most painful way, that Sharon was not alone in suffering the effects of local disapproval. As was usual on Boxing Day, Carol called round at her Uncle Jackson's farm at Ravenshield to take the cards and presents she had bought for the family and receive the ones they had for her. She took Sharon with her, but not her mother, who would neither have been welcome nor wanted to come. Arriving at teatime, she expected to stay for the meal, to catch up on gossip, to share the remaining celebrations with them all. She was looking forward to it, as a happy time which she and her daughter would enjoy, a chance to meet with all her cousins at once, since they would certainly all be there. She stood in the bitter wind outside the kitchen door, waiting for an answer to her knock, and heard faint sounds of laughter from inside and saw the glow of lamplight falling on the frosty ground. She was already, in anticipation, smelling the good warm smells of mince pies, rich cake, sausage rolls, home-produced ham, all underlaid with the scent of pine from the great tree that would stand, as always, in the far corner of the kitchen.

Then the door opened and her uncle stood there and something in his stance immediately warned her that things were not, after all, as usual; that something had gone badly wrong. "Yes?" he said, curtly.

She stepped forward, holding out the bag containing her gifts. "Happy Christmas, Uncle Jackson."

He glanced at the bag, but made no move to take it. "I'd have thought you'd have realised. You're not welcome here."

She stared at him, feeling a chill that had little to do with the winter evening. "But – why?"

"All the years my Dad had the business, all the years your father and I had charge, there was nothing like this. It's taken you and your mother to bring the good name of Armstrong's into the dust. Well, we want nowt more to do with you. I'm sorry, but there it is." And then, abruptly, he shut the door.

It seemed very dark out there in the yard, and perishingly cold. Sharon tugged at Carol's hand. "Mam!" Her voice was soft but full of anguish. When Carol looked round she saw that her daughter was silently crying.

"Let's go home," said Carol, trying to sound cheerful. They walked back towards the car left parked in the lane, just outside the gate. "We'll go and see Nana if you like. We'll make toast by the fire, and maybe have a game of Monopoly." Sharon liked Monopoly, and was good at it, but tonight she seemed unimpressed by the offer, for she made no response.

"Why does no one like us any more?" she asked instead. "Why do they think we've done wrong?"

"Now you know not everyone thinks that. Only stupid people."

"So Uncle Jackson's stupid? And Rachel, is she stupid too?"

"Just at the moment, yes. So we won't think about them." They drove home in silence. The game of Monopoly failed to do more than fill an otherwise empty evening.

Later – past Sharon's usual bedtime – mother and child returned to their little terraced house, unlocking the front door just as the phone started ringing. Carol dropped her bags on the doormat and ran. "You get yourself to bed!" she called to Sharon.

The voice on the other end was crisp, youthful, shaped by an expensive private education. "Caz? Hope you're not in the midst of lots of festive fun. I'm going slowly insane – all these aunts and uncles braying away. Too much food and not enough air. Ugh! I've got to do something more interesting or I'll strangle one of them before the night's out. Thought a good gossip with you was just the thing. Now, Caz, tell me, this business with the lorry in Wolverhampton – how are things? Any developments?"

Carol, initially glad to recognise Daphne's voice, was suddenly aware of warning signals. For the second time today she sensed betrayal, the failure of friendship. "Hang on! Are you speaking to me as my cousin, or as a journalist?"

"Not quite a journalist, if I'm honest. Cub reporter's nearer the truth. And your cousin. Oh come on, Caz, I'm on your side, you know that!"

"Not if you try to get inside information for your paper, so they can print more lies."

"Oh, my paper's not interested in anything but the Women's Institute Christmas concert and who married who at St Laurence's last week. National news takes half a page somewhere inside, and you've had your paragraph there – you'll not get any more. Don't worry. I'm just taking a friendly interest."

So they talked, not just about the impending court case – for it was clear there was going to be a court case, and that Diana, as the senior partner, would have to face serious charges on behalf of the firm – but also about relatives and Christmas time and their love lives. Daphne, once the naive schoolgirl, sometimes seemed to have a different man each week, though at present she was besotted with a senior journalist who had just moved from her paper to a more prestigious one in Birmingham. Carol, who had no opportunity these days to meet any of the three or four drivers who, like Dave, had become her occasional lovers, was feeling miserable and frustrated, on top of everything else. "You'll have to take up with someone in the Dale," suggested Daphne. "How about that nice Bruce?" Daphne had got to like him when working for the firm during her university vacations.

"I'm not taking up with anyone local, especially someone who fancies me and hasn't any other ties. I don't want to be tied – didn't we agree that was the best way?"

"Mm." Daphne sounded less than convinced. "That's what I thought, until I met Duncan."

"So much for freedom! Still, it wouldn't do for me. But I don't like not having anything." She glanced round quickly to check that Sharon was not within earshot and was relieved to hear the sound of running water from the bathroom. "No work, an empty bed, just me and Sharon. It's not much of a life. And we haven't any friends left either. Or not many."

"So life's not good?"

"It's foul. Mam says it's just like when she fell pregnant and had to get married and all her family's friends turned against her, wouldn't even speak when she saw them in the street. Well, now I know just how she felt."

After Christmas, things got even worse. Just as the police seemed to have completed their relentless trawling through the firm's documents, the Inland Revenue – presumably tipped off by the police – moved in to carry out their own investigation. "There's nothing for them to find," Diana consoled Carol, who drew no comfort from the thought at all. It was the process she hated, the fact that they seemed to have no privacy any more, no escape from the endless prying into every aspect of their lives. Further, they had both believed that by now the newspapers would have grown tired of the story of the accident – especially with so much other more nationally significant news to distract them – but there was no sign that they had. They were now full of pieces about greedy hauliers who demanded the impossible from drivers and vehicles as a way of ensuring ever greater profits. Many then went on to demand that, when accidents happened, the haulier not the driver should automatically be called to account – and heavily punished. "Much more of this," Diana said to Carol one day, "and we'll be found guilty before the case ever comes to court."

The government changed – to a Labour government under Harold Wilson with a tiny majority – the three-day week ended, miners and railwaymen went back to work, spring crept in. But still the unpleasantness hung over them, still the offices at the garage and the two depots were full of men scouring through files and documents, emerging only to ask yet more questions. As for business, they still had the work for which there were long-term contracts, for the time being at least, but the occasional work – which was most of the long-distance work – had dwindled to a trickle. The office phone would stay silent for hours at a time. Two more drivers left to find work elsewhere, since they could no longer make a decent living with Queen of the Road. Shirley stayed, of course, resolutely loyal in spite of all the inconvenience. Whenever they found themselves short of a driver, she left the depot and went back on the road. "Better than staying here with that lot," she said to Carol one day towards the end of March, with a jerk of her head towards the office in which two Revenue inspectors were already at work, though it was only eight thirty in the morning and bitterly cold. They walked together towards the five wagons that would be working today, though one was already moving off; Bruce gave them a wave as he set out on his day's duties. "Had a call from your cousin yesterday," Shirley went on. "The posh one."

The old suspicions surged into renewed life. "What did she want?"

"Funny. Asked about the clearing house – you know, Harry's mate, the one we used to use for backloads. Said it came up when she was first here."

"That would be about the time we decided to give up on them and go straight to the firms. They always did give us lower prices than any other clearing house."

"Aye. Your Mam thought they were ripping us off. So did I, come to that."

"But I didn't think Daphne would have known about all that." Daphne had only ever worked in the petrol station.

"Says you and your Mam used to talk about it."

"I suppose we may have done. But it's none of her business anyway. What did you tell her?"

"Not a lot. Mind, more than I meant to. She has a way of getting things out of you. I know she's your cousin, but I don't trust her. Working for a paper now isn't she? She got the name out of me, but nothing else. Hope no harm comes of it."

"I don't suppose it matters," said Carol, though she feared it might. She knew how ambitious Daphne was as far as her work was concerned. She also knew, because Daphne had continued to phone her at regular intervals, how skilled she was at setting fears at rest for long enough to extract a good deal of information, without her hearer realising until afterwards that any such process was taking place. In many ways Carol found it a relief to confide in someone sympathetic who was not directly entangled in the situation. She just wished that she could have been quite certain that Daphne was not simply using her obvious vulnerability for her own ends. Each time Carol put the receiver down, she would resolve never again to talk so freely to her cousin; and each time she would find her resolution fading, her fears lulled, in the face of Daphne's soothing reassurances and her own need.

She, who had been so happy, so at ease with the world, so trusting, had become a miserable, suspicious, discontented woman, who did not feel she could even rely on those few friends who remained. Sometimes, in the bleakest hours of the night, she even found herself mistrusting Shirley, the one person outside her immediate family who – along with Bruce – had never given her any reason to doubt her loyalty.

Carol, guiltily afraid that her thoughts might be discernable on her face, looked around at her companion, whose own thoughts had evidently moved on to other clearly more worrying matters. "Cowcleugh contract's coming up for renewal."

In previous years, renewal had been automatic. "Do you think we'll be all right? With the court case still hanging over us – will they risk renewal?"

"Don't know. Doubt it myself."

It was a dispiriting prospect, for if that contract went then almost inevitably, when the time came, they would lose the other contracts they had with Dale Industrials. "Do you really think we might lose our licence?"

"No, not really. Your mam does, but I think it'll just mean a fine. And no reputation left."

"Ronnie Shaw rang Mam last night, asking how things were."

Shirley glanced sharply at her. "And?"

"I think he might just be keeping in with her, so he can be first in line if she has to sell."

"Not so sure about that. He's sweet on her."

"Is he?"

"Has been for years. Surprised you didn't know."

"But what about that business with the sugar? Oh, I know he didn't know about it, but he was angry enough about us for his manager to think he'd be pleased."

"Maybe. People act strange when they're thwarted. But you talk to Norman – knew Ronnie during the war. Says he worshipped your mam, reckons he still does."

"And Mam?"

"He's an attractive man, isn't he? Even I can see that."

Was he? To Carol's eyes he seemed old, though when she thought about it she realised her mother was probably even older. Certainly he was vigorous, muscular, and had a charming smile. It was possible. The intriguing thought stayed with her all her working day. She tried to recall signs that her mother might be tempted by what, if anything, Ronnie had to offer, but had seen them so little together that she could not really judge. As far as she knew, the Christmas letter and the recent phone call were the only contact they'd had for years. Very likely Shirley's view was nothing but idle speculation.

Her return home at the end of the day drove all thoughts of

Ronnie and romance out of her head. It had been arranged that Sharon should go to her grandmother's after school, so Carol bathed and changed at home and then went round to the flat to join them for supper. There was no sign of her daughter.

"She's at Rachel's. They're friends again."

"Oh, that's good!"

"Is it? This'll soon put a stop to it." Diana handed Carol a dauntingly official-looking document. Carol saw then how grey and tired her mother looked, as if all the burdens of the world had been laid on her shoulders. "It came this morning."

It was a summons to appear in court in May to answer a whole list of charges, including failure to maintain the firm's vehicles in a fit state. "Oh dear," said Carol, inadequately.

"I've spent the day with Mr Simmons."

"What does he think your chances are?"

"He still thinks I should plead guilty, then put in a cringing letter saying how very sorry I am."

"No way! You haven't done anything wrong. Harry's the one in the wrong, even if it's only his word against ours."

"That's just it. Mr Simmons thinks he'll be the one they believe. So do I, come to that."

Sensing the depths of her mother's despair, Carol reached out and drew Diana into her arms; where, to her dismay, her mother, head resting on her daughter's shoulders, burst suddenly into tears.

The next week was a horrible one, the worst since the whole unpleasant business blew up. The newspapers, quiet on the subject for some weeks now, were full of it again, and Carol and Diana both heard the suddenly ended conversations when they entered a shop or passed a group of people on a street corner. The only small consolation was that this time Rachel made no move to drop Sharon from her circle, as she had before; in fact, she even invited her friend to spend a whole weekend with her. "Sharon says they had a long talk about loyalty," Carol explained to her mother the following Saturday, over a lunch of sardines on toast. She grinned. "I can just imagine Sharon giving her a solemn lecture."

"It seems to have done the trick. Maybe I should get her to plead my case in court."

They ate in silence for some time, while Carol tried to find the courage to pass on to her mother what Shirley had phoned this morning to tell her. In the end, she decided there was no gentle way of putting it and simply said baldly, "Shaw's have got the Cowcleugh contract."

"I know. Ronnie rang and told me." Diana sounded resigned rather than bitter. Carol was outraged.

"How dare he gloat over us like that! I hope you told him what he could do with his contract."

"Why should I? They weren't going to give it to us, were they, with this hanging over us? Anyway, he wasn't gloating. He was very nice about it, and said he'll drop out if we're cleared."

"It won't be that easy, will it?" She gazed at her mother's weary face. "It'll be ages before the case is over, you said that yourself. By then we'll be lucky to have any sort of business left."

"We shan't be cleared, shall we?"

Carol felt like shaking her mother. "Don't give up, Mam! Otherwise you might as well have pleaded guilty in the first place." She picked up the empty plates and carried them through to the kitchen.

The doorbell rang. Diana gave an exclamation. "If that's another journalist I shall scream!"

"Oh, they don't call – too much like hard work. They phone." Carol put the plates on the draining board. "I'll go."

It *was* a journalist, a young female one with long blonde hair, wearing a close-fitting brown roll-neck sweater, flared cord trousers and a patterned fleecy jerkin; no hint now of Brigitte Bardot. She carried a bulging shoulder bag and was smiling broadly, as if sure of her welcome. "Hi!"

"Daphne! What are you doing here?" Carol kept the door half shut, barring her cousin's entrance.

Daphne, no longer the diffident schoolgirl, pushed her way in. Her expression was oddly triumphant. "I'm aiming for investigative

167

journalist of the year. The nationals'll be falling over themselves to hire me after this."

Furious, Carol followed her cousin, grasping her shoulders, pulling her round to face the door. "You're not using us to further your career, that's certain! Now get out and leave us in—"

Daphne was making soothing noises, waving a hand in her cousin's angry face. "Just hear me out." She freed herself and sat down on the sofa, thumping her bag down on the coffee table and beginning to pull papers from it. She glanced at her aunt. "I tell you Auntie Di, if I don't get an award for this, then there's no justice!"

"If it's justice you want, then don't hold your breath," advised Diana bitterly, from her seat at the dining table.

"Oh, but it is. And you'll get it, believe me." Swiftly, Daphne spread the papers – and notebooks too – into neat piles, while her bemused relations looked on. "There it is – the evidence – or my rough notes anyway. The fair copy's gone to the police, all typed up, with the evidence attached."

Carol sat down in the armchair, facing her. "What on earth are you talking about?"

Daphne leaned back, expansively, looking from one bewildered face to another. She was clearly enjoying herself. "It's like this. When I heard about the accident and how Harry's version of events differed from yours – you know, his claim that you made him take on extra work, cash in hand, no questions asked; all that sort of stuff. Well, I've worked here, I know you – I didn't believe a word of it, naturally. But proving it – that was obviously going to be difficult. Anyway, I fell to thinking about where the accident happened, how you said Harry shouldn't have been anywhere near there. I seemed to remember that the clearing house, the one where his friend was – that was Wolverhampton way too."

"But we've had no dealings with them for years now!" said Diana. Yet some faint sense of hope must have risen in her, for she moved to the sofa, closer to her niece.

"*You* haven't. But who's to say Harry hasn't? Never did care for him. Anyway, I went to see them. Didn't tell them I was a journalist, of course. I said I was a novelist – romances, Mills & Boon sort of thing, but very careful about my research. I had this hero who was a hunky lorry driver and I wanted some inside information. I think he was flattered, Harry's friend. Well, I did lay on the charm a bit too. I think he thought I was a bit dizzy – I went blonde on purpose – you'd never believe the difference it makes! Anyway, that's beside the point. I was amazed how much he told me, more than I ever needed. Not that it was evidence, of course, and I'm damn sure he'd not talk in court, but it gave me more than enough to follow it up elsewhere. I looked up all the contacts he mentioned, all the people Harry was said to have done work for. Tried a few approaches – student looking for vacation work, the novelist again, oh, you name it, I tried it. By the end, I had enough on paper and in my notes to make sure Harry was up to his neck in it."

"Then – just let me get it right – he's been working on the side, just as we thought, is that it?"

"Part of it. Whenever he can, cash in hand of course. But you know why he recommended his old friend to you, all those years ago? Easy – any job you got, any backload you carried, he got a rake-off – commission, if you like."

"So that's why we got so little, compared with the other clearing houses! Not that any of them were that good . . ." Diana stared at her niece in fascination, as if she was striving to understand, to believe.

"Hang on a minute," Carol burst out, "are you saying we're off the hook – cleared?"

Daphne spread her arms along the back of the sofa, her expression thoroughly smug. "That's just what I'm saying. You see, I've found someone who'll talk – well, more than one, but one to begin with. I don't think he'd have talked, except I told him Harry had brought his name into it, as being behind the fiddling. That panicked him. His name led to another couple of firms too, and they named Geoff and Brian as well. Anyway, I gather they've now made their statements to the police, not only about what Harry and Co were up to, but also confirming that you'd never been involved, that they'd never even heard of you till all this blew up."

Carol gave a cry that mingled amazement, joy and exasperation. "Daphne, you wretch, why didn't you tell us what you were doing? All those questions – there are times I've thought the very worst of you!"

Daphne shrugged. "Oh, I thought you might not approve – you might have tried to stop me, told me to leave it to the police or something."

Carol studied her face, speculating. "I think you just like worming things out of people without their knowing."

Daphne grinned, as if acknowledging the charge. "Well, any good journalist needs to be able to do that doesn't she?"

"Then – then, is it over?" Daphne nodded vigorously at her aunt. "I can't believe it's that easy. How can you be sure? There's still the matter of the brakes."

"They've no evidence they failed because of poor maintenance. Besides, Harry shouldn't have been on the road so long anyway. They overheated, I think, going down a hill, but he was going much too fast. Something like that." She laughed. "I'm not much good at all that technical stuff, but I did get chatting to one of the men on the case – not bad, for a policeman. Not very bright though." She stretched luxuriously. "Now, where's my fatted calf?"

They tried to celebrate, and thanked Daphne for all she had done, but it was not until the following week, when they heard through the solicitor that the case had been dropped that Carol and Diana truly believed it was over. All that remained then was for Diana to appear as a witness for the case against Harry, who was found guilty of dangerous driving and given a short prison sentence as well as a disqualification. Afterwards, Diana's solicitor advised her to lodge a civil action against him for defrauding the firm, but she decided against it. "He's finished anyway," she said to Carol, when her daughter asked her why not. "Especially now Daphne's piece has got into so many of the papers. And it'd probably cost us more in legal fees than we'll ever get back. Besides, I want to put all this behind us, if we can."

"Of course we can," said Carol. "We'll be on our feet again in no time, you'll see." She fingered the tulips and daffodils standing in a vase on the coffee table. "See, even Ronnie Shaw still wishes us well." The flowers had arrived the previous day, with a congratulatory note from Ronnie.

Diana looked ruefully at her daughter. "I don't know if I've got the energy to fight for business any more. Because that's what we're going to have to do. I'm almost tempted to sell up and just stay with the garage here."

"Oh Mam, you wouldn't! What's the point? We'd never make a living from that, not by itself."

"We've still got plenty of funds behind us, and if we sell up we'll have even more."

"Then we've got funds to start building up again too! I'm much too young to retire – so are you. Besides, I want to get back to full-time driving as soon as possible, for our own firm in our own wagons. I've had enough of sitting around doing nothing for half the day. If I don't drive, I'm not alive. There's one thing though—" Her mother looked at her questioningly. "I think we should get those tachographs fitted, at least to the artics. I think we could do with a spy in the cab. Just in case." She stood up. "Come on, Mam. Let's have a sherry and drink to the future." Not waiting for an answer she went to the sideboard and took out glasses and a bottle of Harvey's Bristol Cream. She brought her mother a glass. "Here!" She took her own glass and sat beside her mother on the sofa. "Do you remember that night I left Kenny? We drank to the future then. We've come a long way since that night."

"A very long way." Diana sipped the sherry and already began to feel cheered, though more by Carol's obvious optimism and energy than the sherry. That had been the case that night long ago, she recalled then. She raised her glass, smiling suddenly. "And here's to the way we still have to go, longer and better than ever!"

Thirteen

"Thirty years old! It's ancient!" Carol was staring at herself in the mirror over the mantelpiece, inspecting her features for signs of decay. There were faint lines at the corners of her eyes, she thought, and surely, too, on her forehead, where the thick tumble of curls usually hid them. She'd thought giving up smoking was supposed to make you look younger.

"It looks young from my great age," said Diana, who had called round before work to wish her daughter a happy birthday. She studied the slight figure before her, as slender now as at twenty, more so perhaps, a little too thin, consumed by nervous energy. Though it was that energy, and her tireless enthusiasm, that had kept them all going through the two years that it had taken to rebuild the business after the disastrous winter and spring of 1974. Carol had never allowed her mother to give up, to slacken her efforts to succeed, though Diana had often been close to it.

It had been hard, at a time when many businesses found it difficult to survive at all. Their eventual success had been built on relentless hard work, steady nerves and an avoidance, as far as possible, of debt. Diana had been forced – by the sudden dent to their reputation – to set herself, once again, to go out and deliberately seek business, talking to managers in their offices, making approaches wherever there was the slightest hope of work. It had been harder because she refused to consider using the savage tactics that were becoming common in the haulage industry, just the kind of thing that she had been accused of at the time of Harry's accident. She wanted Queen of the Road to have a reputation for reliability, fairness and good service, no matter what the cost. The strategy had been exhausting and time consuming, but it had succeeded.

Success had also brought its own problems, one of them an old one. Thinking of it now, Carol asked, "Is it today you're going to see Forest Roadstone about the Deepburn site?"

"Yes, this morning." She felt weary just to think of it – would they never be able to say: "This is it, we've arrived"? "Keep your fingers crossed. I don't quite know what we'll do if they say no. It's the only remotely possible site for a depot that's come up in years." Their fifteen vehicles were still straddled between the two isolated and inconvenient sites at the head of the Dale.

Carol, continuing to peer at the mirror, licked a finger and smoothed an eyebrow with it. "Maybe we should look for something outside the Dale."

"I don't think we'll have much choice if we don't get this. We just can't manage without more space." Diana reached into her bag. "Anyway, here's your present."

Sharon, overhearing, came running down the stairs. "Let's see, Mam – what is it?" She was washed, tidy, fully dressed in the scarlet and grey uniform of Meadhope Comprehensive school, where she was a second year pupil.

Carol pulled the paper off the parcel and held up a leather jacket – to Sharon's disappointment, though not to her mother's. "Thanks, Mam! Just what I wanted. Not that I'll be wearing it today." Once again the day was sunny and promised to be very hot.

"It's eight o'clock," said Sharon pointedly. Her school bus left Wearbridge at quarter past. Already, she had her school briefcase, packed with books, in her hand.

They left together. "Do you want Sharon to come to me tonight, in case you're late back?" Diana asked.

"I shouldn't be that late – it's only Teesside today. Sharon's got a key." They rarely made use of Anne Nattrass these days, though Sharon still visited her a good deal, being as much at home in her house as she was in those of her mother and grandmother.

"Well, don't forget I'm cooking tonight."

That evening, over steak and chips followed by a cake which Sharon had baked with her grandmother's help, the birthday was rather overshadowed by the news Diana brought with her. "They didn't actually turn us down flat," she told her daughter, when Carol asked about the morning's visit. "But I had the feeling they've got something else in mind for the old quarry."

"Stan Forest has just taken over that caravan park across the river. Maybe he thinks Deepburn would do for another one."

"It's possible. I can see the attraction." She sighed. "Oh well, we can't do anything more just now. We've made him the best offer we can afford. It's up to him now. Anyway, I've got some other news for you. I had a call from Meadhope Steel this afternoon. It's a good thing you got a passport last year." It had been bought for a package holiday to Spain, their first proper holiday ever. "How does a trip to France appeal to you?"

Carol's excitement was palpable. "A work trip?"

"Yes. Meadhope Steel have some parts to go to a British shipbuilder in Bordeaux. He does small luxury craft – they've been supplying him for years. Anyway, they sent the last lot of parts for him by sea and had all kinds of trouble with them. They want them to go overland this time. In our care."

"By Queen of the Road? Wonderful! When do I go?"

"As soon as we can get the paperwork sorted."

Carol, whose knowledge of geography had always been hazy, went in search of Sharon's atlas, in which her daughter quickly found Bordeaux. Carol gave a whistle. "That's one heck of a long way. I hope they're paying well."

"Top rates, with a bonus for safe and prompt delivery."

"Just as well. There'll not be much chance of a backload from there."

"Ah, but there is!" Diana looked triumphant. "I managed to get in touch with the shipbuilder and he was kind enough to make some enquiries for me – and it seems there's a vineyard nearby with some old equipment that it's sold to one of these new vineyards in Kent."

"Vineyards? In Kent? Are you sure? He's not having you on?"

"Quite sure. This one was planted about three years ago, it seems. Anyway, they liked our price for the job. We're to collect and deliver. It's not far from Bordeaux, I gather."

"Do we get free wine as well?"

"I doubt it. But it sounds interesting anyway. I almost wish I could come with you."

"Why don't you? It's ages since either of us had a holiday."

"Don't tempt me! No, I want to be here in case there are developments on the Deepburn site. But you should have someone with you – Jean's got a passport."

Jean, a year younger than Carol, had joined the firm the previous year. Shirley had met her when away on holiday and tempted her to leave her existing – and undemanding – driving job and come to work for Queen of the Road. A small, pretty, dark woman, she had moved in with Shirley, whether for convenience or for more personal reasons Carol was not sure, though they clearly got on well and both seemed happy with the arrangement. Not that it mattered – Carol liked Jean, who was a cheerful, competent addition to their driving force.

They loaded up the newest Volvo artic and set off on the following Monday, supplied with a formidable wodge of documentation, a guide book and road map of France and the most comprehensive French phrase book that Carol had been able to find – she had only dim recollections of a reluctantly scraped O-level in the language; Jean spoke no French at all.

The journey south to Dover was hot and dusty, and complicated as they reached the edge of London by Jean's sudden indisposition. By the time they neared Dover she was clearly in the throes of a violent stomach upset. "I should never have had that meatloaf!" she exclaimed, as Carol made an emergency stop in yet another layby so her companion could stagger towards the inadequate shelter of a hedge. But it was too late to do anything about the suspect meal they had eaten in the service station yesterday afternoon, and it was quite obvious that Jean was in no state to travel any further. By mutual agreement, they found a B&B in Dover with a landlady who agreed to look after Jean until she was fit to make the journey back to Wearbridge. Then, having phoned her mother to let her know what had happened, Carol made her way, alone, to the Cross Channel ferry port. Jean's absence would inevitably mean the journey would take a little longer, with no one to share the driving, but Diana had agreed that to wait for another driver to reach them from home would only make the delay worse. Carol had heard the worry in her voice at the thought that her daughter should travel all that way alone.

In spite of the bad start to the trip, Carol loved every moment of the night crossing, eating with other wagon drivers in their own café, sleeping in the specially provided bunks, where she was teased but otherwise left unmolested. France, in the darkness of early morning, was full of unaccustomed odours; the sun rose, hazily, on a gentle landscape, so like that of southern England, yet so different, for where were the hedges, the shrub-filled gardens, the village greens?

Carol halted for breakfast in a small settlement where the café was already doing business, though it was not half past eight, and was pleased that she managed to order coffee successfully, and bread and jam. She watched in amazement as a man in overalls, presumably on his way to work, paused to enjoy a cognac before cycling off into the mist.

As soon as she could, she joined the autoroute as far as Paris, but from there followed the long straight secondary roads where there was blessedly little traffic and she threaded through villages and small towns which offered cafés and little shops where she could buy bread and ham and fruit for a roadside picnic. That evening she parked up in a village just south of Tours and found a tiny restaurant full of local working people where a pot of soup was brought to her table, and a basket of bread, followed by the day's dish of veal and potatoes with a green salad, and then a platter of cheese. A carafe of red wine – something local and cheap, she gathered, though she enjoyed it – was also brought to her. There was no choice and no pudding, but she had rarely eaten food that tasted so good, simple though it was. She slept soundly in the cab that night, looking forward to the next stage of her journey.

She reached Bordeaux late in the afternoon and made her delivery to the astonished shipyard owner; it was a relief to speak English again, discuss places they knew. Once having recovered from finding her to be a woman, he took her to dinner at a nearby restaurant, for which his French wife joined them, and then he directed her to a decent *pension* in a quiet street nearby.

Next morning, in heat that was already intense, she set out to find the vineyard with the redundant equipment for the Kentish vineyard; the Château de Flossac, her papers said, dauntingly. She followed the road east from Bordeaux, and soon found herself passing through mile upon mile of vineyards, in which majestic châteaux were planted. In some of them men and women were at work, hoeing between the rows, tying vines to their supports. *Can't be far now*, she told herself, though a glance at the road map told her there was still a long way to go: the vineyard she was making for was almost in the Dordogne, at the eastern edge of the Bordeaux region. Somewhere, she took a wrong turning, and wasted a good hour trying to get back on the right road, in an area where there seemed to be few villages and few people anywhere from whom to ask directions. When she did find someone to ask, he spoke no English and seemed quite unable to understand her clumsy French. The map was not a great deal of help either, for it failed her when it came to the narrow side roads down which she found herself travelling.

By the time she knew she was back on the right road, it was close to lunchtime, and she had been warned by the shipbuilder to avoid lunchtime deliveries. "Everything stops for lunch in France," he told her. "You won't find anyone about anywhere between twelve and two." It was now twelve, and the map told her there were only five kilometres to go before she reached her destination. She would have stopped for lunch herself, but she had seen neither shops nor cafés since well before she lost her way.

The heat came fiercely through the wagon's open window. She was hungry, hot and tired, and she wished she might happen upon a convenient motel with showers and a cold drink, or even a shady wood. But there were few trees and fewer houses, only the long rows of vines stretching either side of the road, over the undulations of the landscape, as far as the eye could see. By now, there were no workers visible, except once, in a group beneath a knot of trees, eating what at home would have been their bait – she glimpsed long loaves of bread, and bottles of wine.

At the end of a straight dusty road, so white and dazzling that it made her head ache, she rounded a slight bend beside a spinney and saw ahead of her a solid stone mansion, not as large as some she had seen, but with all the grace of a castle in a fairy tale. A narrower road led to the right of the house, then on through an archway into a courtyard surrounded by low buildings. She parked the wagon, finding relief in the sudden silence, broken now only by the rhythmic chatter of cicadas, the cooing of pigeons from a small round tower on the further corner. There was no other sign of life.

Nearby, one of three stalls housed a chestnut horse. On the further side of the courtyard a shadowed doorway invited her in; the door was half open. She pushed it wider, looked inside. Long ranks of barrels stretched into the dimness and it was blessedly cool. The air smelt earthy, faintly damp, with elusive odours of alcohol and fruit. She wandered a little way inside, but still found no one about. It seemed only too likely that everyone was at lunch.

She went back into the heat of the courtyard and wondered what to do. Find a door into the house and knock on it, risking the anger of its occupants at being disturbed at such a sacred time? Sit down and wait in the one shady corner of the courtyard until someone appeared, or she could be reasonably sure she had allowed them a decent lunchbreak? Drive away again in the hope she could find somewhere to eat, and come back later, by which time they might actually be pleased to see her?

She was just about to decide on the latter course when she heard a distant murmur of voices from somewhere beyond the furthermost buildings of the courtyard. Feeling very nervous, fearing that she was about to be thrown off the premises as an uncivilised intruder, she went out by the archway – that being the only way out – and made her way round the back of the buildings in the direction from which the voices came.

In the shade thrown by the courtyard wall, a long trestle table had been set up, around which were gathered about half a dozen people, men and women, many wearing overalls or other working clothes, their attention centred on the food that was spread on the white cloth – cheeses and fruit, salad, bread, wine, even soup in a tureen with a great ladle curving out of it.

As soon as she saw them Carol halted, feeling awkward and embarrassed. This was quite evidently the vineyard workers' lunch, and she was an intruder. At that moment someone looked round, said something to one of the others. She saw heads turn – eyes watching her, comments being made. A man at the far end of the table pushed back his chair and made his way towards her.

She braced herself for anger; then, instead, found herself taking in the way he walked, his graceful catlike litheness, the easy arrogance of his bearing. As he came nearer, she saw a lean face beneath soft brown hair, and dark eyes appraising her. She felt very odd, dizzy with the heat, confused, unable to know what to do next.

As soon as he was within earshot he made some greeting, in a soft voice, with warmth in its tones. Not having the least idea what he'd said, she stammered out, "Bonjour, monsieur," and wondered what on earth she should do or say next.

"You are English, perhaps, madame?" he asked then. She had only a moment in which to feel offended that he had so quickly detected her accent before he smiled, and she forgot everything except to think how dazzling that smile was. There was a little silence, during which he must have been waiting for her to admit he was right, even explain herself. When she said nothing, and simply went on staring at him, he prompted her, "May I help you, madame?"

What was it about English spoken with a French accent that

made it the most sensual sound on earth? She felt herself grow hotter still, her colour rising. What to say now?

Then she recalled, belatedly, why she was here, fumbled in her shoulder bag for her papers and thrust one towards him, saying, "Caz Armstrong. I've come for the equipment, for England."

He looked a little puzzled, examined the paper with close attention, then looked at her again. "There was to be a – how do you call it? – *camion*, lorry."

"I parked in the courtyard. I hope that's all right?"

"You! You are the driver? You alone, a woman?"

It was a long time since she had met with such a degree of astonishment. "Yes. Have you any objection?"

He smiled again, immediately overturning the slight prickle of indignation that had begun to rise in her. "Of course not." He gestured towards the table. "You will join us perhaps?"

It had been impressed upon Carol, by the guide book she had read and by her host of last night, that the French did not readily welcome strangers into their homes, still less invite them to meals; a private and individualistic race, so she understood. Yet here she was being ushered towards the table, where the occupants shuffled along the nearer bench to make room for her at the end nearest to the young man, who had introduced himself as they went as "Luc Maury, proprietor of the vineyard." *And of this grand house too, I suppose*, added her mind, with some astonishment. He introduced the others too, but she completely failed to take in any of their names.

In a daze, she ate and drank, aware that the food was good, though not really tasting very much of it; more aware of the man beside her, of the warmth and laughter that surrounded her, the sense of welcome. She wondered if any of the other people about the table were members of his family, though she saw no family resemblance; or if any of the women were married to him, though none seemed especially proprietorial. If he singled anyone out it was her, including her in the talk, occasionally asking her a question, but nothing too probing, nothing that might make her feel uncomfortable or invade her privacy, should she wish to keep it.

The meal ended at last, the workers went back to the fields, and Luc came with her to the courtyard, exclaiming again that she should be the sole driver of the great dusty articulated lorry parked there – as if only when he actually saw it for himself could he quite bring himself to believe that this was how she had come to his vineyard. In any other situation she would have delighted in her sense of superiority, the sense of defeating all the obvious expectations of a man about the things women did. But today something odd was happening to her; she was interested in the reactions of the man beside her, but only because she was interested in him. No, interested was the wrong word; she felt as if he and she were the only people in the whole world, as if suddenly she had no meaningful existence at all, except in relation to him. She seemed to see every detail of his face, his body, his manner, but not so much with her eyes as with her whole self, as if by some process of absorption. She felt him rather than saw him. Yet when he spoke to her, questioned her, she could not think of anything coherent to say. All her usual assurance, her calm control of circumstances, seemed to have vanished without trace. She could no longer even think clearly about the reason for her journey, and though she followed him to the building where he said the equipment she had come to collect was stored, she seemed unable to take in what he was talking about. She could only gaze at him, mesmerised by the dark eyes, the mobile mouth, the graceful way he walked. *It's the heat*, she told herself. *I'm not used to it. It's too much for my poor brain.*

At that moment he turned to look at her, smiled, reached out a hand and touched her briefly on the elbow. She was not even sure that he intended to touch her, or whether his hand simply moved too close. But the touch sent a shock running through her body, from tingling scalp to feet that suddenly felt as if they might at any moment lift off from the ground and carry her dancing away. She felt drunk, exhilarated, weird.

"*Les voici!*" he said, opening a door. Before her in the cool darkness of the cavernous outbuilding lay two great metal objects and a succession of pipes and other things that made her think of the chemistry labs at school, though on a much larger scale.

She found herself asking questions about the equipment, though she really did not care very much about it; but she wanted to prolong the moment. He answered, describing what it all used to do, while she listened, watching his face for every changing expression, hearing every shade of meaning in his voice; observing the way his supple mouth formed the words, struggled, sometimes, with the unfamiliar English words. "I shall show you what we have in its place," he told her, enthusiastically, and led her into another outbuilding, scrubbed clean, full of shining stainless steel tanks. "This is the most modern equipment, the very best. My fellow *vignerons* say I am mad, that the wine will be spoiled. It is not traditional, you see."

He led her past the tanks, on through low cavernous rooms full of barrels, or tiered rows of bottles, all carefully labelled; and all the time he talked, his long graceful hands gesturing, his eyes shining, his voice warm with enthusiasm. He talked of wine as a living thing, of its unpredictability, its potential to be both the most wonderful thing in creation or something fit only to be thrown away. Now and then – if he happened to pause in his talk, which did not happen often – Carol asked him a question, just in case he might be about to bring their meeting to an end. She must have sounded intelligent and interested enough, because he always answered her, in full, and seemed convinced that she was listening avidly to his replies – as she was in a way, because she could happily have listened to that voice for ever.

Inevitably, the tour did come to an end, and they found themselves once more out in the heat of the courtyard. "You will have need of men to put these things on your lorry," he said. "But I should prefer that they should not do it until this evening. There is much to do while it is day. Must you make haste?"

She shook her head. "There's no hurry at all," she said, wondering at herself as she did so. She had no definite time or even day for delivery, having only promised to give as much notice as possible by phone before arriving at the Kentish vineyard. But she knew her mother would worry until she was home again, and she had intended to set out this very afternoon, to cover as much ground as possible in the day, with a view to getting on the earliest available channel crossing tomorrow.

"Then you will rest here today, as my guest, until tomorrow perhaps?"

Oh joy! "Thank you. I should like that." *That must be the understatement of the year,* she thought with some amusement. *I'm getting as bad as my mother.*

"I regret I must work this afternoon, but this evening we shall meet again." He led the way into the house, where he handed her over to the care of Madame Fourcaud, his housekeeper, a calm and stately woman whom Carol found rather intimidating. She was relieved when, having shown Carol to a cool and simply furnished bedroom, pointed out where she could find the bathroom, and brought her clean towels, the woman left her alone. The bed looked comfortable. Carol went to it, felt the mattress, thought she'd try it, stretched full length; and what with the heat and the long journey fell suddenly, deeply, asleep.

She woke, abruptly, to a moment or two of bewilderment; then recollection, a flood of emotions pouring through her. The slant of the sun through the long window told her it was already nearly evening. She leapt up, grabbed the towels and found her way to the bathroom.

Later, dressed in her spare cheesecloth shirt and her second pair of jeans, with excitement and nervousness churning inside her, she descended the wide staircase to the tiled hallway below. Doors led off it on all sides. Where to now? Disconcertingly, as if conjured by her thoughts, Madame Fourcaud appeared and ushered her into an exquisite light-panelled parlour, where she set fresh lemonade on the table – it was still very hot, though the gilded clock on the mantelpiece showed it was already after seven. The housekeeper said something in French, in which the word "monsieur" featured, but nothing else that Carol understood. She smiled nervously, said "thank you," and was glad when she was alone again. The lemonade was delicious, though she was ravenously hungry, too, by now.

Then, at last, Luc came into the room, changed from his work clothes into slightly more formal wear, though nothing to make her feel too embarrassed about her jeans. Now, the working day over, he gave his full attention to his role as her host. He proved to be the most enchanting of companions. She had known nothing like his attentive concern for her. Were all Frenchmen like this, she wondered, or was he special, unique? If so, then what astonishing fate had brought them together? And was he aware – as she was – that something momentous had happened today?

"Do you live here all alone?" she asked, as he led her into the huge dining room. It was, she knew, her way of asking if he was married. It was a question which, in her relations with men, had never troubled her much before. In fact, if the men she singled out were married, then so much the better, for she had never wanted to risk being tied in any way. She had never wanted commitment, on either side. But suddenly it mattered very much that this man, whom she had met only a few hours previously, should not have a wife.

"My sister is often here, with her family. Always in the vacations. But she lives in Paris, and that is where she is now. Our mother died last year. So there is now no woman of the house, save for my sister. You feel the need of a chaperon, perhaps?"

She thought of the vast house, empty of everyone but the housekeeper – and perhaps other staff she had not seen – and their two selves, and looked into his impishly smiling face and felt no need at all of a chaperon.

He pulled a chair out for her, and she sat down. Two places were set at one corner of the ancient oak table, and a tureen of soup stood ready for them. He ladled out the soup and they ate, though she could not have described the meal afterwards, only that it tasted wonderful, better than any meal she had ever eaten in her life, just as the wine was a revelation, though she only sipped at it, feeling as if she needed no stimulant to make her light-headed. Strangely, in spite of the hugeness of the room and

184

its furnishings, in spite of the occasional unobtrusive presence of the housekeeper bringing another course for them to eat or another bottle of wine, it was an intimate meal. In fact, it was astonishing how little awkwardness there was between them. The talk flowed easily, and she found herself confiding in him as she did in few people; but laughing too at things he said to her, fascinated by stories he told, by what he revealed of himself and his work – though she quickly learned that to him the vineyard was not so much his work as his life; rather as driving wagons was to her, she supposed.

Except that this was the first time she had ever felt there was something in her life that could absorb her more than driving, more than life on the road. She felt this evening as if she were isolated in some magical place from which she had no wish to escape. She wanted this to go on for ever, without end.

Once the meal was over they sat on at the table for a long time, with no impulse on the part of either of them to move, as if by suggesting such a step they might break some spell that had woven itself about them. But at last there came a break in the talk, a moment of silence, and she turned her head enough to catch sight of the ornate gilded clock on the huge stone mantelshelf. "It's nearly one o'clock!" How could so much time have passed without being noticed?

"And you have many miles to drive. I am sorry to have kept you so long from your bed." For the first time this evening, he sounded like the conventional host. The next moment, he reached over and laid a hand over hers. "I have met no one like you in all my life."

It was a trite remark, one she had often heard. But this time she believed it; after all, the circles he moved in must be very different from any she knew. She guessed, though, that he meant more than that. She felt a shiver of excitement, read in his eyes a tenderness, a suggestion, that she would have taken for granted from anyone else; but not from this man whom she so much wanted to be attracted to her. "I haven't met too many people like you," she said in an attempt at lightness that merely sounded unconvincing.

She sensed rather than saw that he had moved nearer to her. She moved too, and felt his hand brush her cheek, caressing; and then they were kissing.

Somehow, smoothly, without further words, they were in his bedroom. She had made love to many men before, to meet a need, for enjoyment. Mostly – especially compared to sex with Kenny – the experience had been entirely pleasurable, much as a good meal satisfied hunger. This was completely different, not simply because Luc was a good and considerate lover – though he was – but because somehow it was a momentous happening, something that she knew would change her for ever, whatever might come after.

It was beginning to grow light before drowsiness overcame them and the caresses and soft talk faded into silence. Luc slept at her side, while Carol dozed, and then woke and lay watching the window take on form and definition with the increasing daylight.

It was then in the silence of the dawn that reality began to creep over her. That something overwhelming had happened to her she could not deny; and through the long lovely hours together she had not questioned that Luc felt as she did, that what they had was shared and equal. Now, while he slept, she found herself looking coolly, sensibly at the situation, seeing it as it truly must be. All that tenderness, all those words, the compliments, the attentiveness – surely they were simply his manner, his way of getting a girl to go to bed with him? It was certainly an effective method. After all, he had never met her before yesterday. What had he seen when she came walking into his life? An unusual young woman, modern, independent, someone not likely to be bound by old-fashioned ideas of morality and convention; someone quite different from the doubtless proper women of his acquaintance? Naturally, finding her attractive – as it was obvious he did – he would take his chance, especially when he found her so willing. Because he was French, a foreigner, living in a mansion, he had seemed different; but in reality he was exactly like other men.

She turned to look at his sleeping head on the pillow beside

186

her – her insides seemed to somersault with desire and longing – and told herself to be sensible. What if he did see her simply as a casual bedfellow, a one-night stand? That was how she must look on him too; she belonged to a life far removed from here, far removed from the life he led. Their paths had crossed, strangely, unpredictably, but must now move on in opposite directions. They were unlikely ever to meet again. Whatever she might feel, they could never be anything more to one another than this. She would have the memory of it to carry with her into the reality of her life in England, but that was all. The pain of that thought was so great that she could no longer bear to stay lying where she was. She slid out of bed and walked to the window and looked out on the vineyards, already touched by the first sunlight.

"Caz!"

His eyes were open and he was smiling at her, holding out his arms. She went back to the bed, and even after a night of love, even with so little sleep, they came together again, and for that time the pain was driven back. "Must you go today?" he asked at the end of it.

She wanted so much to stay here for ever, never leave, never part from him. She wanted to lie here in bed beside him and leave the world to turn without her. What else mattered as this did, what could life ever offer that would mean more to her than this? Beyond the boundaries of this place there seemed nothing left of importance to her; all she needed lay here, within them.

Except that to think like that was to delude herself, for even if she were to stay she knew it would not, could not always be like this. A day or two perhaps, even a week, and then he would tire of her, wish to return to some kind of normality. And she would be left, more enmeshed by him than ever, but forced to go back, alone, bereft, to the life she had left behind. So she drew away from him, just a little, and gave him her answer. "Yes, I have to go."

He tried to persuade her to stay, promised her picnics and visits to local sights, invited her to taste foods she had never eaten before, drink the very best wines, to spend hours in bed, like this; but she forced herself to refuse, again and again, until he accepted that she meant it.

After that, all too soon they had dressed and breakfasted and the wagon was loaded with the equipment for Kent, and they stood together beside it and were suddenly tongue-tied. Luc had sent the men away once the work was done, so they were alone, but it was a moment or two before he took her in his arms. "This must not be all," he said when he had kissed her. "You will come again, soon?"

She knew that was unlikely, but she answered from the longing in her, ignoring all common sense. "Yes, yes of course, as soon as I can."

He held her a little way from him and looked earnestly into her eyes. "You and I, Caz, we are designed one for the other."

It was a beautiful thing to say, beautifully spoken. She wanted to believe it. Yet – he had a way with words, she knew that, even words of another language than his own. With those eyes looking at her too, he must have known he was impossible to resist – almost. She smiled, and said with a shaky attempt at lightness, "It's true, everything they say about Frenchmen."

She thought he looked almost hurt – was that because she had not been taken in, as he had hoped?

If it was, he made no comment, simply kissed her again for what seemed a long time and then stood back as she climbed up into the wagon and drove away on the hot and dusty road.

Fourteen

C arol had thought that as she drove home across France she would be able to put Luc behind her, as the distance lengthened and the miles increasingly separated them. *It was just a fling,* she told herself; *like Dave or any of the others, except that because he was French and lived in a château and was better looking than any of them, I got more excited about it.* Yet try as she might she could not get him out of her mind. She felt as if he had possessed her, taken her over. At every turn of the road she saw the way he turned his head, the way he looked at her, heard his voice, even when other French voices speaking English to her intruded into her consciousness, and should, she thought, have obliterated that first voice.

He was still with her as she crossed the Channel, and even as she drove through the narrow hedged roads of Kent, so unlike the place he came from, peopled by such different individuals – this country which he had never visited and almost certainly never would. Tomorrow, perhaps, she thought, when the equipment from France had been delivered and she had left vineyards and everything to do with them behind her, then she would leave him too. The English vineyard, when she reached it, seemed very different in its lushness and greenery, its hilly landscape, from the wide-skyed vineyards of Luc's homeland. The owner, a broad aristocratic-looking man – surely public-school educated? – with fair hair and the countryman's high colour, was nothing like Luc, though she supposed that in a way he had a similar background to his French counterpart. Yet still she had not left Luc behind. She told herself that once she was beyond London, once she had spent a night in an English B&B and was setting out on English motorways with a full English breakfast inside her, then she would wake to reality, putting that blissful interlude behind her. She woke next morning to a creaking bed with a dip in the middle and a greasy, unappetising breakfast, and still he was with her, as he was all that day as she drove home through the baking heat.

The journey somehow seemed to take hours and yet go by, unnoticed, in an instant, as if time had been thrown into confusion by what had happened to her. She stopped for her midday break at a familiar transport café on the A1 – one that, long ago, Shirley had recommended – and there she found Dave eating his way through steak pie and chips. The sight of him jolted her: so normal, so ordinary, so much a part of her life; but it was her past life, before Luc. Once she would have felt a tremor of desire, would have considered finding some quiet place with him, even now in the middle of the day, allowing herself an enjoyable moment of indulgence. Today, she felt nothing, only wondered how she could ever have wanted to go to bed with someone who had so little effect on her. He saw her, waved and called out, and she joined him, with her toast and tea – since leaving France she seemed to have no appetite – smiled vaguely at the things he said, while taking in very little of it. "You're in a funny mood," he commented at last. "What's up?"

"Nothing," she lied. "Nothing at all."

He shrugged with obvious disbelief, and a moment afterwards said, "They say Shaw's has gone bust."

Even that momentous piece of news failed to catch her interest, though she did make a mental note to tell her mother about it. In the end, Dave gave up and left her before she decided not to eat the last piece of toast.

She reached home after the depot had closed for the day, so parked up in the usual layby just beyond Wearbridge and walked home from there. Sharon, of course, was at her grandmother's, so Carol had the house to herself, which was a relief. She bathed, changed, made herself some cocoa – sadly inferior to the hot chocolate she had drunk for breakfast at the château – and then steeled herself to telephone her mother. "Hi Mam, I'm home."

She heard the sighing relief in her mother's voice, though Diana as usual tried to conceal it; she knew how irritated Carol was by her anxiety. "Carol! All well then?"

Was it? "Yes. No problems."

"Are you coming round?"

"I'm tired. I'll see you tomorrow." She could feel her mother's disappointment, though Diana said nothing at all. Anxious to distract her, Carol added, "I heard Ronnie Shaw's about to go bust."

The silence was different now, the silence of someone so amazed and dismayed that she could not think what to say. Then Diana questioned her daughter, trying to find out if the story could be true. At the end, she said, "Poor Ronnie! I hope it's not true. It's been his whole life. What will he do?"

Even in her present obsessed state, Carol, hearing the genuine concern in her mother's voice, recognised that she was more distressed by the rumour than could be explained by the simple fellow-feeling of another haulier.

For tonight, the news had staved off any further questions about her trip. But the next day, facing her mother in the office at the quarry depot – Shirley was needed to drive today – she could not escape so easily. Reluctantly, she handed over the delivery papers from her journey, one of which had been handled by Luc and had his signature on it. She felt almost as if she were giving up a part of herself.

She watched her mother look them over. Even through her own preoccupation, she noticed, as she had often lately, that Diana looked tired, and that there were new lines about her mouth and on her forehead, and more grey hairs than dark ones on her head. But when she looked up, her words abruptly returned Carol to the events of the past week. "How was the trip. Did you enjoy it?"

"Some of it," was all she said. How could she begin to explain? She wanted to go back, now, at this very minute, to turn on her heels and walk out of the office and drive away towards the south and that haunting, distant happiness. Instead, she sat down, rather abruptly, on the stool by the desk and asked what she always asked on her return from any longer trip than usual. "How's things then? Any news?"

Perhaps Diana missed something in her tone, some element of real concern, real curiosity, for instead of answering she said, "Something's wrong. What happened?"

"Oh Mam, you do worry! Nothing's wrong. I didn't sleep too well last night, that's all. All the travelling, I suppose." Diana must have known, as she did, that travelling had never made Carol sleepless before. She forced herself to recall what had been uppermost in her mother's mind before she left on her journey. "Any word from Forest Roadstone?"

"Nothing," said her mother ruefully. "But it's too soon yet to be chasing them up." Then she began to talk of small things that had happened in Carol's absence, having apparently put aside her momentary anxiety.

Carol wished she could as easily ignore her constant obsession with Luc, her need to go over and over in her mind all that had happened, all that they had said and done and shared. She wanted to return to normal, to be again the woman who lived for her driving, who set out each day with complete enjoyment, asking nothing more of life than that. She wanted never to have met Luc, never to have known this volcanic disruption to a happy life. At the same time she wanted only to be with him, to return to what she had turned her back on and could never have again.

Then, on a Saturday morning two weeks after her return from France, when she had begun to find that, now and then, a moment passed without a thought of Luc, a letter arrived, addressed to her in a distinctive neat black handwriting, with a French stamp. Standing in the hallway in her housecoat, she tore it open and pulled out the folded piece of paper inside, covered in that same angular writing.

My most dear Caz,
   You mock me when I say you we are designed one for the

other. Did you not believe me, did you think I make a joke?
Indeed that is not so. I know that what I say is true, for I can no
longer breathe without you. You are for ever a part of me.
Come again here to France. Here I shall make you believe
I am sincere. I know you are as I, that you love too. Please
come!
I embrace you and wait for you. Luc.

Carol read the words again and again, while her heart thudded so
that she felt it set her whole body shaking, and her mind exulted,
pushing aside all her doubts, all her fears. He would not have
written like this if she had been no more to him than a passing
fancy, the amusement of a moment. His ardour, his conviction
reached her through every passionately written word.

"Mam! You said I could go to Rachel's this morning. It's
nearly eleven o'clock – it's nearly not morning any more!"

She had forgotten all about her daughter, who had already
breakfasted and dressed and now came downstairs, impatient to
be on her way. Carol tried to shake herself out of the trance of joy
that had enveloped her since she read the letter and concentrate
on what had to be done, now, today.

But she knew that in the days to come, somehow, she had to
find a way to go to France, to see Luc again, to discover if it
really had been as he said, for him as for her; if it had been
more than just a momentary fling. Part of her simply longed
to accept what he said, wholeheartedly, to go to him, here and
now. Another part warned her to be wary, to keep her feet on
the ground, to recognise that in many ways he knew very little
about her, less even than she knew of him.

The next day she had a proposal to put to her mother. "Mam, I
was thinking – Sharon breaks up in four weeks. You were saying
it was time we had a holiday together, me and her. Could you
spare us for a fortnight – no more, I promise. I never told you,
but that vineyard I went to in France – I've got an open invitation
to go back." She spoke casually, standing in her kitchen with her
face turned away from her mother; Diana had come to the cottage

193

for Sunday tea (Sharon was, as usual, deeply absorbed in a book). "They were nice people," Carol added, hoping that Diana would visualise a welcoming French family, husband, wife, children even. "I thought it would be really good for Sharon's French." And Sharon would make sure she kept her feet on the ground, that she kept in touch with reality; and would also show Luc that Carol could never simply be a person alone, that she had a separate life, which meant something to her.

So it was that a few days after the school term ended she found herself driving back to France, in her Mini this time, and with her quietly happy daughter at her side. She had written to Luc, telling him she would be passing his way with Sharon, asking if they might stay for a day or two – better not to push it! – and had received a brief letter in reply, which told her she would be welcome, but said little else. Now that the moment had come, she felt anxious – even fearful – about the whole thing. Would it be a disaster, the greatest mistake she had ever made, to try and revive last month's idyll?

After two years at Meadhope Comprehensive, Sharon's French was already impressive, her accent good, and she showed a solemn readiness to try out what she knew on every possible occasion. She surprised her mother, too, by her interest in everything around her, all the things that were different and remarkable about France. She was eager to try new food, to explore new places. Through her solemn eagerness Carol had a new outlook on this country she had so momentously visited.

The further south they went the more she began to dread her arrival at the château, the meeting with Luc. She could scarcely now recall the joy with which she had made the arrangements. She was simply afraid of what would be waiting for her at the end of the journey.

This time she took no wrong turns and found herself earlier than expected driving into the remembered courtyard, while Sharon exclaimed at the grandeur of their surroundings. Even though it was mid-morning rather than lunchtime there seemed to be no one about, though eventually she found a man she did not recognise in one of the buildings, and was able to summon up enough French to ask him where she could find Luc. He said something, and then disappeared.

The next moment, Luc was there, in his work clothes, coming smiling to greet her, his hands outstretched. In a daze, she felt his cheek briefly against hers – one side, then the other – then he had turned to Sharon. "So, this is your little girl!"

"*Bonjour, monsieur,*" said Sharon carefully. Luc laughed. "Ah, *bon,* she is an excellent pupil, I see." He kissed her too, to her obvious delight. "Now, come inside. You shall see your rooms and then we shall eat."

He was so calm, so correct. From the first moment of seeing him, Carol had felt all the old emotions cascading through her, but he looked as if he were simply welcoming an acquaintance to his house, someone he liked well enough, but no more. Was he concealing his feelings, or had they changed since he first wrote to her? Or – worse – had he never felt anything much at all, so that his cool manner was no disguise but an open display of what he felt? Her legs felt leaden as she walked beside him into the house, with apprehension churning inside her. Then he turned to glance at her, and she saw, unmistakably, the warmth in his eyes, the tender little smile. For the first time happiness surged up in her.

He showed them to separate but adjacent bedrooms, pleased at Sharon's struggle to express her delight in his own language. "She is an original, that one," he said quietly to Carol. "You must be proud of her."

Am I? wondered Carol. After all, the things that were so striking about Sharon were not things she had gained from her mother, either by inheritance or by example. She was indeed an original. And at least, so far, Luc seemed to like her.

Sharon enjoyed the lunch and afterwards showed great interest in everything to do with the vineyard, asking perceptive questions, observing, taking note. Once, watching her, Carol was suddenly reminded of herself as a child, looking on in the garage, eager to learn everything there was to learn about lorries and cars. That evening, Sharon enjoyed the grown-up dinner too, though by the end of it she was clearly exhausted. Carol packed her off to bed, where she quickly fell asleep.

Then she and Luc went to bed too, in his room, in that bed where Carol had found so much happiness last month, and it was as wonderful as she remembered – better perhaps, because of the fear and anxiety that had gone before, and which it dispelled.

Some time after midnight, as they lay sleepy and contented, he said, "My sister comes on Saturday. I hope you will stay until then, to meet her."

"You want me to meet your sister?"

"Of course. You will like her and she you, I am sure. But if she does not, that is no matter. She must accept you, as my wife."

What was he saying? Surely she had misheard. "What did you say?"

He kissed her, gently, then said, "I know it has been for you as for me. To be apart – that is intolerable. Even before, I knew. Now, it is certain. We are meant to be together. That is how it is, is it not?"

She struggled to find words for what she was feeling, which was impossible, because she did not know what her feelings were. "I don't know. I had not thought . . ." Oh, but she had: she had thought of nothing else but Luc, of their lovemaking, his voice, his whole self; of seeing him again. But marriage – that was something quite different, something that had nothing to do with them; or had not until now. To her, marriage meant Kenny; it was something that, with relief, she had put behind her. "I'm divorced," she said baldly.

"I know. You told me. If it does not matter to me, why should it to anyone else?"

She realised then how little she knew about him in reality. "Aren't you a Catholic?" Having herself been a pupil at a convent school, she knew a good deal about Catholic attitudes to divorce and marriage.

"After a fashion, yes. You were married in a Protestant church perhaps? Then I believe that marriage is not, in the eyes of the

Catholic Church, fully valid. I think the divorce would make no difficulty. But if it did so, I would not care. We may still make a marriage by French law at the *Mairie*." He held her closer still. "Come, Caz, I know you feel as I do. Say you will be my wife! I wish for no other."

What could she ask of life, except to stay with this man for ever? She had doubted him, suspected him of shallowness, of looking on their relationship simply as a casual fling; yet here, now, he was demonstrating unequivocally that his feelings for her were as strong as hers for him, as real, as enduring. "Yes," she murmured into the darkness. "Yes, I will be your wife." It was so easy, so right. Yet a little later, she was not quite sure why, she heard herself say, "Don't tell anyone, not Sharon, not your sister – not yet anyway, not at first."

He laughed, teased her. "You want first to be sure she is worthy to be your sister-in-law! Oh, very well, *ma chérie*. But before she goes home again, I wish that she is told."

In twenty-four hours his sister had arrived, with her three children – their father had remained behind in Paris. Marie-Laure was beautiful, assured and very well-bred, as were the children. She treated her brother's guests with perfect courtesy. There was nothing in her manner to which anyone could have taken offence. But Carol recognised at once that they had nothing whatsoever in common. Their upbringing, their experience, their view of life – everything was completely removed the one from the other. This woman who had shared much of her life with Luc demonstrated only too clearly to Carol, by her very presence, how unlike the man she loved she in fact was. She had known that, of course, before he had ever commented on how he had never met anyone like her. She knew that this was for him part of the attraction. Perhaps it was for her too; she was not sure. But now she found herself beginning to wonder if this attraction was enough to make her give up everything she had left behind at home and move to France and live here in this château – what did she know about life in such a place? – giving her support not to a haulage firm, which she understood from the very marrow of her being, but to a vineyard. And what of Sharon?

They had little time to themselves now that there were so many people staying at the château, but one evening, before dinner, she and Luc managed a walk together through the vineyard. "Now," he said, as soon as they were out of sight of the château's windows, "we must decide. When do we tell Marie-Laure? We shall celebrate with a special dinner." She said nothing, only continued to walk on at his side in silence. "You are very quiet."

"I've been wondering. Where shall we live?"

He was clearly astonished at the question. "Here, of course."

"You wouldn't consider coming to live in England?"

"But my life is here, the life we shall share."

"And mine is in England."

"That is what marriage is, to give up the old life for the new."

"For the woman to give it up – that's what you're saying?"

"Of course. Has it not always been so? For it is the husband who must provide for the wife, and the children."

Conscious that they were both becoming irritable, that this was on the verge of developing into a quarrel, still Carol took the risk of pursuing the argument. "But what if the woman has good work that she loves doing?"

"There might perhaps be a situation where one would find a wife who must support the husband, because he is unable to support her. It would be unusual, perhaps unnatural. I think for a man it would be very difficult. But you must know that when I ask you to be my wife, it is to come here and live with me."

"And Sharon?"

"She is your daughter. She will come too, of course, and she will be my daughter too. That is no difficulty for me. I love her already!"

"And if she doesn't want to?"

"Would that be enough to change your mind?"

No, for Sharon could stay with her grandmother, if she wished.

In any case, Carol suspected that her daughter, already quite clearly an ardent Francophile, would be delighted to come and live in this place. But before she could say anything, Luc suddenly came to a halt and took her hands in his and stood looking into her face, his eyes full of reproach. "Caz, you are unsure. You do not love me as you said you did."

"Oh, I do, I do!" She reached out to clasp him to her, wanting to feel his arms about her, shutting out doubts and uncertainties. But though he held her, it was lightly, at a little distance, and the doubts remained. "It's just . . ." She drew back so she could look at him. "When it was just us two, without anyone else. Even with Sharon here . . . But now your sister's here . . ."

"I know – there is so little time that we can be private. But that will pass. My sister comes only a few times a year. What is left shall be for us alone."

"It's not that, not altogether. It's that – oh, I like your sister, but she's so different. Not like anyone I'm used to. I suppose I hadn't thought about what it would be like to live here all the time, what your way of life is like. I love you, I want to be with you. But I think I want you and *my* ordinary life, not you and your life. Do you see what I'm saying?"

She knew he did before he spoke, because his eyes had a look of desolation. "I see, too well. When you do not answer my question, when to tell my sister, it is because you do not wish to tell her. You do not wish to marry me after all."

She bent her head, not wanting to see the hurt she was causing, which she felt too, for herself. "I don't know," she said, which was true.

He did hold her then, passionately, kissing her with a fierce entreaty that seemed to melt every part of her. But though for those moments she felt as if they were fused into one body, all else shut out and forgotten, it did not help. When it was over she was as unsure, as full of doubt, as ever.

Five days later she drove away from the château, with Sharon at her side. Leaving her children in her brother's care, Marie-Laure had gone back to Paris without being told anything she had not already seen with her own eyes – that her brother loved the odd young Englishwoman, that they were lovers. Nothing had been resolved. Luc had cajoled, implored, raged, beguiled, but still Carol's doubts had lingered. They remained doubts, not certainties, not a complete repudiation of what Luc offered, or what she had so easily agreed to. "Perhaps when I'm back home I'll be able to see things more clearly. Will you give me time?"

At last, sombrely, he said, "A little time, if I must. I want you, Caz. But I shall not wait for ever."

She tried another approach. "Come with me, see where I live, see what my life is like!"

"You hope I shall wish to give up all this, to come to England and share your life?"

"Perhaps. I don't know." All she knew was that somehow her old life had to be meshed with his, in some way that made a satisfactory whole. Whatever her ultimate choice, she could not wholly cut herself off from her past.

"One cannot wonder for ever. One must decide, at last. I shall expect your answer by—" He paused, considering. "By the New Year, the first day of 1977. Which I hope will be the best of years. But if I have not heard from you by then, I shall know you do not wish to see me again."

"I could never wish that, never," she said sadly, because she knew that was what her ultimate choice might bring upon them. "And whatever I decide I shall let you know. I owe you that much at least."

They slept together, as usual, the night before they parted, but their lovemaking had a kind of desperation about it, and the next morning the same gloomy sense of foreboding hung over their parting and settled itself over Carol's mood for most of the journey home. "I don't know what's the matter with you, Mam!" Sharon observed more than once. "You're in such a bad mood."

"It's the heat, that's all," was Carol's excuse, though the ache at her heart had nothing at all to do with the relentless sun.

Diana noticed her daughter's mood, too, almost as soon as Carol returned. After more than a week during which she had gleaned almost nothing about its cause – except what she could deduce from Sharon's contrastingly enthusiastic account of their holiday – she decided the time had come to tackle her daughter about it. She found an excuse for calling on Carol late one evening, when she knew Sharon would be in bed. Carol was sitting gloomily in front of a television programme she could not have found remotely interesting, but opened the door for Diana to come in. "I'll make us some tea," Diana said, since Carol simply sat down again, saying nothing. She brought the two mugs to the sofa, where she sat beside her daughter. "I had a call from Stan Forest today. Apparently there's a letter in the post. They're turning us down. It's as we thought. They're planning to turn the quarry into a caravan park."

Carol shrugged. "Oh well. We expected it."

"I wondered if you had any thoughts on what we should do instead."

"No," was Carol's unequivocal reply. Silence closed in again.

Diana felt as if she were pushing a heavy stone up a hill that was too steep ever to be climbed. She drew a deep breath. "I did wonder, now we know Shaw's are definitely selling up – there's the Meadhope depot."

"I suppose there is."

"It's just what we need. But I don't want to make things worse for Ronnie." Diana had thought of phoning, or writing to him – after all, he had written in support when she had most needed it. But that had been different. What he was facing now was the certain destruction of everything he had worked for all his life. And she was a fellow haulier, a rival. How would she feel if she were to write from the security of her own success, and then add the final insult by buying up one of his earliest depots? No, at the moment she felt she could not do that to him; unless Carol could convince her that it would be all right.

Abruptly, Carol put down her mug, stood up, turned the television off, turned on her mother. "Oh, Mam, what does it matter! I couldn't care less what Ronnie Shaw thinks. Can't this wait till our next meeting?" She took a few restless steps about the room and then sat down again, on the armchair this time, some distance from her mother.

"If that's what you want." After a few moments of not-very-comfortable silence, Diana said gently, "What happened in France, Carol?"

"You know. I told you."

"You told me hardly anything. I thought you were going to visit some friends."

"So I was."

"A good-looking young Frenchman, so I gather – from Sharon, not from you. She seems to have had a good time at least. But you didn't, did you?"

Carol shrugged. "You win some, you lose some. Now leave it alone, Mam. I don't want to talk about it." She got up and snapped the television on again. Then she slumped back on the sofa and said suddenly, "All right, you win. He wants to marry me. I said yes."

For several moments Diana could not think what to say, though a momentary panic shot through her – *What will I do, if Carol goes to France?* Aloud, she said at last, "Then what on earth is the problem?"

"When you love someone, it's supposed to be enough. You're supposed to want to give up everything for them, no matter what."

"But you don't want to give up everything and go and live in France?"

"I don't know. I don't think so. But I don't want to give him up either."

It had been painful enough to face that dilemma for herself; to see her daughter going through it too was unbearable. Diana laid a hand over Carol's. "It's much easier if you're a traditional woman, with no real life of your own. Then marriage is the answer to everything, the obvious thing."

"That's what I thought when I married Kenny. I know better now."

"Yes," said Diana. "A bad marriage quickly teaches you that there are worse things than being alone. And a marriage can turn bad even if you marry someone you love, if you're not wanting the same thing from life."

Carol gazed at her mother with some surprise. "I suppose you know that, from Dad."

"Not just from your Dad. I do know about loving someone yet feeling it's not right to marry – about not wanting to give up your independence. Because that's what it is in the end, isn't it?"

Carol did not answer directly, because her mother's remarks, spoken in a voice rough-edged with pain, had jolted her out of her gloom. "Who was it, Mam – who wanted to marry you? Someone did, didn't they? And you loved him? Is it someone I know? Someone local?"

"Yes, you know him. And he's local, sort of. Sometimes."

Carol studied her face, full of curiosity. Diana could see that she was running over the possible candidates in her mind. "It's Ronnie Shaw, it must be – it is, isn't it?" She suddenly hugged her mother. "Oh, Mam!"

They both cried then, just a little, and then told each other their stories, sharing experiences that were in so many ways alike, finding comfort in the depth of understanding.

Much later, Carol said, "Would you ever change your mind and marry him?"

"Who knows? I don't suppose I'll get another chance, especially not now. You have to take that into account when you decide."

"What do you think I should do?"

"I can't choose for you. No one can but you. Whatever you decide it's going to be hard. The only thing is, when the choice is made, you have to stick with it, make the best of it, try and put everything else behind you and get on with what you've decided is best. Time does heal, you know, if you let it. It's no good living in a constant state of regret and looking back."

"No," said Carol thoughtfully. "No, I can see that. Whichever way I choose." Then she smiled. "Thanks, Mam." She stood up. "I fancy some toast. How about you?"

Fifteen

Queen of the Road took possession of Shaw's Meadhope depot in the last week in March the following year, two weeks before Easter, so as to allow time to sort everything out during the holiday period.

For weeks beforehand, work had been done on the yard, repairing buildings, installing new equipment, refurbishing the offices, repainting the fencing and altering the sign on the gate. Yet still, on this spring morning, Diana thought it looked much as she remembered it, when she had first come here on a September day nearly sixteen years ago.

The office where she stood this Thursday afternoon had been transformed, with new paint, new furniture, new shelves and a modern filing system; and Shirley, her Transport Manager, had already added her own touches – a photograph on the wall of Jean and herself standing beside her favourite old wagon, a row of succulents in pots on the window sill. Yet the ghost of that day still seemed to hang about the room, even while Diana tried to concentrate on the business matters Shirley was discussing with her. She could still feel Ronnie's presence, almost see him perched on the edge of his desk, leaning towards her. She tried to push away the memory of his kiss. She tried, too, to tell herself that there was no need to feel guilty. In coming here she had taken nothing that Ronnie had not already lost; in fact, in paying a good price for the depot she might well have helped to ensure that he was not left destitute once his entire business was sold off.

She did not know, of course. She had heard nothing from

204

Ronnie since last year, when, before putting in an offer for the yard, she had set her scruples aside and written to him, offering her sympathy and asking if he would mind if she were to buy it. She still worried, recalling that letter, in case she had allowed any kind of triumphant note to creep in – the gloating of a fellow businesswoman over a defeated rival. Not that she had felt anything of the kind. She had known the sort of pain Ronnie must have been suffering over the loss of this enterprise that had been his whole life, and she had tried to tell him that she understood. But who knew what he might have read into it? Though he had answered without showing any sign of taking offence, and even written that if he had to lose the yard, he would rather it went to her than anyone else he could think of, she had still never been able to feel wholly reassured. She found herself often thinking about him, wondering what he was doing now, what he felt.

"Are we moving the wage accounts down to the bank here?"

It was a moment or two before Shirley's question reached her. "Oh – yes. Yes, I think that would be safer. At least, no, the accounts stay at Wearbridge, but I've arranged to collect the cash from here. But the sooner we can persuade everyone to open a bank account the better."

"You know drivers – all for cash in hand," Shirley said. She turned as Carol came up the stairs and entered the office. Diana saw again, with thankfulness, that her daughter appeared to be restored to her old cheerful self. The misery of the New Year seemed at last to have gone for good. Her renewed energy and enthusiasm had helped to keep her mother going during the days of the move, which was just as well, for Diana found herself feeling increasingly tired lately. Sometimes, she would ask herself if the day would ever come when they could simply enjoy their success, without always having to change and move on.

"This looks nice!" Carol looked approvingly around the office. "Kind of homely."

"Shirley's touch," said Diana, pulling herself together. After all, today was a new beginning. She ought to be excited, full of hope for the future. "Are the wagons all in the right place now?"

"No, there's still the old Volvo artic. We're just off to get it – I'm giving Bruce a lift up there." It had been a complicated matter, to make sure that each vehicle was where it ought to be. The original depot was, appropriately enough, to remain the base for the heavy duty wagons used for (mostly local) stone and mineral transport, while all the rest – including all the newest artics, the tautliners, everything that was used for long-distance haulage – were to be housed at Meadhope.

"I'll see you later then. Do you want to eat at the flat this evening – you did say Sharon was staying over in Meadhope after the performance?"

"With Rachel, yes. I still can't see Sharon acting in a play. But I suppose Mrs Walton knew what she was doing, choosing her."

"Mustardseed's a very small part. What does she say? 'And I'? Even Sharon can't go wrong with that!"

Carol laughed. "And, yes, Mam, I'd love to come for my tea. But I'll cook." Diana did not argue. Carol was the better cook; more to the point, Diana recognised that her daughter sensed her own weariness and was trying to take some of the load from her shoulders. She was grateful, but a little depressed that such support should be needed.

Up at the depot, once Bruce had driven away in the Volvo, Carol spent some time tidying up, and then set off back to Wearbridge in her Mini. She still did not much like her own company. Where, in the company of others, she could put Luc out of her mind, on her own it was not always possible. Unless she was behind the wheel of a wagon. That had been her salvation, she thought; her love of driving was, in the end, a stronger passion than the love of any man.

Three months ago, when she wrote to refuse his offer of marriage, she had thought her heart was irrevocably broken, that it would never mend. She thought that in the future she would always associate Christmas and New Year celebrations with the choice she had made, the sleepless nights that had preceded the writing of the letter, the tears she had shed while she struggled to find the right words, the exhausted misery of the days that followed, while she wondered if Luc would write to give her his reaction, half hoping, half dreading that he would do so; then heartsick because she heard nothing. For a long time she had found it impossible to believe she would ever be happy again. But with the spring came hope and looking forward. From now it could only go on getting better.

She was vaguely aware, as she passed the petrol station, that two people stood on the forecourt: one of them Kevin, now senior mechanic, probably on his way home, the other a man who was evidently asking directions, from the way Kevin was gesturing. It was only after she had been home for just long enough to have put the kettle on, run a bath and undressed to her underwear that she discovered who the enquiring stranger had been. There was a rattle on the brass doorknocker. Carol swore – the bathwater would get cold again if this took too long – pulled on a dressing gown and went to see who was there.

For a long time she stood quite still, staring, unable to speak, almost unable to breathe. Yet for a moment on opening the door she had not recognised him, this man she had never thought to see in Wearbridge, so far from the sun and the vineyards, all those things she had rejected as the old year ended.

He, in his turn, looked unsure, anxious, watchful for any hint of what her reaction was, whether she was pleased to see him or no. In the end it was he who spoke first, his voice hoarse, stating the obvious. "Caz. I am here."

She stood aside to let him in, but still could not speak. She closed the door, while he looked round the small front room, cheerfully papered, simply furnished, its few shelves filled with Sharon's books; the cheap ornaments on the mantelpiece, the family photographs. Carol suddenly saw the room through his eyes, contrasted with the ancient elegance of the château. Was he asking himself, *How could she choose this before me?*

At last he turned to look at her. She felt very conscious then that under the flowered orange robe – a bit scruffy now – she was wearing only briefs and a greying bra. Even in this most awkward and painful of moments, she felt the familiar lurch of the stomach as his eyes met hers. She thought she had remembered everything about him, she had seemed to see him clearly, yet even so she saw at once that in the flesh he was much more attractive, much more handsome than her memory allowed him to be. All the old hunger returned, with breath-stopping force. "Caz, you asked that I should come."

She tried to clear her throat, but her voice was still beyond real control. "That was before – before I wrote."

"You did not say in your letter, 'Don't come'."

"I didn't need to say it. I told you it was over."

"I know. I tell myself it is what you want, that I must accept. I try. But I cannot. I must hear from you yourself. Tell me, is it what you really want?"

He took a step towards her, and she ached for him to reach out and hold her, longed for him to carry her up to her small bedroom, to make love to her as he had done in his own huge antique bed. "It has to be. I can't come and live in France."

He gestured around the room. "You cannot leave this?"

There was disbelief in his voice, and she felt herself colouring; even felt a sudden invigorating surge of anger. "You may be rich and live in a château, but that doesn't give you the right to sneer at the rest of us!"

It was his turn to blush. "No – no you are right. I apologise. I came to try and learn why you had written as you had, what it is you cannot leave behind. You wrote that you love me, and I thought that would be enough. But you say it is not. I wish to understand, that is all."

That is all. No more. Or was there more, a tiny glimmer of hope, for her, for both of them? "And if you find you do understand, would you consider coming here to live?"

"I think it unlikely." His mouth had a wry twist. "But let us see, shall we?"

Carol realised she had been twisting her hands together like some agitated woman in an old film. She forced them to fall to her sides, straightening her shoulders, as if she were calm, in control of herself. "What do you want to do then?" This time her tone was detached, impersonal.

"Tomorrow, to see you at work, to stay at your side for a day, for longer if necessary. To watch and listen and learn. Tonight," and here his voice deepened and softened, "to lie in your arms, as we did in France."

Her whole body urged her to agree, and she had to force herself to stay where she was, with that little distance between them. She knew how it would be if she were to give in; she would become ensnared again, faced with the likely prospect of having to make that anguished choice all over again, when she had thought it was over and done with, that the worst of the pain was over. "No," she said. "It'll make things worse. I'll only go to bed with you again if we can sort this out, for good." She saw how he flinched at the rejection, and fought an urge to offer him consolation; after all, there was only one kind of consolation that would be acceptable. "You'll get a room at the Queen's Head," she said as coolly as she was able. "If you come here tomorrow morning at seven, then you can spend the day with me."

He left soon afterwards, without one kiss or caress, and Carol went to have her bath, too exhausted to make the effort to add new warmth to the cooling water. Later, she phoned her mother and said she would not after all be coming round. Some time, when this was over, she would perhaps be able to find comfort in confiding again in Diana, but for now it was simply too soon for talk; she was still too much in the midst of everything, too overwhelmed by what was happening.

If, when she first met Luc, Carol had thought of what it would be like if he were to spend a day with her, learning all he could about her work, she would have thought of it as a delightful prospect, certain to add an extra dimension of excitement and delight to what she already loved doing. But that spring Friday was not like that at all. It was perhaps the most dreary and exhausting day she had ever experienced, though she was doing the work she loved

– three relatively local deliveries, this time. She recognised that he tried to understand her enthusiasm for the work, for he asked questions until her head spun with them and listened earnestly to her answers, and he helped her where he could, showed an intelligent interest in everything. But she sensed that, try as he would, he could not really understand how this business might mean more to her than what he had to offer, could not see how she might love the Dale more than his own land. She was increasingly conscious of despair, both hers and his. Perhaps if they had slept together last night it would have been easier, because the whole day would not then have been complicated by the pain of unsatisfied desire.

When, that evening, the wagon had been returned to the depot and the two of them stood by her car, discussing what to do next, he said, "This is not good, is it? I should leave, I think."

That dismayed her, though he was perfectly right of course; it wasn't good at all. Last night she had told him she wished he had not come; now, illogically, she did not want him to go, because she knew it would be final, for ever. "You haven't met my mother." Until now she had not particularly wanted him to meet Diana – after all, she had made her decision and told her mother what it was. Now, it occured to her that Diana's knowledge of the business, of longer standing and probably more articulate than her own, might win him over where hers had so far failed.

Certainly, when they sat at supper at the table in the flat, to which Diana had readily invited them, Luc seemed charmed with his hostess. Carol knew, too, that her mother, equally charmed with Luc, understood why her daughter loved him and was now exerting all her most subtle persuasive skills to win him over. Where Carol's happiness was concerned, Diana could be ruthless. Her enthusiastic yet detailed account of how the firm had been built up must, Carol thought, have made him understand better Carol's own unwillingness to leave it all behind. After the meal, as they sat drinking percolated coffee from the chunky blue earthenware cups that Carol had given her mother last Christmas, Diana suddenly said, "It wouldn't be easy, I know – there'd be all kinds of complicated formalities to go through, lots of new rules and regulations. But we could look into the possibility of opening a branch in France."

Carol caught her breath. Why had she not thought of that? It was the obvious answer, the wonderful, shining solution to all the heartache. She wanted to hug her mother, for she guessed that Diana must shrink at the thought of all the work such a development would involve, and recognised that the suggestion came from her love for Carol, nothing else. "Oh, Mam, of course! Then I could run it." She glanced at Luc. "Oh, I'm so glad you came, otherwise it might have been too late!"

Luc smiled, but the smile was faint, far from the enthusiastic response she expected to see. "Perhaps," he said. "Let us not go too fast." Then, swiftly, with scarcely a pause, he changed the subject. "Have you ever eaten at the Queen's Head? You would not believe how terrible is the food. Indeed I have not enjoyed one decent meal since I came to England – until tonight, of course." The last point seemed to have been added as an afterthought, a hasty correction, which angered Carol, though she would once have agreed with him, wholeheartedly.

Later, as they walked through the quiet streets to her house, she challenged him, "You wouldn't talk about Mam's idea – about opening a branch in France. You must see, it's the answer, the way we can be together!"

"We should not be together that way, Caz. You would be in your office, or at the wheel of one of your wagons; I should be at the vineyard, at my work. We should scarcely meet. And what of our children? Who would care for them? You do want children?"

Did she? She loved Sharon, but was glad she could organise her life so the child in fact made few demands upon her. If she had to go through the business of childbirth again – and she was not sure she really wanted to – then she would want similar arrangements for any children that resulted. But would Luc allow her to make such arrangements? His manner now suggested otherwise. He halted and turned to face her. "Caz, I want to share my life with you. For me, the wife is the mother of our children, the mistress of our house, the partner, sometimes, in the vineyard. She is not a businesswoman whom I scarcely meet, who has in her heart an enterprise that is nothing to me. I am sorry, but that is how it is. That is how it must be."

"Then I don't think I can be a part of it," said Carol quietly. "I love you, I want to be with you. But not by giving up everything. I cannot do that."

"You would not give up everything. You would have the love that is between us, a beautiful home, children, much to interest you."

"I know. I'd give up quite a lot for that; I'd even leave the Dale and my mother. But not everything, not my work."

After a long horrible silence, Luc said, "So that's it then? You will not change, your mind is made up?"

"Yes." The word came in a near-whisper, as if she could scarcely bear to speak it at all.

"There will be no going back," he reminded her, relentlessly. "If we part now, I shall not return. We shall never meet again."

Carol shuddered. "Then please go, soon! I can't bear dragging it out, on and on. It only makes it harder."

"If your mind is fixed . . ."

"It has to be. Because yours is – it always has been."

"Do not accuse me! I want only what any man would ask of the woman he loves. What to any normal woman would be sufficient."

"You always said I wasn't like other women," she said sadly.

They parted outside her house without kiss or caress, and the next day he left the Dale without calling to say goodbye. Carol knew she would never see him again.

The following evening Carol and Diana had tickets for the Meadhope Comprehensive School production of *A Midsummer Night's Dream*. Apparently, the play had gone well on the three previous evenings, but tonight was to be the crowning evening, when the cast would be especially good, so Sharon assured them, and the performance would be followed by a party for all who took part.

Diana arrived, as arranged, to pick them up and take them to Meadhope. She took one look at Carol's face, said, "He's gone then?" saw Carol nod, and let the matter drop, to her daughter's relief.

Sharon, who on the previous evenings had been silent with nerves before the play, was now confident and happy, looking forward to the evening. She recounted all the excitements of the earlier performances, the things that had gone wrong, what had gone gloriously right. "I can see we've a budding actress in the family," said Diana, during a pause in the girl's unaccustomed volubility. "What is it to be, stage or films?"

"Oh, Nana, you know I'm not going to be an actress!"

"Do I? What are you to be then?"

"A partner, of course. In Queen of the Road. I'm going to be good at computers and law and accounts and all those things, and then I'll run everything, when you and Mam get too old."

Diana said drily, "There, and I thought you were ambitious!" Sharon chuckled. Carol felt a sudden surge of optimism. Everything was going to be all right after all. Life would go on. It had been a bad two days, but she would get over Luc, as she had begun to do before he had so suddenly intruded on her again. There would be other men in her life, and if they did not mean what Luc had meant to her, then it did not matter. She would still have her work, the Dale, her daughter, her mother: the adventure that was her life.

They enjoyed the play, and both thought Sharon performed excellently.

The following Monday, they found they had left a box of essential papers at the Quarry depot, and since everyone else was busy Diana offered to go and fetch them. She was glad of the excuse to get away from the questions everyone kept asking her, the constant need to make decisions, small and large. She wanted time to herself.

It was mid-morning when she reached the depot, and there were few people about. Most of the wagons were out making deliveries, though one or two of the men must be in the workshop; she could hear singing coming from there: Steve, she thought, one of the site's three trusted mechanics. She had given up on Colin years ago; married with two children, he was now employed in a small factory in Wearbridge.

She made her way towards the office, seeing that the door stood a little open. As she reached it, an excited mongrel pup came rushing out, leaping at her, all tongue and paws. From inside, Bruce called sharply; the dog was his replacement for Smokey, who had died a year ago. Diana patted the animal as she negotiated her way past it. "It's only me!"

Bruce, now managing the Upper Dale depot of Queen of the Road, rose to pull back a chair for her, offered to make her a cup of tea. "Thank you, but I'll have to get back," she said, though she sat down, glancing round the office as she did so.

"This what you're after?" Bruce reached into a corner and lifted the missing box on to the desk. He studied her face. "You're looking tired, Mrs Armstrong," he said. "You need a holiday."

"It would be nice, but this is hardly the moment."

As she drove away she thought, "He's right. A holiday is precisely what I need. Some hope!"

Reaching the depot entrance, she turned right, towards the west, instead of east, in the direction of Meadhope and the many duties that awaited her. There was no likelihood of a holiday for some time to come, but she could at least extend this small break that had offered itself.

The trouble was, she was beginning to wonder if a holiday would be enough; if what she needed wasn't something more permanent, retirement even. It was now thirty-seven years since, a girl of nineteen, she had first begun to work for the business that was now Queen of the Road. Her enthusiasm for it had scarcely dimmed since then, but the last years had taken a good deal from her and she was weary, often finding herself wanting to leave the responsibility to someone else. She had already noticed how Carol often took on tasks she would once have done, to relieve her; Shirley did the same. But it was not enough. She recognised that there had been bad times before, when she had wondered if she would be able to find the energy or enthusiasm to keep going, when her confidence was low, when everything seemed an uphill struggle. But this was different. This was a time when she should have been feeling exhilarated, a time of adventure, hope, new beginnings. Everything was going well, the business was secure. They were able to expand without over-extending themselves, as Ronnie had clearly done. Why then did she feel like this, as if she wanted to put it all behind her? *Perhaps I'm just getting old*, she thought ruefully, imagining how Carol would have responded to such a suggestion, how she would have urged her to new efforts. After all, fifty-five was not so very old and she was in good health.

At the top of the hill, where Durham became Cumbria, there was a layby, allowing drivers to rest their vehicles and admire the view. It was a good place for thinking, and Diana pulled into it, noticing with regret that there was another car already there – the occupants were probably just sitting inside, drinking from a Thermos, admiring the view. Then she saw that a man stood by the fence that marked the boundary, staring into the valley below. She wondered whether to move on somewhere else, but in the end she got out of the car and only then, as he turned to look at her, saw it was Ronnie.

She had not seen him for seven years, and his dark hair was now fully grey, his face lined, his eyes tired; more tired than hers, she guessed. He did not look old exactly – he was after all not much over fifty – but she guessed that the past few months had taken a deeper toll than any of the years before. Diana hesitated. Should she return to the car and drive away after all? She was afraid her coming might seem an intrusion to him.

Then he smiled, and the look of strain diminished a little, though it was not quite the old transforming smile. He came towards her. "What are you doing here?"

"I could ask you the same question." Absurdly, she felt her colour rise.

"I've been to look at a cottage that's to let on the edge of Alston."

"For you? To live in? That's a long way from home."

"I don't know. Where is home, after all? This is the place where I felt most at home. I've always had a hankering to live round here. But there was always you. Now that you're based at Meadhope – well, I thought I could live up here without bumping into you all the time."

She felt a need to excuse her presence. "I came up to the quarry for something. I'm not likely to be up this way much. This is just a coincidence."

Perhaps she had sounded anxious, flurried, for he seemed to read more into her words than was there and said wryly, "Don't worry, I'm not going to propose again. I know I've nothing to offer now."

She had never heard that note of bitterness in his voice before. She felt as if a hand had clutched at her heart. "You have exactly the same to offer as you always had. I would never have married you for your business. Only for what you are."

"Which wasn't enough." He shrugged. "I know. That's the way it is."

"No, don't think that. It was just – well, my work, the business . . ."

"You were afraid I was after your business, not you – oh, not entirely, I know, but partly."

She recalled that once that had been precisely what she'd thought. "It's not as simple as that. I feared I'd lose my independence. It's the way men are – they have to be in charge. You'd be no different."

"Perhaps that's true. Or was once. Do you still feel the same?"

"I thought you weren't going to repeat the proposal."

"I'm not. I just wondered."

"To be quite honest, I think I've had enough – or that's how I feel at the moment. That's why I came up here – to get away, and think." She studied his face. "You too, I suppose. How are things?" Then, swiftly, she amended, "I'm sorry. That's a stupid question. It must be awful."

"Oh, I think maybe I'm past the worst. I hope so. But, yes, it's been bad." He gave a faint rueful smile. "Remember that talk we had, before . . . ? When I told you how much I liked taking risks? Bad timing, I suppose. Your way's proved best after all."

"Maybe we just have a more helpful bank manager," Diana said gently, though she knew he was probably right. "So, what are you going to do? Retire to the country?"

"Does that sound my style? No, this cottage has a good bit of land—"

"Farming!"

He laughed. "God no! This is yard sort of land, with outbuildings, for workshops. I'm still a good mechanic. They can't take that from me. Oh, I've no illusions about starting again and building back up to what I had. But it'll give me something to do, and time to think."

There was a little reflective silence. They turned together to look at the view into the valley where, before long, Ronnie might be living a life very far removed from the excitements of the past. The hills, full of the greened scars of leadmining, folded away into the distance, their creases darkened with tangled growths of hawthorn and scots pine, alder and birch, the air filled with the calling of curlews and peewits, underlaid with the softer sounds of rushing burns and the ceaseless wind. After a time, he said, "What I said, about not proposing again. There's one other reason why I won't – not just that I've nothing left to offer." She waited, saying nothing. "You know what they'd say, if we got wed – that I'd married you to get my hands on a business again. I'll not have anyone say that about me, no matter what. I do have some pride left. So even if I knew you'd say yes, I wouldn't ask."

She was astonished at the pang of regret that shot through her then. "So there's no hope until I've retired, is that it?"

He swung round to look intently into her face. "You're sorry!" His expression was full of wonder. "You *want* me to ask again?"

"I don't know. I just don't know. But since you're not asking, it doesn't matter, does it?"

He grasped her by the shoulders, gently yet firmly. "I once said it had to be marriage or nothing. I was a fool – I know that now. Half a loaf and all that . . . Is it too late to take it back?"

"You mean, for us to meet sometimes, like we did in Sunderland?"

The faint smile was back. "Now and then, when you want, when I want. No ties, no commitments. Or not yet anyway."

She moved closer to him, felt his arms hold her. "Of course it's not too late."

"And when you retire, if you ever do? Do I get a hint that you might say yes after all?"

She looked up at him, into his kindly eyes, and smiled. "Could be," she said. "Who knows?" But she did know, though she would not tell him yet. She suspected he had already guessed. In any case, she knew now that she was still a long way from retirement. The tiredness seemed suddenly to have left her. It would come again, of course, from time to time, but in future she would have something else in her life, someone who would offer her an escape, an adventure that had nothing to do with work. She had thought she needed a holiday, but this was better, for it wouldn't end. It was based on a love which had endured for more than thirty years, for all of Ronnie's adult life – and most of hers, she acknowledged.

Overhead, a pair of curlews hung on the air, calling and calling. The wind lifted her hair. Behind her lay the Dale, with all the richness life had offered her. Before her, a future that was unknown, probably different, but could yet offer riches of quite another kind.